Passer by would have already
arrived and began according to his own words

1. Hears dog barking
2. Enters Brices burning house
3. Removes Trudie from bathtub
4. places her on porch
5. Performes resuscitation outside
6. places Trudie back in tub
   All in 2 Minutes
7. Leaving Brice house

All in 2 Min 72

3:09

Passer by returning to Brice house!

way to Shackley house
FF OK, if Me

Passer by arrive 3:08

Passer by if dog barkofous

Passer by if dog barkofous

Shock House

Fired & call to 3:08

South

*

At 3:11 or 3:12
Fire fighter & passerby
should be on murder
scene

found Trudie Face down
found Trudie Face up

East

scene (Brice house)

Davenport finds door unlocked (he in Kitchen
when he enters sees bathroom door open

For chief Braglia
Best regards
Tomas

THE PASSERBY

a novel by
Thomas Ray Crowel

$ Success
Press

Success Press, Highland, IN 46322
Copyright © 2008 by Thomas Ray Crowel

All rights reserved under International and Pan-American Copyright Conventions.
Published in the United States by Success Press, Highland, IN 46322

Library of Congress Catalog Card Number: 2008907498

ISBN-13: 978-0-9669917-6-5

Printed on recycled paper.

SECOND PRINTING

And whosoever shall offend
one of these little ones that believe in me,
it is better for him that a millstone
were hanged about his neck,
and he were cast into the sea.

Mark 9:42

For the angels that guide us

The old two-story farmhouse sits alone at the bend in the road. Its porch wraps from front to side. It was built in a day when there was neither electricity nor any of the things that go with it. It was designed to be cool in summer and warm in winter with minimum human intervention. Its builders are only names now. The people who put up the house and their children and grandchildren are gone now — all of the people who lived there.

On that day — twenty years ago — it probably looked well lived in. The newly decorated Christmas tree was visible from outside, through a large picture window.

If you had gone inside you could have seen, beneath the tree, three wrapped gifts next to a handmade nativity scene. There was a dog's chew bone tied with a big red bow and tucked up in the branches; a dog lived in this house. You would have also seen a family portrait on one of the end tables. Sitting between her parents in the photo is a young girl, her blonde hair resting on the shoulders of her Sunday School dress. Her smile is a pixie's smile. That's their daughter, Trudie.

The firemen who came into the house later that afternoon were in a hurry. They probably didn't notice the tree or the photo. They didn't see the family dog, which should have been there, guarding things, but mysteriously was not.

They did a quick check; it was important to check every room. Around the corner is the kitchen, just off of it, a bathroom. The bathroom door was wide open.

In the bathtub was a naked body, face up, eyes and mouth open, stringy wet hair floating atop the water. Two distinct purple marks compressed the girl's skin deep around her throat. That's their daughter, Trudie.

CHAPTER 1

In our imagination, catastrophes don't happen in small-town America. We associate insanity and cruelty with big cities. But we've learned to see, those of us with long memories, that villages decay, and the social fabric rots. Hampton, like many small country towns, fell victim to the modern quick-food marts and strip malls that ringed the town. The franchises and chains choked out local business the way weeds choke out healthy plants. There was once a Main Street business district in Hampton. It included a drugstore where the pharmacist, like a druggist in an old-time magazine photo, dressed each day in a starched white coat and splashy tie and greeted every customer. The pharmacist was someone a neighbor could count on to give the best remedy for a cold, a bellyache, or other minor aches and pains. Toward the back of the drugstore was the marble-topped soda bar, where the young and old alike popped in from time to time for a healthy scoop of ice cream, a cup of coffee, or the blue-plate special, usually served up with the local gossip as a free side-dish.

The drugstore outlasted the boarded up theater. Over time, the theater had become so dilapidated that it was only recognizable by one-time moviegoers, townsfolk who still remembered the taste of warm, buttered popcorn, waiting to be eaten once the MGM Lion roared on the big silver screen. Most now preferred the convenience of DVDs, microwave popcorn, beer and chips. Children used to pack the seats on Saturday afternoons, waiting for the "Hi-yo, Silver, away" of the Lone Ranger and the "That's all, folks," Looney Tunes. Now they opted for the Sunday afternoon comfort of Internet chat rooms.

Down the street had been the doctor's office. The doctor too was a local guy. After medical school, he had decided to come back to the town he grew up in. After all, the regular doc was getting up in age and mainly had fishing on his mind. Of course, the old doc could always be counted on if his young colleague needed help, or advice — especially advice.

Most every household in Hampton had a piece of furniture with the Shones' Furniture Store logo stamped on it in some hidden away place. Shones' itself is gone.

As travel by horse and buggy phased out, a long time

ago, most townsfolk bought either a Ford or Mercury from the models displayed inside the showroom of the Hohms' Motor Company. The car dealership replaced the old blacksmith and livery stable — different building and different times, but the same family name, with Mr. Hohms' son and grandson to carry on. The Hohms' name stands for transportation. Some member of the future Hohms' family will probably be selling the next unimaginable vehicle.

The lawyer's office was another few steps down the street. Hampton's only lawyer also served as its judge. His law practice mainly dealt with land squabbles and wills. As judge, he lowered his gavel on more dramatic issues — street fights and larceny. The judge was involved in many political debates, most of which took place in the back room of the local pool hall and tavern amidst poker games and after-hour beer drinking. Storytelling was always the main course in the tavern.

What helps a small town survive are the people on and about its streets. For instance, the one remaining barbershop still has a bench outside where folks can sit and talk on a warm day. The homegrowns still know each other and each other's family's family.

A final telltale sign of what the earlier Hampton once was is the little stone drinking fountain that still stands at the four corners downtown. It hasn't produced its cold water for years, and no one seems to know why or when it stopped. That's just the way it is.

What particularly defined Hampton, of course, were

not just its buildings and businesses, or even the most remarkable accomplishments and crimes of the locals. The character of the town was a result of the summing up and averaging of its citizens' quirks and personalities. One might view the locals as one big extended family — folks who fought, made up, and then fought all over again.

They all, at some time or another, attended the one school building together and eventually grieved together while standing at the gravesides of their loved ones, all in the same cemetery, saying their goodbyes. One small town cemetery may look like another because everywhere people are born, live, work, have children, weaken, and die. But look closely and, of course, each graveyard has its own unique roster of the dear departed.

For most of its citizens, even into modern times, it was basically impossible to escape from the Hampton families, their histories, and their almost tribal values. There was really no place to go outside Hampton, no place you'd be understood. Every member of the Hampton community knew that.

In a general sense, these folks didn't have significant differences that set them apart from city people. It was their way of living together, of being enmeshed, that made the country folk of Hampton different from the city folk of anyplace else.

The social contract was maintained by commonly understood rituals and gestures. The squabble, followed by the handshake, was the rule of order. After all, there was only one drugstore, one soda bar, one movie theater, one doctor's office. You couldn't get along without any of them.

In fact, there was only one of most everything, except for churches. Hampton had an abundance of churches, every major denomination. More than one faded white-washed steeple still sat along Main Street. The churches offered different prisms through which to look at the world — Catholic and Protestant. You could find differences, but if you stressed those differences you'd puncture, maybe even tear, the social fabric.

So, how was it that an out-of-towner like Ray Krouse could blend in with the folks of Hampton? He would not have drawn attention to himself anywhere in America but he was a good fit in Hampton because he was raised with the same values. In the long run, he hadn't been able to escape his background either. Ray's kin had once been neighbors, kin who settled in Hampton long before it became a town. They lived in and farmed the countryside at the same time the Potawatomi Indians were still trying to save their villages and hunting grounds from the white man. The Potawatomis were eventually driven out.

Ray was able to buy back farmland his relatives once toiled, land he intended on keeping just as it was over a hundred years ago. Though Ray didn't live in Hampton, the fact that he owned four farms that totaled over five hundred acres made his name one worth knowing. Farmers were always in search of land to cash rent and grow their crops.

In time, some of the farmers and townspeople who came to know Ray began to accept him. And, when his time came, Ray decided, Hampton was where he would one day rest amongst his ancestors and friends.

Nevertheless, it can't be overlooked that Ray had been away. He had more than one prism through which to look at the world. By Hampton standards, for example, he was unusually curious.

Willow Grove Cemetery is well cared for. Like many country graveyards, it is surrounded by old trees and tucked in amongst crop fields on all sides except for the unpaved gravel road that leads in, loops, and carries you out again. As visitors entered, a weather-beaten bluebird house resting on a fencepost marked the curve leading to the water spigot.

The driver parked where they had parked before and the two got out. Ray Krouse stood next to Kick Jetton overlooking a heart-shaped grave marker. Ray's eyes fixed on the name and age of the girl lying beneath the headstone. Kick remained quiet, her tall shadow cast over the gravestone, waiting for him to speak. When Ray turned toward her for a second, he noted that the summer sun made her olive skin appear even darker.

Ray pulled his eyeglasses from the collar of his sweater and knelt down, reading the small inscription on the stone. "Kick, have you noticed that this grave always looks as if someone has visited?" he said.

"Most of them have something on them," Kick answered. Her eyes scanned the flowers, flags, and keepsakes on the nearby gravesites.

"She died in 1986, only eleven years old," Ray said.

Kick shook her head. Her eyes saddened.

"I wonder what she died of," he added.

Kick knew Ray intended on finding out. She sighed.

Kick jumped behind the wheel of Ray's pickup. Ray climbed into the passenger seat and when they reached the road pointed in the direction that led away from town, Kick slowed to make her turn. "Drive over to farm one," Ray said.

Kick grinned and turned to the left. A mile down the road, at the last mailbox before farm one, was Del Pitt's place. Del sat outside in his front yard swing, watching a new batch of barn kittens run and jump one another. The mother cat looked on from underneath the front porch. Del spotted Ray's truck and waved.

Del was a retired farmer. His thick, calloused hands were a giveaway. "Retired," for Del, meant overseeing several farmhands who never did anything the way he wanted. It was more work than working itself.

Ray liked Del from the first day they met, not long after Ray came back to Hampton.

Ray and Kick got out. Ray sat down next to Del. Kick knelt on the grass. The kittens started toward Kick; they knew a cat lover when they sensed one. Kick played with them, keeping an ear to the conversation.

"Del, that little Brice girl in the cemetery, what did she die of?" Ray asked.

Del paused a second. He liked Ray back, but Ray had been away a long time. "She drowned in the bathtub," Del said finally.

"Was she epileptic?" Ray asked.

"No, she was basically healthy. Nice little girl, so far as I know. She was home sick from school that day. A lot of the kids were. Flu epidemic back in 1986," Del said.

"Home alone?" Ray asked.

"Yep," Del nodded, pointing to a pitcher of iced tea up on the porch. He motioned for Kick to get herself a glass.

The next hour went by quickly. Ray would circle the question of the girl's death. Then, when it was clear that Del preferred to leave the issue alone, they'd slide off into a discussion of crops and weather, or baseball, or even politics. Ray always managed, though, to come back to the Brice girl. He kept asking for Del's personal opinions. He smiled when Del finally told him the rumor was the little girl was killed by a Guatemalan who couldn't speak English and lived in a trailer park near the high school. Del said the Guatemalan left town shortly after the murder. Sure looked like he was running away.

"Were there any other suspects?" Ray asked.

Del said he was out of town at the horse track that day, along with a couple pals. So as far as he was concerned, everyone was a suspect except him and his buddies. Del then mentioned Michael "Junebug" Davenport who used to be a Hampton police officer. Del thought

Junebug was probably an expert on the case and told Ray that Junebug was now a Sergeant with the Keysville Police Department. Kick wrote his name down on her notepad.

Del didn't seem the nervous type, but while they talked he smoked three cigarettes to the nub. When he settled into his last and longest silence, Ray stood, held out his hand and pulled Kick up. She set her empty iced tea glass on the porch and shooed the kittens back into the yard.

Ray and Kick headed back toward Ray's lake house, a few miles out of Hampton.

Ray had been successful in the "city." It was not a large place, only a city in comparison with Hampton. But Ray needed to get away from time to time, mostly on weekends, and buying the lake house gave him a way to come home. As he counted on his sons and managers to run his businesses, he spent more and more time writing. The lake house became a kind of a beachhead. From there he started buying up local farm properties.

Kick was used to chatting in the car but Ray remained unusually quiet as they drove through the countryside.

"What's up, Boss?" Kick asked.

Kick always called him Boss. It was hard for her to call anyone who'd been in charge anything else. She worked for Ray in his various businesses and when he started writing books, it seemed fitting that Kick would become his publicist. Also, Ray was a take-charge kind of guy, a boss by nature. They were also best friends.

Ray was comfortable having Kick do research with him. She had not only learned quickly over the years, but had actually picked up some of his habits and sayings. This was mostly okay with Ray, but at times, to tell the truth, it could be an irritation when she read his mind. He thought it was mostly up to Kick to figure out the right times to speak up and the right times to lie low.

"I don't believe that a healthy eleven-year-old girl could die while taking a bath, Kick," Ray said. "I don't think that Del ever believed it either."

He raised his eyebrows as he looked at her. She remained silent. "Hell," he said, "when I was eleven, I damn sure wouldn't have been taking a bath when I was home alone."

"Girls are different, Boss," Kick said, playing Devil's advocate.

Ray looked at her over his tinted glasses and smiled.

Kick waited for Ray by the main desk that sat just inside the front entrance of the nearest and largest library in the city of Riverside. She had already had a conversation with a soft-spoken, grandmotherly type who showed her to the genealogy section where the city newspapers were kept. Ray followed the women to the room. Kick told the woman she needn't stay.

Ray gazed around the musty smelling room. He began browsing old high school yearbooks that were neatly placed next to other reference books in the room. Kick went to work at the clunky microfiche machine, running records of *The Riverside Press*. The elderly librarian peeked in on them from time to time. Each time she opened the door her perfume scent announced her presence. Ray wondered how often people looked into these records. Not often, he thought.

"Here it is, Boss," Kick said. "'Girl Found Dead After Fire.'"

Ray looked over her shoulder as she read: "In rural Hampton, a girl's death is being investigated as a homicide. A fire, which began on the second story of a private residence, may have been started to cover up evidence."

Kick glanced up at Ray, her eyes wide.

"Big story," Ray said.

The crux of the article, dated December 12, 1986, was that the fifth grader was staying home from school due to illness. Trudie Brice was last seen alive when her mother, Ronda Jo, stopped at home over her lunch hour to check on her. The apparent murder was discovered when a passing motorist noticed smoke and flames coming out the roof of the house. He went to a neighbor's home and asked them to call the fire department. He then returned to the burning house, the article said. He entered and found the family dog, which he let outside. He said he found the girl's unclothed body, face down in the water-filled bathtub on the main floor of the house. The motorist was reported to have taken the girl from the house and tried to revive her but was unable to do so.

Kick replaced the roll of microfiche with another and began to turn the crank on the machine. Ray continued to scan the bookshelves, finding nothing of interest. He walked back over by Kick, whose next find was from a few weeks later. Trudie's death was now being investigated. Investigators believed the fire was deliberately set on the second story of the rural Hampton farmhouse to cover up what they suspect was evidence of child molestation. A police official was refusing to release the name of the passing motorist pending further investigation; but the Prosecutor did use "he" and "his" while describing the series of events. The passerby had never been a suspect, it was reported, because he had been talking with Sheriff's deputies only minutes before discovering the fire. The Hampton Fire Department alarm went off at 3:09 p.m.

Ray's mouth dropped. This wasn't adding up to him. He told Kick to go back to the first article.

"What's wrong, Boss?" she asked.

Ray just shook his head. Kick swapped out the reels, found the first article, and cranked down the page.

Ray pointed to a line buried on the inside of the paper and read aloud. "An autopsy on the body was scheduled for 5:00 p.m. today, County Coroner Ron Sellars said, during the press briefing."

Kick leaned back and rubbed her hands, wriggling her fingers.

"They let the passerby go before they got all the facts," Ray said.

"He wasn't a suspect," Kick said. Maybe she was playing Devil's advocate again. "I don't see why they didn't print the hero's name."

"They didn't have the time of death, cause, anything," Ray said. "They ran this story less than twenty four hours after the murder."

Kick photocopied the article. For another two hours, she and Ray skimmed later references about the case — interviews with and statements by the prosecuting attorney, as well as editorials. The more they looked, Kick noticed, the quieter Ray got. When something bothered him — especially when something made him angry — he could go way down deep inside himself.

Ray didn't say a word as they crossed the parking lot and hopped into the truck.

"How 'bout I buy you lunch?" Kick said.

"Pull the truck in front of Morrow's Real Estate Office," Ray said. The office was really an add-on room to the Morrows' house.

Ted Morrow was one of Hampton's senior citizens. More, he had been the town's unofficial mayor for twenty years, and going way back, his day job was as a trade embalmer for several funeral homes. He still held a political office and was never short on stories to tell. Ray and Kick had spent some interesting afternoons swapping yarns with him since they came back to Hampton. Kick referred to him as "Godfather."

Ray and Kick sat down in front of Ted's desk. Ted's

phone rang. Ray reached over and put his hand on top of the receiver. It was sometimes best to get right to the point. Ted saw that this afternoon Ray was interested in something more than local color.

"Ted, can you recollect anything of interest about the Trudie Brice murder?" Ray asked.

Ted paused before answering, the same way Del had. Partly he wanted to think about his answer, and partly he wanted to remind Ray that though he was almost a townie, Ray been away for a long time. Ted said he believed that he knew who killed the little girl. He paused again. Ray waited until Ted spoke.

"A local preacher name Billy Jack Hummock," Ted said.

Ted leaned forward to tell Ray how he knew. He said that Trudie's mother, Ronda Jo Brice, attempted to pick her daughter up from the casket in the Methodist Church. The preacher told her not to because Trudie's bruises might show if her dress didn't remain in place. Ted understood; he'd gotten many a body ready for burial over the years. And he'd seen Trudie's bruises himself.

"How do you know the preacher said that?" Ray asked.

"Because I was standing next to the casket when Reverend Hummock took Ronda Jo by her arm," Ted said.

Ray leaned forward in his chair. "You must have a reason to suspect him, right?" Ray said.

"You betcha," Ted said. "How did the preacher know

about the bruises, unless he was the one who caused them?"

But there was more than circumstantial evidence. Ted told Ray there was also talk about the Reverend and Ronda Jo being sexually involved with one another.

Kick wrote as Ted spoke.

"You know, Ted, it's not going to be easy for me to get folks to talk about the murder. Many see me as an out-of-towner," Ray said.

Ted nodded.

Ray continued. "But I think the real reason is because most everyone has a skeleton hanging in their closet. If I start sniffing around, I just might accidentally open someone's closet door and rattle the bones."

A boyish grin appeared on Ted's face; he laughed. "You betcha."

Ted walked over to the door leading into the interior of the house and cupped his hand, "Doris," he said, "Doris, come here."

Ted's wife, Doris, walked in, holding the magazine she'd been reading. She backed up Ted's theory. Doris had been working at her family's gift shop, located across the street from Sauers' Hardware Store back in the 1980's. Ronda Jo Brice worked at Sauers'. Doris recollected that Ronda Jo usually went home sometime around noon to check on Trudie whenever the girl stayed home from school, or wasn't over at the babysitter's house.

Doris said that on the day of the murder, if her memory served her right, Ronda Jo left the hardware store soon after the town fire alarm went off. Doris thought it would have been sometime after three o'clock.

Talk was that Ronda Jo drove down to the house alone. She became angry when the officials at the scene wouldn't let her go into her home. Doris heard that Ronda Jo, for whatever reason, threw a rock through the picture window.

Ray wanted to know how Doris remembered so many details. Doris said she had gotten the story from someone who overheard it from Ronda Jo's husband, Stan. Doris also mentioned Betty DeHaan, the Brices' neighbor. Betty said Stan had arrived at the fire by himself. Some folks at the scene heard Stan turn to Ronda Jo after she threw the rock and tell her that she better have her purse handy to pay for a new window. Ronda Jo didn't answer him. She turned on her heel, got into her car, and peeled out, yelling and screaming from the car window. She headed back to the hardware store hysterical, leaning on the car horn and weeping.

Ray took the opportunity to ask Doris if she knew who the passerby was — the one who saw the fire in the first place.

Doris said she knew all right; it was a man named Cleve Hauser. She believed then, as she did now, that he didn't kill Trudie, because he was a schoolteacher, married with three children of his own; but there were plenty of people in town who believed that Cleve knew more than he had ever let on. Doris also repeated something Ted had already mentioned to Ray — that Ronda Jo had some kind of "entanglement" with Reverend Hummock.

"Whatever happened to Reverend Hummock?" Ray asked.

"That's another reason I think it was the preacher," Doris said. "He left town in a hurry." Ted grunted in agreement.

"Who could we see that would have pictures of Trudie, other than her parents?" Kick asked.

"Well, Dorothy Johnson, would — the school librarian. She'd be the person to see," Ted said. "I'm sure they have yearbooks for the middle school."

"The main library only had high school yearbooks," Ray said.

"Go see Dorothy Johnson, Kick, she'll have them," Ted repeated.

Ray sat back with his feet propped up on his office desk. He reread the newspaper articles, and then closed his eyes, resting his head on his hand. Ray knew that listening to all the rumors could be tricky business.

For the most part, he agreed with the statements made by law enforcement who'd spoken out about the story for weeks after the girl's death. But one of them was quoted as saying that rumors were getting in the way of their investigation. That's where Ray disagreed.

He believed that a rumor about the murder, repeated enough, just might be something worth following up on. Ray also knew he had to listen to rumors not connected with the Brice family in order to get people to eventually tell what they knew or heard about the murder. He was going to have to get real familiar with the social fabric of Hampton. He was going to have to wrap himself up in it.

"Kick, get Michael Davenport on the phone," Ray said. "The guy Del Pitt called Junebug."

"He's not in. I already left a message at the Keysville Police Department," Kick said.

Ray looked down at the list of questions he had made that needed answers. He'd gotten up at four in the morning — he couldn't sleep — and written the questions sitting at the kitchen table. He was always prepared for interviews. There were clearly going to be a lot of them.

Kick was used to this. She would either listen in on Ray's conversations, or type out responses from Ray's rough notes. After twenty years, Kick had acquired the knack for deciphering Ray's obscure or indistinct doodling. Still, she was thankful that most of the time Ray's mind was like a steel trap. In every interview, even every phone call, Ray would begin by exchanging pleasantries and only then get down to business. Despite his casual banter, Ray remembered every important detail. A single line or a name would jog his memory, even months later.

They had a quiet morning. Ray gave Kick a couple of new ideas about his list of questions. She typed them up. Then they made a list of people who, at this early stage of the investigation, might have some information. They agreed that some of them had a lot to answer for.

When they came back from lunch, Kick found a message on the answering machine. She set down her coffee cup and played the message. Ted Morrow had managed to arrange a telephone interview between Ronda Jo and Ray. Ray pulled out a notepad and propped up the list of questions against a stack of books at the corner of his desk. Kick sat in the second chair in Ray's office. She grabbed her notepad so she could jot down notes. She was surprised to realize that she was a bit nervous. She dumped out the remainder of her coffee. After they went over her notes, Ray was ready.

When Ronda Jo answered the phone, Ray told her that he was a writer and that he had gotten interested in the circumstances of Trudie's death. He didn't want to reopen old wounds but said that he and many others thought there was more to the story. After he had gained Ronda Jo's confidence, he said he wanted to investigate her daughter's murder again. He let that sink in and then said he believed the murderer could be found. The phone went quiet.

"Hello? Hello," Ray said.

"What business is it of yours?" Ronda Jo asked.

Ray explained to her that murder — if that's what it was — was every citizen's business. He reminded her that her faith, as well as his own, taught that her Trudie was in a better place. But here on earth, Trudie's murderer still had to face the consequences of what he had done. Ray thought that society required this, but also that it was the murderer's only hope for redemption.

Ronda Jo asked what Ray might gain from his investigation. Ray explained that he wanted to write the true story, and bring closure to her and her husband. It wasn't a money-making proposition, he said. He just wanted to clear the record.

Ronda Jo continued to object to Ray's best efforts. The anger in her voice gave Ray an indication that their conversation was coming to an end. Ronda Jo finally said if she was interested in future communications with Ray, she would let Ted Morrow know. Ray thanked her.

Ray hung up the phone and looked over at Kick. He held out his hands.

"It's hard for me to believe a mother wouldn't want to know who killed her daughter," Ray said. "When I asked her if she didn't want the truth, she said *they* know. Who do you think *"they"* might be?"

"The police, maybe?" Kick said. "Sounded like she sure didn't want you in the police files. Or maybe she thinks everybody already knows. She couldn't stop you could she?"

"Not officially," Ray said. "When I told her what Ted Morrow said about Reverend Hummock's comment to her, next to Trudie's casket, she got all defensive and snapped, 'That had nothing to do with Reverend Hummock's reasons for leaving town.'"

"Why'd he leave then?" Kick said. The question hung in the air.

"Maybe she's one of those people who don't believe in justice," Ray said. "Or maybe she can't live with truth.

I was just thinking if someone killed my dog, or cat, I'd sure like to know who did it, and why. And why doesn't Ronda Jo want me to see the police files?"

"You can look at them anyway," Kick said.

"I'd prefer to respect her wishes on that," Ray said. "It doesn't matter, Kick, we can investigate the murder without the files."

Kick could tell by the tone of Ray's voice that he was disappointed. He had been hoping for a breakthrough.

Ray went on. "She asked what made me think that I could find out who Trudie's killer was when the Sheriff's Department couldn't."

"She doesn't know you," Kick said. She smiled. It was an old joke between them — Ray's perseverance.

"She'll never get over her bitterness until there's closure," Ray said.

"I bet she knows more than she lets on," Kick said.

"She's so angry, I feel sorry for her," Ray said. "I told her that I understand that she'll never, ever, forget, but still, I believe if she would talk to me, I could help her."

Kick took a deep breath. Ray was jumping on the Brice murder case and there would be no stopping until he found out who did it.

Ray handed Kick a piece of paper he'd made notes on, then helped her fill in her notes. He wanted to make certain she had down the main points of interest that might eventually have a bearing on his investigation.

Ray got up and stretched while Kick went over the notes. "Okay, Kick, we've got to dig deeper into this," Ray said. "Run this Reverend Hummock down."

Kick looked down at her notepad. "Call Hummock" was underlined twice.

"What are you smiling at?" Ray asked.

"Nothing, nothing at all," Kick said. Sometimes Ray didn't like to be reminded that she read him like an open book.

CHAPTER 2

Kick came into the office early. She made herself a cup of tea and got on the phone. After a few calls, she shuffled her notes and began entering them on the computer.

Ray came in a couple of hours later. He'd gotten a haircut and read the newspaper.

They went for a drive down a country road, taking their time. It was getting hot out. Even if you rolled up the windows you could smell the grass and the cattle manure. It was a sweet smell, not entirely different from the smell of a brewery.

Ray put his hand on Kick's shoulder. "Kick, pull over. I believe that's Paul Pitt," Ray said.

"It's not deer season for months. What's he doing out

on farm two?" Kick asked.

Paul Pitt was Del's youngest son. Ray had an arrangement with Paul to keep an eye on his farms, mostly to run off poachers. Paul was at the far end of a field, attaching a camera to a tree in a wooded cove.

Kick pulled over to a wide place in the shoulder of the road. She turned on the radio and laid back. Ray got out and carefully bent down, stepping between the lines of barbed wire that ran next to the road. He wasn't wearing the right shoes to cross the field but he paid no attention. Ray kept an eye out, watching for coyote holes.

When he got to the tree, the two exchanged greetings and then Ray watched Paul getting the angle of the camera just right. Out of respect for his work, Ray remained silent.

When Paul was satisfied, he stepped back to permit Ray to admire how nicely he'd rigged up the camera. An avid deer hunter, Paul told Ray that he took pictures to determine the size of the herd. Ray believed it was also his way of seeing who was coming and going on the property. Ray approved.

He asked Paul if he knew anyone on the Hampton Police Department who served during the time Trudie Brice was murdered. Paul repeated what his father already told Ray about Junebug Davenport. Ray asked if Paul knew Cleve Hauser. Paul knew Cleve was once a teacher at Hampton High School. Ray wasn't learning anything he didn't know or hadn't figured out.

Paul pulled some old branches from around the tree

trunk, then brushed off his pants. Then he told Ray that Hauser was also involved with the Future Farmers of American (FFA) organization. Paul said he had no idea who the passerby was.

Ray asked Paul how old he was back in 1986. Paul said he was a senior in high school and admitted that he didn't pay much attention to the Brice murder; what he thought about mostly was graduation and hunting. They talked about deer for a while, about how there were fewer and fewer of them because of poachers, and too many vehicles, and too much development. It was a common enough topic in the country, like the weather. What was that line of Mark Twain's? "Everybody talks about the weather but nobody does anything about it." Same with the disappearance of wildlife.

Ray got back into the pickup. Kick thought he still smelled of the field. She turned off the radio and started the engine. Ray looked back as they drove off. Paul was posting a "No Trespassing" sign on a large utility pole aside the road.

Back in the office, Kick got a couple of bottles of iced tea out of the little refrigerator in the corner. Ray had been unusually quiet on the way back to town and she was a little annoyed to be excluded from his thoughts. She was glad when he started asking questions again.

"Kick, what other names of interest do you have?" Ray asked.

Kick thumbed through some papers. She picked out

one sheet she'd jotted some notes on while they were at Ted Morrow's. On it were three names each with a question mark beside them:

Chip Wiersma, Sheriff?

Dorothy Johnson, School Librarian?

Betty DeHaan, the Brices' neighbor?

"Maybe you ought to get a binder, Kick," Ray said.

"Funny you say that," Kick said. She opened the lower right drawer of her desk and pulled out two big, heavy ring binders.

Ray laughed. "You know I want you to find Reverend Hummock. Did you contact anybody at the Hampton Methodist Church?" Ray asked.

"I spoke to a woman who said she was the wife of Reverend Gary Hitt, the current pastor. She also told me that the Reverend's sister babysat for Trudie at one time," Kick said. "She said that Gary's parents might know Reverend Hummock's whereabouts, they've been members of the church forever. She gave me their phone number and I'm still waiting for their call back." Ray didn't answer. He was mulling it over.

"Betty DeHaan returned my call," Kick said. "One of the neighbors a farm over from the Brices."

"Did Cleve Hauser stop at her house?" Ray asked.

"No," Kick said.

"Well then, what did she have to say?" Ray asked.

"She said she was home the day of the murder with a sick child of her own. Her kids were younger than Trudie, not even school age yet. Betty heard the sirens, then saw

the fire truck go speeding past her house in the direction of the Brice home. She went to the window facing
the Brices' place and noticed the flames shooting out the
roof. She said she felt bad seeing the fire, but remembered thinking, It's a good thing Trudie's still at school. It
was a little after three o'clock."

"How'd she remember the time?" Ray asked.

"Because the school bus hadn't been by yet," Kick
said. "Mrs. DeHaan told me that the passerby went to
Ben and Jeanne Shackley's house to report the fire. Then
I asked her if she knew who the passerby was."

"Well?" Ray said.

"Mrs. DeHaan hesitated, so I came straight out and
asked her if it was Cleve Hauser. She said it was, but
said she didn't know if she was supposed to say," Kick
said. "She told me again, though, that Cleve didn't stop at
her house. It seemed important to her that I understood
this."

"Are you beginning to see how these interviews play
out, Kick?" Ray asked. "We aren't going to get the folks
to answer our questions until we tell them all we know.
That's the way trading information works."

"She was nice," Kick said. She didn't know if his
approach to questioning would work for her. She wasn't
sure what to reveal and what not to — Ray always knew
though.

After lunch, Kick went back to making calls. She was
finally able to reach Sergeant Michael Davenport. He'd

moved from Hampton to Keysville and was now assistant chief of the Keysville Police Department.

"Boss, pick up the phone," Kick said. "Sergeant Davenport says he was never on the Hampton Police Department."

Ray squinched up one eye and gave her a funny look. Kick looked back at Ray and shrugged.

Ray got on the phone and began the conversation with small talk, then told Davenport he called because he was looking for information on the Trudie Brice murder case, but since Davenport wasn't a Hampton policeman at the time, Ray told him he wouldn't take much of his time.

A couple minutes later, Kick heard Ray hang up the phone.

"What's going on, when are we going to meet Junebug?" Kick asked.

"Pretty soon, I guess," Ray answered.

Ray came out of his office with some papers in his hand.

"What are those," Kick asked.

"Newspaper clippings," Ray said.

"Where did you get them?" she asked.

"You gave them to me," he said. "You left them on my desk."

"That was days ago, Boss. I had them sent from the Keysville library."

"Did you read them?" he asked.

"No," Kick said. "I haven't had time yet."

"Well, I just made some time." He handed Kick a newspaper article from *The Keysville Press* that came out the same day as the copy in *The Riverside Press.*

"See the difference?" Ray said.

"You want me to read the whole article?" Kick asked.

Ray pointed to the name of the passerby.

"Cleve Hauser," Kick said.

"Why did a town fifteen miles away from Hampton include the passerby's name when a newspaper from the very county where the crime took place omitted it?" Ray asked.

"Maybe they didn't want to alarm the community," Kick said.

"So it's okay to alarm the folks of Green County instead?" Ray said. "And look at the picture beneath the article."

"It's the Coroner, the Sheriff, and the Prosecutor all from Penn County," Kick said.

"Don't you find that strange?" Ray said.

"What do you mean?" Kick said.

"The Sheriff from Green County's not in the picture and one of the newspaper articles that came out later mentioned that he was assisting them," Ray said.

"Why do you think they didn't keep him involved?" Kick asked.

"I'm sure it wasn't because they couldn't use the help," Ray said.

"You believe there was a cover-up by the Penn County

Sheriff's Department?" Kick asked.

"Hold that thought," Ray said. "Right now I don't have the slightest idea."

They drove out to Junebug's house not knowing what they might find. Junebug was in his driveway. He had his tractor, a John Deere, on a trailer and he was doing something to the hitch mount.

Junebug was a tall, well-proportioned man. Ray couldn't help asking him how he got the nickname, "Junebug."

He said that when he was born, his grandfather held him in one of his hands and exclaimed, "Why he ain't no bigger than a Junebug." With that, the ice was broken between Ray and Junebug.

Junebug explained that though he wasn't a police officer at the time, he was the first fireman on the scene. He said that back in 1986 he was still living with his parents who lived only about a mile from the Brices' house. It took him and his partner only two or three minutes to get to the scene.

"And the police were there already?" Ray asked. "That was quick."

"No lawmen. We were the first ones there. Firefighters are usually first on the scene," Junebug said. "A lot of people don't know that. Other professionals didn't show up right away."

Junebug said he entered the house through the unlocked front door, the kitchen door. Passing into the kitchen, he spotted a bathroom where he noticed the body of a young, nude, girl face up in the bathtub — Trudie. He could tell she had been dead for a while.

"How did you know she was dead? Did you touch her?" Ray asked.

Junebug told Ray he didn't have to touch her. The color of her skin and her clouded eyes told him that life had taken its leave. Her body had already started to stiffen with rigor mortis. Junebug recounted seeing the two deep marks around the girl's small neck. She was dead all right, he repeated. Somebody had made sure of that.

Junebug said he called the Penn County Sheriff's Department since it was in their jurisdiction. Ray asked if he used the Brices' telephone. He said he used his two-way radio.

Junebug stayed with the body, guarding the bathroom door while his partner went upstairs to the master bedroom and began hosing down the fire. He said that it took approximately twenty minutes before the first deputy from the Penn County Sheriff's Department arrived and he turned the scene over to him. Junebug thought the deputy was a man named Chip Wiersma. Wiersma was now Sheriff of Penn County.

He said other firefighters began arriving. Bud Lackey, the Police Chief of Hampton, was next on the scene, even before the Sheriff's deputy. Junebug did not remember seeing a dog on the scene.

Ray wanted to know if Junebug could tell him anything about the passerby. Junebug started pawing through a cigar box looking for a nut the right size for a bolt he was installing. He said he had heard rumors that someone returned to the Brice house and tried to revive Trudie, but he didn't know how that could have happened.

Junebug said he never read any published newspaper articles at the time, though he remembered his mother saying that she believed the killer was someone that Trudie knew. He also said rumor was that Ronda Jo wasn't cooperative with the Sheriff's Department for some reason.

"Do you know that the newspaper didn't mention the name of the passerby?" Ray asked.

"Wouldn't surprise me," Junebug said. "Like I told you, I didn't read the newspapers."

"One paper did give his name though." Ray paused to let that sink in. Junebug said nothing. "It was the newspaper in Keysville," Ray said.

"Really," Junebug said. "Must have had a crack reporter there."

"Or maybe the passerby talked to a reporter from Keysville," Ray said.

"And not to the Riverside reporter?" Junebug said.

"Might have been too upsetting to the local people," Ray said. "Of course, maybe the local paper just didn't want to publish the name of the passerby."

"Isn't that what they're supposed to do at newspapers?" Junebug asked. "Protect their sources or something?"

Junebug tightened up a bolt on the hitch. Ray noticed that he was putting a little extra muscle in it — more than was necessary. Junebug started sweating; his face reddened.

"If I were to tell you who the passerby was, would you know him?" Ray asked.

Junebug said that almost everyone in Hampton knew each other.

Ray told Junebug the passerby was Cleve Hauser. Junebug's eyes widened. He said Hauser had been his shop teacher at Hampton High.

"Would you remember if you'd seen any civilian, especially Cleve Hauser, either inside or outside, at the crime scene?" Ray asked.

Junebug assured Ray that Cleve Hauser wasn't there. Junebug said he didn't even know who called in the fire. It didn't matter to him at the time. He was in his early twenties he said. He liked the action and the responsibility of being a firefighter, but since he wasn't a policeman back then, he wasn't so interested in the criminal aspects of arson.

Ray understood. Life goes on full speed for the young. Death had to wait its turn, except in instances when it came too soon, as in Trudie's case.

When they got back, Ray went into his office and opened his desk drawer. He took out a plain piece of copy paper and began to draw a map of the crime scene and other key locations, then he added in time frames.

Ray replayed the conversation in his head. One of Junebug's answers had struck him. When Ray asked Junebug if anyone from the Sheriff's Department interviewed him at the time, or anytime after, he said they had not.

Ray scratched his head and thought about this. It made him suspicious about what the police were up to and what they weren't checking out. They were hiding something, or somebody. It wasn't luck that got Ray this important piece of information. It was what the map before him was starting to reveal. Ray's contact with Junebug was serendipity.

Sam Toner was the reporter who covered the Brice murder in *The Riverside Press.* Every lead, according to Ray, had to be checked out, so Kick invited Toner to Ray's lake house for an interview.

Ray and Kick drove out to the house first thing in the morning. Ray chased a flock of geese out of the backyard, then filled the birdbath and put some raisins out on the bird feeder. The bluebirds loved the fruit. The grass needed cutting.

In the house, Kick got out some snacks. Toner arrived a half hour later. Ray greeted him and introduced Kick and himself. Toner had that reporter's kind of curiosity. He took in everything.

Ray motioned for Toner to take a seat on the couch. Kick sat at the opposite end. Ray plopped down in his leather chair.

"You're younger than I thought," Ray said.

"I was only thirty when I wrote the Brice story," Toner said. "I'd just come to work for *The Riverside Press.*"

Toner continued with the details. He said he was told back in 1986 by the chief prosecuting attorney, Frank Smith, that he was not to interview any officials about the murder case, that every piece of information had to come through Smith's office. Toner thought this was an unreasonable request — maybe even illegal. But he was new to the job and he didn't protest. Toner recollected that Smith was difficult to get along with. He believed that, like many of the officials involved, Frank Smith wanted to protect the passerby's reputation since Cleve Hauser was a schoolteacher and they didn't want the folks in the small community — as Toner put it — to freak out.

Toner believed the lead detective on the case, Lou Skipper, was now residing in Florida. He said the current Sheriff, Chip Wiersma, would probably know Skipper's whereabouts if Ray wanted to speak to him.

Ray nudged Toner to remember any image, any impression, anything at all, about the day of the event. Toner seemed to want to be helpful. He thought about it for awhile then said that one thing he did remember was seeing a burnt mattress lying on the front porch of the crime scene for quite a while — if that was of any help to Ray's investigation.

Toner said he left the newspaper in 1987. Newspaper reporting wasn't as exciting as he'd hoped. It wasn't like in the movies.

After Toner left, Kick went into the kitchen to rustle up some supper. Ray did his best to help out but he kept drifting off in thought. "Do you think Toner might have second thoughts about the way he reported the murder back then?" Ray asked.

"He was a cub reporter. But I also don't think he had much of a choice in how he did the newspaper write-up," Kick said.

"Why?" Ray asked.

"He was an outsider," Kick said.

"He isn't what you'd call a forceful personality," Ray said.

"Nice enough," Kick said. "But kind of a pushover."

Ray thought she meant it as an indirect compliment to him.

The next day, out of the blue, Junebug called Ray's office to say that he had talked to another firefighter over the weekend. Junebug said the firefighter was willing to talk to Ray.

Ray wanted to know if the firefighter was the one who was with Junebug on the fire truck the day of the murder.

"No," Junebug said. "But sooner or later my partner's name will come to me." Junebug reiterated he was the first firefighter on the scene.

That afternoon, Kick found Ray at his desk scribbling

away on another piece of copy paper. He seemed to be perfecting his map. Now and then he would double check one of the newspaper accounts. Once he called to Kick, "How long do you think it would take for a fire truck to leave the station after a call came in?" There were several sheets of paper in play, in fact. Ray would draw something then wad it up and toss it in the wastebasket and start all over. She knew better than to pry. At last he looked up.

"Take a look at this map, Kick," Ray said, pointing at his rough sketch.

It was a complicated drawing, partly map and partly timeline. Kick read aloud: "Passerby spots black smoke and flames shooting from the Brice house at approximately 3:05 p.m. He arrives on the Shackleys' doorstep to report the fire around 3:06 p.m. Mrs. Shackley calls in the fire reported to her by Cleve Hauser at approximately 3:08 p.m. Hauser tells Mrs. Shackley that he is going back to the Brice house. Town fire alarm goes off at 3:09 p.m. Junebug's fire truck leaves the station. Junebug and his partner arrive at the Brice house by 3:11 p.m. Junebug enters the burning house and finds Trudie in the bathtub about 3:12 p.m. He immediately secures the murder scene until a Penn County Sheriff's Deputy arrives at around 3:30 p.m."

Kick hesitated and looked up at Ray. "If what Hauser said in the newspaper was true, he would have been back at the Brice house at 3:11 p.m. That was the same time Junebug got there," Kick said. "He had to have spent more than a few minutes there, what with the dog and the body and whatnot."

"And Junebug said no one else was on the scene. He was positive about that," Ray said.

Ray picked up Kick's binder. It was already getting heavier. There were notes and Xeroxes and a few computer printouts. Kick had carefully punched holes in everything and inserted dividers. It was in her nature to make things neat. Ray appreciated this quality though he wasn't particularly tidy with busy work himself. Ray found the section of printouts from the microfiches, flipped to Toner's first article and studied it for a moment.

"It's just what you were saying," Ray said. "Hauser says he hears a barking dog and lets it out of the house. That would have been at approximately 3:09 p.m. Then he enters the Brices' burning house, removes Trudie from the bathtub, and begins artificial resuscitation.... This all would have had to take place while Junebug was guarding the bathroom door. It would have been impossible for Hauser to do what he said he did."

Ray walked over to the window and looked out as he cranked the window shut. They had started laying a new line of pipe in the street and the noise was aggravating.

"According to this map, Kick, it's an undeniable truth that Cleve Hauser would have been on the scene at approximately the exact same time as Junebug," Ray said. "If you told me you got out of bed, I can say that before you got out, you had to get in. This time frame is the same kind of logic."

Kick whistled softly and took a deep breath. She

knew Ray was on to something. Something big.

"Rule number one in basic crime detection is to investigate anyone who puts themselves in a crime scene," Ray said. Part of that he knew from reading newspapers, partly from reading books. Most of it was common sense.

"Where do we go from here?" Kick asked.

"Call the Shackleys and see if they'll talk to you," Ray said.

Ben Shackley answered Kick's call. Though Kick asked for his wife, Jeanne, she didn't want to come to the phone. She was attending to several children in her home daycare. Kick heard her in the background telling Ben, "I don't know anything; I just called the fire department." Ben was kind enough to be the middleman in answering Kick's questions.

Ben confirmed it was his good friend and one-time colleague, Cleve Hauser, who stopped to report the fire at the Brices'. Ben said he didn't remember if Cleve had been in school that day, or if he'd left early.

Jeanne said Cleve was on their doorstep only momentarily and then told her he was returning to the Brice house. Cleve said no one was home. Kick asked if she saw him double back. Ben told her that his wife said she did.

Kick was ready to end the phone conversation when Ben said, "I don't know if I should mention this ... but ..." He proceeded to tell Kick about an old vacant house that used to sit across the road from the Brice home. Some curious things had happened there.

Ben farmed the land around the house and when the owners moved out of town, they asked Ben to keep an eye on the house for them. Ben said the house would be broken into regularly.

"Do you mean vandalized?" Kick asked.

Ben said, No, just that he could tell that someone would go inside pretty often. Around the time of the murder, Ben noticed that a curtain had been purposely pulled aside in a front window, the window facing the Brice house across the road. Ben said he reported this to the Sheriff's Department, but he never heard back from them.

Ben now owned most of the farmland surrounding the property where the old house once stood. The owners cut three acres out where the old house had been and sold it to folks who presently lived in a brick house they built after having the old one torn down.

Kick told Ben if he could think of anything else that might have anything at all to do with the case to please give her a call.

As soon as Kick got off the phone, Ray called Ted Morrow. Ted confirmed the existence of the old house across the street from the Brices'.

It had been owned by a farmer and his wife, who both died while still occupying the home. They had several children who inherited the property. One of their children sold it and moved out of town. Ted said it was more like a dumpy old shack that sat close to the road. Ted remembered that it had some outbuildings around it.

Ted gave Ray a couple more names, suggesting that they might be of interest in his investigation. Ted was a good source of information. And anyway, wasn't the Godfather a man who could be trusted?

Ray relayed to Kick what Ted shared with him about the old vacant house. That's when Kick searched some old plat surveys that Ray had in his office. Kick verified what Ted had said, plus she discovered that the Brice house was originally built and lived in by Ray's great-great-grandparents. When she told Ray of her find, Ray believed now, more than ever, that he was being guided by divine intervention.

Kick arranged a meeting with Dorothy Johnson, the librarian at Hampton School. As Ray and Kick walked into the school library, Kick spotted a middle-aged woman walking up to the front desk, with some papers in hand.

"I'm Kick Jetton and this is Ray Krouse."

"I have a meeting in twenty minutes," Dorothy said, "I got these for you." She handed Kick some photocopies — Trudie's class pictures for grades 3, 4, and 5.

Dorothy explained the notes she made on the pages. She underlined Trudie's name and made comments as to the other children in Trudie's class — notations as to who was still around, who had moved out of town, who was no longer living and the circumstances of their passing. Dorothy looked at her watch.

"That's everything I know," Dorothy said.

Kick took the copies from the desktop and looked

over at Ray.

"Could we sit down with you for ten minutes?" Ray asked. "I only have a couple of questions for you, Dorothy."

Dorothy frowned and pointed to a table with four small wooden chairs surrounding it.

"It's been quite a while since I sat in these," Ray smiled.

Dorothy glanced at her watch again.

"My first question is, who were Trudie's closest friends?" Ray asked.

Dorothy pointed to one of the pages from the yearbook. She began rattling off more tidbits of information.

"This one died of some kind of blood disease, this one moved away." Dorothy put her finger on one of Kick's copies. "And this one," Dorothy said, pointing to one of the pictures, "lives over in the trailer park across the highway."

Kick made her own notes on the copies, circling the pictures of three of Trudie's classmates — Dina Schwin, Sherry Marshall, Leeann Petty. She underlined Dina's name and wrote "trailer park" next to it.

"Here's the way I see it," Ray told Dorothy. "Trudie was about to take a bath when she heard someone entering her house. She knew who it was. She fled upstairs, he chased after her. Once upstairs, he raped her. She started screaming and pounding her fists at him. She broke free and ran down the stairs, grabbing the phone on the kitchen wall, crying, 'I'm telling my mommy,' something like that. The intruder picked up a thin rope ... maybe the telephone cord. He whipped it around her neck, squeezing it tighter and tighter. That's what made the bruises. Trudie fought until her body went limp. She dropped to the floor. Next, the murderer carried her into the bathroom, placed her body face down in the tub of water, then went back upstairs to start a fire on the bed. To try to cover up evidence of the rape."

Dorothy's eyes widened. Even Kick thought Ray was a little more graphic than necessary. What was he talking about?

"A passerby said he spotted the fire in the house and went in to try to revive Trudie," Ray continued.

Dorothy swallowed hard.

"Now I can tell you something else," Ray said. "Do you want to know the passerby's name?"

Dorothy whispered, "Cleve Hauser ..."

Kick, still writing, looked up as Ray leaned across the table, looking into Dorothy's eyes.

"Can you imagine how terrified that little girl was? She was probably thinking of Christmas being two weeks away — Christmas vacation, parties, presents," Ray said.

Ray leaned back, his face stoic.

Dorothy looked around the library, then whispered with deliberation that Cleve Hauser was a creep. She told about how he would come into her office at the library on some pretext — to ask for information or report a bit of gossip and how he then would sit in silence, staring out her office window, watching the children. Dorothy's mouth twisted as she described him as useless and a pest. "You know how I eventually got rid of him?"

Ray looked at her.

"I moved the extra chair out of my office," she spouted.

Dorothy got up to go to her meeting. Ray had shaken her up and she couldn't hide it. She surprised herself by sharing something with Ray that she had kept locked up for twenty years. Ray and Kick were also standing, about to take their leave, when Dorothy made a suggestion. She gave them the name of the current principal and suggested that he might know something since he was also the principal back then. She then told Kick to call her if she had any more questions.

Ray started the truck as Kick hopped in the passenger side.

Kick gave him an inquisitive look when she sat down on the seat beside him. "How did you know about the rape?" she asked. "Nobody I talked to mentioned a rape."

"Me neither," Ray said.

"But you told Dorothy ..."

"I wanted to catch her off guard. Got her attention anyway," Ray said.

"You mean you made the whole thing up?" Kick said.

"I didn't make it up. I made an educated guess. There must be some reason people are keeping their mouths shut about this case. Here's what I've noticed. Not just on TV but from just reading the papers." Ray reminded her of the newspaper article. "If a victim hasn't been raped the police and the papers say, 'there was no suspicion of rape.' If they don't say anything at all, it's pretty sure that there was."

Kick took a deep breath. Ray was never mean or untruthful, but sometimes he could build whole fantasy arguments just for the intellectual exercise. She knew, though, that this wasn't one of those times. Ray felt that some unimaginably bad things had happened to that little girl.

Kick pulled the truck door shut. "Do you think Cleve Hauser is a child molester?" she asked.

"The jury is still out on that," Ray answered. "Do you think it's possible that Trudie could have been a tease?"

"I'd like to think not," Kick said.

The next morning, Ray was up early.

"Kick, find out who lives in that new brick house across from where the Brices used to live," Ray said. "Get on that today."

Ray continued going over the notes pertaining to the investigation. Kick closed herself in her office and went to work.

Kick found the owner's name and made the call. The owner's wife told Kick that the old house sat north of where they'd built their new home, amongst a grove of trees close to the highway. The woman said the old home's driveway impression could still be seen near their mailbox beside the road. She and her husband had the old place, a garage, and an outbuilding that sat behind it, torn down back in the early nineties. Hidden amongst some trees, the corncrib was the only outbuilding that remained.

The woman said she never went around the site of the old house. She remembered seeing raccoons going in it and groundhogs burrowing around it. She said that Kick might ask a neighbor up the road about the old house. He used to be a plumber and he'd taken out some toilets and antiques before the house was torn down.

When she got off the phone, Kick poked her head into Ray's office.

"I left a message for Dina Schwin to call," she said. "Trudie's classmate."

Ray nodded. He liked it when Kick ran with the ball.

Dina called the next day. Ray took the call. "I understand you were a classmate of Trudie's, Dina," Ray said.

Dina told Ray that Trudie was her best friend. She said she was one of four girls who called themselves the "Four Musketeers" — Trudie Brice, Leeann Petty, Sherry Marshall, and herself. Dina said that Trudie was a "good girl" who got A's and B's in school. Trudie was more of a brain; she had big plans for college. "I'm the one who didn't get the grades," Dina laughed.

Ray asked Dina about a few people whose names

turned up, just to get her thinking. Then he asked if Trudie would have had any previous contact with Cleve Hauser. Dina didn't think Trudie was a 4-H'er, or a member of the FFA. She probably didn't take any of his classes. Ray asked if Trudie had ever talked about being molested. Dina appreciated that Ray was being straightforward. She said that Trudie never talked about any such thing, and that she and her friends talked about everything.

Dina confirmed that Trudie had been home sick with the flu on Monday, Tuesday, Wednesday, and Thursday of the week she died. Dina herself had been sick Monday, Tuesday, and Wednesday, but went back to school on Thursday. She said she didn't want to miss being in the Christmas concert, a singing program that was to be on Friday. Trudie was supposed to be in the program, too, but she never made it back to school, Dina said.

Dina didn't have any doubts that her friend had been murdered, and she believed the murderer was someone that knew Trudie. After all, Trudie knew to keep the house locked whenever she was home alone. "Everyone in the group knew this rule," Dina said.

A couple of hours after they first spoke, Dina called back to say that her dad, Nick Schwin, was a firefighter back then and was on the scene of the Brice fire that day. Dina told Ray to call him because he remembered quite a bit about it.

Kick got Nick Schwin on the phone a few minutes later. She transferred the call to Ray but eavesdropped.

Nick told Ray he left work in his own car to go to the fire. By the time he arrived, there were already a couple of fire trucks on the scene. He couldn't remember the exact time, but knew it was still daylight. Junebug's partner hadn't had enough equipment to put out the fire upstairs, so Nick entered the burning house through a second-story window, dragging a fire hose into the flaming bedroom.

When things upstairs seemed to be under control, Nick walked downstairs where he saw a couple of firemen blocking off the bathroom, which sat just off the kitchen. Nick said they yelled, "Don't come in here," or "You can't come in here" — something to that effect.

Nick said he never saw Trudie's body himself, but he knew she was in the bathroom. Nick said that he remembered hearing that a telephone cord was still wrapped around Trudie's neck as she lay in the bathtub.

Ray told him the newspapers said that the murder weapon, the cord, was never found, nor did anybody ever come out and say that it was indeed a telephone cord.

"Maybe someone just told me the little girl had cord marks around her neck," Nick said.

Nick didn't see any dog at the Brice house, inside or out. He also heard talk that the fire was arson.

Nick said he knew Cleve Hauser and was sure he had not seen him at the fire. He recalled that Dick Fowler was one of the Sheriff's Deputies assigned to investigate the murder case. In fact, Fowler lived right around the corner from him.

Nick remained silent as Ray filled him in on his own investigation and shared some of his conclusions. Ray mentioned the map with the time sequences. Nick had apparently been thinking about the murder for a long time. Once Ray finished, Nick gave Ray his take on it.

Nick told of two brothers, the Barkers, who pedaled their bikes around Hampton. Nick said they were meth heads. He explained they even had some sort of a shrine built up in a tree, hung with Christmas decorations and other plastic articles. He said the Barkers never spoke to anyone, but the local kids were afraid of them. Nick said there was a rumor that they even wrapped an old car in tin foil and buried it, for some reason or another.

Ray thanked Nick for his time, but couldn't help mentioning that druggies were usually after money or items that could be sold for drug money. They might have been unsavory, but Ray didn't agree that the Barker brothers should be suspects in Trudie's murder.

CHAPTER 3

Sheriff Chip Wiersma called Ray's office and confirmed his meeting at Ray's lake house. The Sheriff knew the way. He had driven to the lake house several times — times he was pretty sure Ray wasn't around. Sheriff Wiersma would be happy to point out to you that by nature he wasn't suspicious. The Sheriff was three-quarters Dutch and the Dutch aren't suspicious by nature, local people say. Which may be why he paid no attention to the fact that police work was not only about justice, but putting individuals on the right track before something major happened to them. Or maybe even setting a good example. The other possibility was that beneath it all, Chip Wiersma was just too involved in politics to be a good law officer.

Nevertheless, Chip Wiersma was faulty at reading people's intentions. He had suspicions about Ray. There was something in Ray's personality that both interested and nettled him. Ray wasn't a local, not really, though he seemed familiar. Ray was more curious than most people, or maybe he didn't hide his curiosity. Sheriff Wiersma believed his job was to keep the peace. That meant he had a good nose for meddlers who caused a great deal of the trouble in the world. Wiersma suspected Ray of being a pot stirrer.

He'd had to take a phone call from the next county about the time he was due to set out, so the Sheriff was about forty minutes late for the meeting.

Kick noticed that when he came in the door he checked out everything. His eyes scanned the house. Kick worried that the place wasn't tidy enough, though she knew that dust on the sill would escape his attention.

Ray, Kick, and Sheriff Wiersma sat in the living room. She and Ray were having coffee but the Sheriff had refused her offer to join them. Kick laid her binder on the coffee table, full of information on the murder case. The Sheriff was all spit and polish down to his last hair being in place; his boots looked spit-shined. Kick thought he was a nice looking man, one who would fit in quite well at a ladies' afternoon tea party. But as Sheriff, he wasn't setting the world on fire. As one of his former deputies told Ray, "Wiersma's a real stick in the mud."

This morning the Sheriff sat at the couch's edge. He

set his hat close to the end of the table where it threatened to fall off.

Ray began the conversation by sharing a couple of key names with the Sheriff, one being Ted Morrow, the other Michael "Junebug" Davenport.

The Sheriff said he was not the deputy who received the radio report from Junebug on the day of the murder. Wiersma said he was a sergeant back then and was also the fire inspector. He said he didn't arrive at the murder scene until later on in the afternoon. He also said the Brice case wasn't assigned to him, so he wasn't that familiar with it.

Ray showed the Sheriff his map and went into detail on the time frames. Kick wasn't sure he followed Ray's narrative. The Sheriff looked and listened with interest, but kept quiet. As Ray pointed out places and times, the Sheriff scooted forward on the couch toward the coffee table, his eyes following Ray's finger over the map.

"I can't believe we could have missed something so simple," the Sheriff said. Finally, the Sheriff leaned back, crossing and uncrossing his legs, fussing with his car keys. Then Wiersma pointed to the old newspaper article that Ray laid out before him.

"I've been in office since January, and trust me when I tell you that you can't believe everything you read in the newspaper," Wiersma said.

Ray asked if the Sheriff's Department had had any suspects. The Sheriff hesitated, then said they did.

"You mean you had suspects then, or now?" Ray

asked.

The Sheriff knew that this was a trick question but he answered simply. "Had and do," he said. "People still remember."

"Cleve Hauser should be your number one suspect," Ray said.

The Sheriff blurted out that Hauser had been a suspect, but not their number-one suspect. When Ray asked why not, the Sheriff said it was because they had two others that were more interesting to them.

Ray slid down in his chair. "Please don't tell me one's the Guatemalan," Ray said.

The Sheriff tightened his lips. "No, it's not the Guatemalan," the Sheriff said.

"Then I hope it's not the druggie who wrapped his car in tin foil and buried it," Ray said.

The Sheriff said, "No," and added that the Barkers were mentally ill.

"That's what I've heard from others, but they all said the Barkers burned their brain cells out on meth," Ray said. "Now you might call that mentally ill, but that would be a stretch."

"Did you ever think how hard it would be to bury a car?" the Sheriff asked. "You don't call that crazy?"

The Sheriff told Ray that the Penn County Sheriff's Department had gotten the Indiana State Police Cold Case Division, as well as two more prosecutors to look at the Brice case. Furthermore, he indicated that the Sheriff's Department had the FBI crime lab and FBI technicians at their disposal. None of them could see anything that might have been missed. They commended the original investigative team, two Penn County Sheriff's Detectives who were "pit bulls" when it came to investigations. The Sheriff didn't reveal their names, but Ray already knew he was speaking about Detectives Lou Skipper and Dick Fowler.

"I guess you think we're a bunch of country bumpkins," Wiersma said. "You probably think we didn't do a good enough job."

"What would give you that idea?" Ray asked.

Ray knew the Sheriff thought he had spent some years in Illinois since Ray didn't pronounce the "S" in Illinois when he was talking about an investigation that took place in Chicago. Ray knew, that is, that Wiersma didn't think he could trust him.

"Sheriff, I was born and bred a Hoosier, as far back as my great-great-grandfather, so if being a Hoosier earns a person the right to be a bumpkin, then I guess I'm one, too," Ray said.

"I'm proud to be a bumpkin," Wiersma said. He was.

"As a matter of fact," Ray said, "the Brice house? That was built by my great-great-grandparents."

"Really," the Sheriff said. "Maybe that should make you a person of interest." He laughed at his own joke.

Ray knew the conversation was going nowhere. "I'm not sure I've earned the right to be proud to be a bumpkin, but I will tell you that I'm proud to be a Hoosier," Ray said.

Kick was impressed by Ray's diplomacy, how he held his tongue. She held her breath.

"So you say that my map seems too simple," Ray said. Kick knew that he meant the opposite. Wiersma didn't understand the map.

The Sheriff pushed the map toward the center of the table. "That's right," Wiersma said. "It's too simple."

"Have you ever heard of William of Occam, or Occam's Razor?" Ray asked.

"No, but I bet you're going to tell me," Wiersma said.

"Simply put, unknown phenomena many times can be uncovered by simple means. That means the simpler the better. Let me give you an example," Ray said. "You go to turn on your television and nothing happens. You think the worst, a blown picture tube. You're going to get out the manual and troubleshoot or call a repairman, only to find out when you look behind the TV that it's unplugged."

The Sheriff leaned back, glad that he understood. "Why do you think he called it a razor?" he asked.

"Because it cuts through all the crap," Ray said. "That's what this map tries to do." The two men stared at each other for a few seconds, as if they were stalemated.

The Sheriff shook his head. "What do you expect me to do?" the Sheriff asked.

"I'm already working on this case," Ray said. "Doing it unofficially, pro bono."

"Okay," the Sheriff said.

"Deputize me and give me any one of your deputies, or maybe even yourself, and let me reinvestigate the case on the record," Ray said.

"That ain't gonna happen," Wiersma said.

Wiersma held his ground, refusing to discuss any way to bring Ray in. Ray was a meddler, just as he thought. He wanted to get his hands on the records. That was out of the question.

Ray told him he could get information if he had a mind to.

"How you gonna do that?" Wiersma asked. "By making payoffs? You going to buy people's cooperation?"

Ray reminded him that law enforcement had always worked through snitches since way back when. "You ever heard the term 'leaks'?" Ray asked.

"Not in my department," the Sheriff said. "My men are of the highest integrity. They know bribery is unlawful."

"Really," Ray said.

Kick thought the Sheriff was showing a kind of superiority. It was an odd quality in a man with so many limitations.

"I don't want to argue with you, Sheriff. I just want to bring the little girl's murderer to justice," Ray said.

"I think of Trudie every day," Wiersma said.

"Come on. Every day, Sheriff?" Ray said.

The Sheriff shifted his body, his face reddened. It wasn't clear whether he was embarrassed or angry. He was uncomfortable for sure. He stood up and reached down to pick up his hat. He had knocked it to the floor.

Kick picked it up and handed it to him.

"I'll definitely check the timeline, since you mention it," he said. End of conversation.

At the door, Ray shook the Sheriff's hand.

"When we catch the killer, you'll be the first to know," Wiersma said.

Ray smiled. He thought that the Sheriff would be hard pressed to know the whereabouts of the files on the Brice case, let alone what to do with them.

After the Sheriff left, Ray picked up his coffee cup and stood at the sliding glass door looking out at the lake. "I think he was telling us the truth when he said he didn't know much about the case," Ray said.

"At least he said he'd check out the time sequence on Hauser," Kick said.

"He's lying," Ray said. "He's going to be doing the same thing the Sheriff's Department has been doing for the past twenty years." Ray's jaw tightened.

"Ignoring or avoiding?" Kick asked.

"Comes down to the same thing," Ray said. "Though I do think he was telling the truth about two, maybe three, things."

"It's almost as if he came here just to find out what we know," Kick said. "Did you see the look on his face when you said you could put this case together without looking at the police files?"

"I was itching to tell him how Hauser pulled the wool over the eyes of his two pit bulls," Ray said.

"He would have taken it personally," Kick said.

"I'm going to continue to investigate this case, which is just the opposite of what the Penn County Sheriff's Department did. And I'll share everything I uncover with the folks of Penn County, rather than keep everything under wraps," Ray said.

Ray didn't like injustice but what really got him going was ignorance and laziness.

"I'll contact some of the retired deputies," Kick said. She knew that though Ray seemed calm, as usual, this case was something he was determined to get to the bottom of — no matter how long it took.

A few hours later they drove back into the city. Along the road Kick suggested they stop in at the Winners' Circle, their favorite bar.

Even after he had a drink, Ray was pretty quiet.

"You have to admit, it was pretty tense," Kick said.

"Now he's going to put the kybosh on the entire Sheriff's Department from talking to me about anything that has to do with the murder," Ray said.

"Well, he won't make that stick, Boss," Kick said. "You remember Marti Mann?"

"Sure," said Ray. "The woman with the property for sale. You still talk to her?"

"Every once in a while," Kick said. "I mentioned the Sheriff to her and Marti said he's got a handful of adversaries on the force. We'll get to them."

"Those pit bull detectives of his are a joke," Ray

said.

"Don't get me laughing," Kick said.

"I'll tell you another thing that frosts me," Ray said. "The Sheriff says he didn't review the case files, then he argues about my time frames and suspect."

"Did you catch the look on his face when you slid down in your chair, and threw your arms up, Please don't tell me it's the ..." Kick started laughing, then choking. She covered her mouth with her napkin, muffling the end of her sentence.

"I couldn't hear a word you said," Ray said, wiping a small spot of spittle that shot from Kick's mouth, landing on his jacket.

"The Guatemalan," she uttered.

Ray pointed to his lips and flipped his finger. Kick wiped her mouth.

"Not even he believes it's the Guatemalan," he said.

It was the day after the meeting at the lake house. Ray had decided to go back and try to tie up some loose ends. "Any luck finding Reverend Hummock?" Ray asked.

"No, but I got you an interview with Reverend Brett Storm," Kick said.

"Who's he?" Ray asked.

"He was the minister at the Methodist Church before Reverend Hummock," Kick said. "Maybe he can give us a lead on Hummock."

"I see you're on top of things," Ray said.

"I try," Kick told him.

Reverend Brett Storm greeted them in his office in a polite manner. He looked like a young Billy Graham, without any of the evangelist's real charisma. Ray liked this; he preferred pastors with a more humble demeanor. Ray got to the point immediately, asking how well Reverend Storm knew Trudie and whether he'd heard any rumors.

The Reverend offered them a soft drink and they declined. He opened a diet coke for himself and sipped on it through a straw as they talked. The Brices had joined the parish in the early eighties. His wife, Emily, he said, babysat for Trudie at the parsonage. He remembered Trudie being very close with her dog. She talked about the dog as though it were a brother. She kept asking if he could come along whenever she came to the house.

"What was her family like?" Ray asked.

Reverend Storm said that Ronda Jo and Stan Brice were very protective of Trudie; she had been a difficult delivery and they knew that she would be their only natural born. The Brices adopted two children after Trudie's death, but Reverend Storm said that, according to the Brices, they were "mean and ornery," nothing like Trudie. He excused himself, saying he didn't mean to speak harshly.

"Kids aren't all angels," Ray said. "They can be a handful."

Ray asked how Reverend Storm knew the family's personal problems so well. The Reverend said he mostly knew the Brices from his wife babysitting for Trudie.

"I did share in speaking about Trudie at her funeral service," the Reverend said.

Reverend Storm said he understood that Stan and Ronda Jo moved in with Reverend Hummock and his wife, Helen, after the murder. The fact that the Hummocks opened their doors made the Storms inclined to like them and trust them. Reverend Storm and Emily never got close to the Hummocks, but the new pastor told Storm a little about the case later. Reverend Storm repeated what Hummock and several others had already told Ray, that there had been no forced entry into the Brice home. Whoever killed Trudie knew the family. He took a sip of his coke and looked at Ray poker-faced.

"Any theories?" Ray asked. He marveled at how much work it took to get some preachers to open up.

Storm said he had heard talk that a friend of Ronda Jo's named Tammy Lemel had a British boyfriend who lived with Tammy in a trailer park near the school in Hampton. He was a suspect because he went back to England shortly after the murder. Reverend Storm clarified that this was only hearsay.

Kick was taking notes, keeping a low profile. When Reverend Storm mentioned the Englishman, Kick wondered how much truth there could be to the story. Tammy's boyfriend sounded like the Guatemalan. Both of them hightailed it after the murder. Apparently leaving town was enough in itself to bring you under suspicion. No wonder it was taking Ray time to gain credibility. What rumor would float around if Ray ended his investigation?

Tammy attended the church when Reverend Storm was pastor and continued attending when Hummock took over. In fact, Reverend Storm said he had counseled Tammy from time to time on personal problems. Ray wondered if the Reverend knew he was revealing privileged information. Apparently, he didn't think it was a professional breech. In general, though, he did seem reluctant to reveal much detail.

Finishing his coke, the Reverend excused himself. Ray and Kick sat reading the titles of some of the books in the bookcase that sat behind the Reverend's desk.

Moments later, the Reverend returned, holding a thick binder. He said he checked the listing of Methodist ministers. "No Hummock in here," he said, laying the register down.

"Hummock didn't stay in touch?" Ray said.

"He was a man I didn't really get to know or understand," Reverend Storm said. "Maybe he had secrets. That's what it seemed like."

"Why did you transfer to another church?" Ray asked.

"The opportunity arose.... The truth is that Hampton seemed like a strange town to live in," the Reverend said.

"Was it always that way?" Kick asked. She usually stayed out of these interviews but she couldn't stop herself from wondering.

"Probably," said the Reverend.

"Was it weirder after the murder?" she asked.

"It seemed weirder," the Reverend said. "Or maybe I hadn't noticed it before."

"Where did you grow up?" Ray asked.

"Just outside Indianapolis," Reverend Storm said.

"Well see," said Ray, "You're an outsider." He flashed a half smile.

Reverend Storm smiled back.

At the door, Reverend Storm held out his hand and said that he believed that Ray was doing God's work. He gave Ray and Kick another name, Wayne Dumas, a church member who was a Penn County Sheriff's Deputy at the time of the murder.

"I don't know whether or not Wayne was involved in the Brice investigation," Reverend Storm said.

"Mention our conversation to your wife," Ray said. "I'd like to talk to her if she knows anything that might help."

"I will," the Reverend said.

"Call us if you remember anything else," Ray said.

In the car, Ray batted the conversation around in his head.

"Kick, do you remember that quote Reverend Storm used at Trudie's funeral?" Ray asked.

Kick held up two fingers on each hand, displaying the 'in quotes' sign. "The Reverend said, 'Some good will come of this.'"

"I haven't found any yet," Ray said.

Driving back to the office, Ray kept his own council. He parked the car and Kick opened the door when he stopped her.

"Kick, I believe the reason the police never found the cord that was used to strangle Trudie is because it was taken by her killer," Ray said.

Kick waited.

"The cord was attached to the telephone," Ray said.

"So he used the telephone cord and then took the entire phone with him?" Kick said. "How do you know he didn't bring a cord with him?"

"Because I don't think he came in planning to kill Trudie. I think he just snapped when she ran to grab the phone," Ray said.

"But why didn't the newspapers mention a phone cord?" Kick asked.

"Because the whole phone was gone," Ray said, replaying the murder in his imagination. "So nobody gave a thought to the cord. He probably ripped the entire phone off the kitchen wall. But the base was still there, on the wall."

"They didn't mention the phone cord because they couldn't find it?" Kick said, summarizing the conversation. "And they didn't want to make an educated guess because they couldn't find the phone."

"I think they got caught up in looking at the mess the killer left," Ray said.

"Boy, they sure don't like to stick their necks out do they?" she said, half to herself as she got out of the car.

Ray closed the door behind him. He leaned on the roof and stared out into space for a minute. "Nope," he said. "It's not their usual routine."

When they got inside the office, Ray sat down at his desk and thought some more. He remembered an old friend of his from Hampton, one he hadn't talked to in a few years — Les Dupont. Les was once an "honor" cop on the Hampton Police Department and was a cousin of the Hampton Chief of Police.

"I'm going to give Les Dupont a call," Ray said. "He has more tidbits of information than a dozen telemarketers."

"I'm surprised you didn't call him first," Kick said.

"Didn't occur to me," Ray said.

Kick was pretty sure that there was more to the story than that.

Ray met Les in the diner downtown. They took one of the tables in the back, near the door to the kitchen. It was the most private spot to sit. On Friday afternoons that's where the good ol' boys held court.

Ray's guess had been right. Les confirmed that Trudie was strangled with a cord — almost certainly a phone cord — and the telephone had been taken from the Brice home. Les told Ray that immediately after the murder, he and the Chief of Police drove up and down the back roads near the Brices looking for the missing phone in the farm fields.

Les said he was acquainted with Cleve Hauser and

told Ray that the Sheriff's Department had Cleve under suspicion from the beginning. They interrogated Hauser a number of times, but they could never get any solid evidence on him, only a few circumstantial facts, Les said.

Ray asked Les what he knew about Detective Skipper, the "pit bull" detective Sheriff Wiersma had boasted about. Les said Lou Skipper was the Penn County Sheriff's Department's lead detective. He was supposed to be competent.

Ray asked him to describe Skipper personally.

At first Les couldn't think of anything that might set him apart. Finally, he mentioned that Lou had a "raspy" voice. He'd been wounded in the throat in Vietnam, or so the story went. "He spent a lot of time at the American Legion, mostly at the bar," Les said.

Even Kick never saw Ray as discouraged. If he wasn't sure he was getting somewhere, he never let on. Once in a while he wondered aloud if he'd live long enough to track down Trudie's murderer. He decided he needed to stop beating around the bush and go after Cleve more directly.

Kick was afraid this might be another blind alley. "Cleve said he was at the scene, but if he was the murderer, wouldn't he have gotten away from the Brice house as soon as he could?" she asked.

"Follow my logic on this," Ray said. "There are a whole lot of things that don't add up."

"Tell me," Kick said.

"Kick, several people have mentioned that Cleve Hauser's father was a devout Catholic and that he graduated grammar school from St. Mary's Elementary School," Ray said.

"I know his parents are buried at St. Mary's Cemetery, but what's your point?" Kick said.

"It might be nothing, but Paul Pitt told me that he and his wife have attended St. Mary's Church for the last twenty years and neither one of them have ever seen Cleve there," Ray said.

"Paul goes to mass?" Kick was somewhat surprised.

"Only when it's not deer season." Ray raised his eyebrows.

"Maybe Cleve was rebelling against his father," Kick said.

"The word out there amongst a few folks is that Hauser was shell-shocked from Vietnam," Ray said. "That could very well be, however, when I tie the murder together with other things that have been said, I'm beginning to think Cleve's problem started way before Vietnam."

"What makes you say that?" Kick asked.

"Sure, a lot of vets have Post-Traumatic Stress Disorder," Ray said. "You see a lot of that now in vets from Iraq."

"But not Cleve?" Kick said.

"Think back about what people have said about him," Ray said.

"Dorothy Johnson? The librarian? She knew him, that's for sure," Kick said.

"Not only Dorothy Johnson, but Doris and Ted Morrow, Paul Pitt, Junebug.... They all have a story about Cleve," Ray said. "Everyone I talked to said that the Cleve who came back from Vietnam was the same one who left Hampton."

"You're right," Kick said. "Only one or two said he came back changed."

"Give me a one-word description of Cleve based on everything we've heard," Ray said.

Kick gave it some thought. "Weird," she said. "Weird as shit."

"Exactly."

"So?" Kick said.

"So check out who was teaching at the parochial school," Ray said. "We'll just dig a little deeper. Maybe we'll find out about his developmental years."

A few minutes later, Kick stood at the door of Ray's office. "I called that plumber who took the old bathroom fixtures out of the house that was across from the Brice place," Kick said. "His wife answered the phone. She said she felt bad about what happened to Trudie, but she was glad to hear someone was doing something. She wished us luck and put her husband on the phone."

"Did he say anything interesting?" Ray asked.

"Kind of," Kick said. "Of course he said he didn't know anything that could help us. He was working the day of the murder and the cops kept everything under wraps. He said hardly anything was written in the local paper and nobody talked much afterwards. He did say that an old shed and garage were still there when he removed the toilets."

"I always wondered where the killer went after the murder," Ray said.

"He knew where to go all right," Kick said.

"Same place he hid his truck when he was peeping," Ray said.

"You think that he could see inside the Brice house from across the street?" Kick asked.

"Hard to be sure what he could see, but he'd know who was coming and going," Ray said.

"Might be interesting to get inside the Brice house," Kick said.

"In time," Ray said. "Don't want to make a cold call, though. I'd like to be introduced to the owners."

"The Manns. Agnes Mann is on the deed," Kick said.

"You got their name?" Ray said.

"For future reference," Kick said.

Ray handed Kick a sheet of paper where he'd written: CRITICAL FACTS

1. Telephone missing — Brice house. Why did Hauser not stop at Brice home when he noticed the fire? He had taken the phone previously.

2. If Hauser doubled back, as he told Mrs. Shackley, how did he have time to revive a dead body? Besides, — no question Trudie was dead when found in bathtub — Junebug.

3. If Hauser *did* try to revive Trudie, why put her back into a tub? Much less back in a house that was on fire?

4. Why no one saw Hauser at scene. Because he hid his vehicle on the vacant house property? An outbuilding?

5. Could Hauser get past Junebug guarding the bathroom door until the Penn County Sheriff's Deputy arrived? Impossible.

Kick added Ray's notes to her binder. There was a lot in it. Ray was pleased whenever Kick came up with an additional piece of information. He compared the new information with what he had in his head as he would compare loose pieces of a jigsaw puzzle with the part that had already been put together. The piece belonged some-where, but it had to fit.

Ray enjoyed fishing off the pier in the early morning. He yawned and stretched, before sitting down to put a minnow on his hook. He slid the red and white bobber up his line and leaned back, watching the sun peek out from the gray clouds.

"Hi," a voice said.

Ray turned to see a young girl sitting on the edge of the pier. Beside her was a cat.

"Catching anything?" she asked.

"Is that my old cat, Murray?" Ray said. "He's been dead for ..."

"Watch." The girl held out her small hand, as the cat raised his paw to shake. "Now stand up, Murray, and dance," she said.

Ray laughed as the cat stood on its hind legs.

"Who are you?" he asked.

Her pixie smile widened. She giggled.

The clouds parted and the sun spilled from the sky. Gold flecks of dust fell all around the pier. The girl pointed to her feet. She wore a pair of pure white sneakers. Threaded through one of the shoelaces was a small gold safety pin with several tiny colored beads. Her lace was untied.

"Tie my shoe for me," she said.

Ray set his fishing pole down and bent over to tie her shoelace.

"Not too tight," she said.

Ray looked at his watch. It read one-eleven. Ray shook his wrist. The time went to eight-eleven and the girl was gone.

Ray rubbed his eyes as his bobber went under water. He reached for his pole and reeled in the line. A bare hook came up. His minnow swam around the surface of the water then disappeared. Ray blinked his eyes, rubbed them again, then picked up his pole and headed toward the house.

As he came up to the glass door, Kick was inside kneeling on the tile floor of the sunroom. Ray's cat, Junior, stood on his hind legs, holding out his paw to shake her hand.

"Are you okay?" Kick asked.

"I'm fine," Ray said. In fact, he felt a little shaken.

"You look as though you've seen a ghost," she said.

Ray went over to the kitchen sink and splashed some water on his face.

Ray and Kick drove out to the Penn County Historical Museum. It was pretty hot for August and waves of heat off the pavement made you feel like you were looking at the road through water. Ray knew the fish would be down deep, so when Kick wanted to find out what year Hauser left his teaching job at Hampton High School, he was up for the trip. The yearbooks would reveal the answer, plus Ray knew the old basement at the museum would be cool.

The museum had two wings. The exhibit section was in an ugly modern-style building from the '50s or '60s with concrete walls and roofs at angles and a lot of pale green on the interior walls. The other wing, where records were kept, had once been the building that contained county offices. The old building was where they now stored the records. It was one of those big thick-walled brick structures maybe as much as a hundred years old. It kept out the cold and was pretty cool in the summer. In the old days you could open the large Chicago windows and catch the breeze. Now they'd sealed the windows and there was central air.

Old records were stored in the basement. Kick went down to see what she could turn up. Ray stayed upstairs browsing through old photographs that hung on the walls and current displays. Kick went into the stacks containing the school yearbooks. Ray eventually found himself taking the best part of an hour talking to two elderly ladies who were working on various projects and filing. He came up empty, except that they both remembered the Brice murder.

Finally, Ray went downstairs. Kick was sitting at a table covered with reference books and stacks of papers. Across from her sat a female employee on the genealogy staff.

"This is Kay Ledbetter," Kick said. "I was asking her about Trudie Brice and then we got sidetracked talking about Cleve Hauser. Kay knows him."

She flashed him a look that said, Watch your step.

"It seems to me everyone knows everyone out in the country," Ray smiled.

Ray looked over at Kay. "So, how do you know Cleve?" he asked.

"He's a teacher at Bloom where my kids go to school," Kay said. "I also have a son who teaches math there, and my husband is a guidance counselor."

"Cleve was the hero," Ray said. "Right on the scene when that poor Brice girl died." Ray started filling her in on his investigation, the people he'd spoken with. Then he asked Kick to lay out his map. Kick opened the binder she'd brought with her. Kay looked at the map with interest.

Kay was curious and, unlike most people, she didn't mind showing it. She recalled the Brice murder, but was unaware that Cleve Hauser was the passerby who attempted to resuscitate Trudie. She said she thought it was an out-of-towner who committed the murder. Ray let her talk. He didn't want her to know that he suspected Cleve of being involved — at least not yet.

Kay agreed that it didn't sound right that Cleve wouldn't be at the house when the firefighters arrived, or the police, for that matter. Still, she wasn't about to draw any conclusions. Kay said folks in the country were nosy and if they reported a fire, or accident, they'd stay right there at the scene until the authorities arrived. She said her own experience as an EMT for thirteen years told her that. Any ordinary person, she thought, would have stayed around to see the action play out. Still, Cleve wasn't any normal person.

Kay said she believed that Cleve had been out of teaching for a year or so when the crime took place. She thought he was in some farm-related occupation, maybe selling farm implements, or seed.

"More than one person told us that Cleve always seemed to have a lot of time on his hands," Kick said.

"That hasn't changed," Kay said. "I mean, he still teaches, but he's usually out and about the countryside."

Kay said that she thought that at one time Cleve was an overseer for the Interdisciplinary Cooperative Education (ICE) Program, a work-study program in some of the rural schools. She said it was the overseer's job to go out to the workplace of the student and evaluate them. It was an assignment that made it possible for a teacher to move around and about freely, with no one to check up on them.

"You could check with the person who runs the program now. They'd probably know if he was or not," Kay said.

Kay went on to mention that Lou Skipper, the lead detective on the Brice murder, eventually became Sheriff of Penn County. She knew Detective Skipper had spent a lot of time asking folks questions. Nobody thought much about it. In time, Skipper's popularity faded, according to her. Kay said Skipper seemed to be on a "witch hunt" for child molesters. He was ready to think the worst about anyone at the drop of a hat. Kay wondered whether Detective Skipper might have been molested himself as a child.

Kay thought at the time that the detective probably needed some counseling of his own. "Detective Skipper saw a molester in just about everyone, and because of that, he cost a lot of people their jobs," Kay said. Detective Skipper never pinned anything on Cleve. He had a better plan.

Kick caught Ray's attention. She had two Hampton High School yearbooks open on the table in front of her and was looking at the faculty photos. "Cleve's in the 1986 yearbook, but he's not in the one from 1987," Kick said. "He left the year after the murder."

"That's pretty interesting," Kay said. She turned to Ray. "If you wanted to find out why and exactly when Cleve left the Hampton school system, you could visit the Superintendent's office and request to see the School Board minutes. That information is all public record."

Kick and Ray left a little confused. Kay was fickle when it came to her relationship with Cleve. She reminded Ray of a playmate that liked her schoolmate one day, then didn't the next day.

"When I came downstairs, I thought you had already told her about Cleve being the passerby," Ray laughed.

"No. In fact, she was telling me how Cleve's likeable, friendly, and a good conversationalist," Kick said.

"Don't you find it strange that Cleve's never once mentioned to Kay that he attempted to resuscitate a little girl?" Ray said.

"Yeah, but what's weird is that when you were upstairs, she was telling me how Hauser was her good friend. Then after you explained the map, she told you she doesn't know him that well," Kick said. "Maybe she doesn't trust us."

"Do you believe she really didn't know Cleve said he was there? How can someone who tried to do a heroic thing never talk about it to a woman who professionally answered rescue calls? It don't make any sense," Ray said.

"She said she knew someone who might know a thing or two, a woman who had a daughter that something bad happened to about the same time Trudie was murdered," Kick said.

"Yikes," Ray said. "One thing leads to another."

They drove for a while and started to reminisce. "This investigation carries me back to the time when I was a door-to-door salesman," Ray said.

"How do you compare a murder case to knocking on doors?" Kick asked.

"Sometimes the people standing in the doorway spoke to me, more often they slammed the door in my face," Ray said. "This investigation has the same surprises; people make their choices for their own mysterious reasons."

Ray adjusted an air vent on the dashboard. "We're not going to get any cooperation from Detective Skipper, that's for sure," he said.

"I think he'll help," Kick said. "Why wouldn't an ex-Sheriff want the case solved?"

An optimist at heart, Ray thought. Kick was just like him at times. Good thing, too.

Chapter 4

The next day, Kick called Detective Lou Skipper. He wasn't at home but his wife, who answered, gave Kick a cell phone number she could call. Kick told Detective Skipper that she was Ray Krouse's publicist. Skipper didn't know the name. Kick explained that Ray was a writer who was researching the 1986 murder case of Trudie Brice.

She told Ray about her conversation after she hung up.

"I'll bet that made him nervous," Ray said.

"Not really," Kick told him. "Detective Skipper told me the case was still open. I caught him off guard. He said he'd have to think about it, it's been a while."

"All unsolved murders are open, there's no statute of

limitations," Ray said.

"Do you think he thought I'm stupid or something?" Kick asked.

"Who knows, who cares," Ray said. "Did you tell him we'd found some things out? Did you tell him Sheriff Wiersma was out at my lake house for over two hours?"

"Yes, but it's pretty clear he doesn't think about the Sheriff's Department anymore. What did he say? It's in his past? No ..." she corrected herself. "He said that being the Sheriff was in the far past. I guess he feels he's put that part of his life behind him."

"So he don't want to talk to us to set the record straight," Ray said, putting words in her mouth.

"I wouldn't say that," Kick said. "He said first he wanted to contact the current Penn County Prosecutor, Rudy Fisher, to see if he could talk about the case."

"Okay, he's the one who's stupid. The case is over twenty years old. That's why they call it a 'cold case,'" Ray said. "He's retired now. He's out of the loop."

"His wife warned me that she didn't know if he'd talk to us," Kick said. "He said he'd get back with me."

"I wouldn't hold my breath if I were you," Ray said. "In the meantime, call my attorney and have him get me the statute on confidentiality of retired law officers. He'll verify what I already know from watching cold case murders on television, that retired officers are only silenced by a Judge's gag order."

Kick rolled her eyes. "You want to prove to Detective Skipper something he already knows? Or maybe get him to admit he's not any more interested now than he was way back then in the first place?"

"You know better," Ray said. "I'm only interested in bringing closure to Trudie's murder, so call the counselor and get a ruling if there is one."

"I'll call Dewey, Cheatum, and Howe tomorrow," Kick said.

"Very funny, Kick," Ray said.

"You're golfing with your attorney next week," Kick said. "Ask him then."

"No. On the golf course, I golf," Ray said. "Plus I want a written opinion."

The next day Kick was at her desk trying to transcribe pages of smudgy photocopies she'd gotten in the library. The phone rang and it was Dorothy Johnson. Dorothy had clearly been mulling over her previous conversation with Ray and Kick. She wanted to know if she could be of any further help. It wasn't clear what her reasons were, or what she might have to offer.

Kick mentioned to Dorothy that Ray hadn't had an opportunity to talk to the present Principal of Hampton School, as she had suggested. Dorothy told Kick that she already had had a conversation with the Principal. "I wanted to fill him in on the meeting I had with Ray and you in the library," she said. Dorothy told Kick the Principal was glad someone was taking an interest in the murder, but he didn't have anything to add.

Kick liked it that Dorothy had taken an active part.

The word would get around. And, after all, Dorothy was a respected person in the community.

Kick wondered if she should tell Dorothy about how Ray ran into one of the school custodians who had said a few things about some of the teachers to him. Ray listened as the custodian told of a teacher who wasn't where he should have been. "I saw Cleve Hauser coming out from the girls' restroom one time. I didn't think anyone was in there, but just the same, what was Cleve doing inside?" the custodian said. When Ray asked him his name, he walked away.

Instead, Kick told Dorothy about Ray's conversation with the woman in the County Museum. "Who would I call about seeing the School Board minutes?" Kick asked.

Dorothy gave Kick the school Superintendent's name, as well as the Superintendent's secretary's name.

Kick took a shot and asked if Dorothy was familiar with anyone at the trailer park near the school. As Reverend Storm had told them, the trailer park was where Tammy Lemel lived, the best friend of Ronda Jo Brice. To Kick's surprise, Dorothy rattled off the phone number of the park manager. "I used to live next door to him," Dorothy said.

"Does Hampton High have an ICE program?" Kick asked.

"They do, but I don't know how long they've had it and I don't know if Hauser was involved in it," Dorothy said. "You can call Josie Kreps, though, she would know everything."

Kick jotted the name on her notepad. She ended by telling Dorothy that Ray had also heard from the woman in the museum that Cleve was the same as ever, a man who always seemed to have time on his hands, even at the school where he now taught.

Dorothy laughed. "Now he's bugging the school librarian there, too," she said. "He must have a thing for librarians."

Ray didn't have a lot of faith in the Hampton Police, or the Penn County Sheriff's Department. He thought somebody who had some connection with the Brice investigation was hiding something. Kick liked working with folks who didn't have an ax to grind — people who knew bits and pieces but never came forward for fear of retribution. They remembered things.

"Good luck on getting me more interviews," Ray said.

"You got any advice for me?" Kick asked.

"You do just fine, Kick," Ray said.

"No advice then," Kick said.

"Drop names," Ray said.

Kick made an appointment to speak to the Hampton School Superintendent's secretary. Kick looked the part as she entered the Superintendent's building, briefcase and all. She wanted to look official.

It was interesting that in the School Superintendent's office there was nothing to remind you of education. It was a corporate suite that could have housed any small office. Kick thought it was purposely planned that way.

She took Ray's advice, telling the secretary that Ted Morrow and other members of the community were helping Ray with his investigation of the Brice murder. It turned out that the secretary's niece was married to a man who was a friend of Ray's.

Kick filled her in on what she was looking for. She wanted to know when Cleve Hauser terminated at Hampton High School and why. Kick didn't say she thought he might be the murderer, but told the secretary he was the passerby, he'd nearly saved the day. And he probably knew things nobody had ever asked him about before.

The secretary confirmed that the Superintendent said the School Board minutes were public record, but asked if Ray would mind waiting a few weeks to see them. The new school year had just gotten underway and the secretaries were swamped.

Kick was disappointed. She hadn't accomplished as much as she would have liked.

Ray didn't say anything when she came in, though she believed she detected a raised eyebrow. "I'll get an appointment after the school year begins," Kick said.

"The School Board members would have to have given us access to the School Board's minutes under the Sunshine Act," Ray said.

"It's better to be nice," Kick said.

Ray smiled. She was right.

Over time, Ray and Kick came to be friends with a couple bartenders and waitresses who worked at another of Hampton's hangouts — a bar and grill called Aftermath. It was only a few blocks from the high school.

Every day at four o'clock the owner set out some sort of complimentary snack bar. Some days it was pizza, other days there'd be meats and cheeses, or peanuts and chips — free food, the kind that drew a regular drinking crowd.

Ray asked one of the bartenders if any of the teachers frequented the bar.

The bartender laughed. "Teachers and free food?"

Ray mentioned he'd been interested in talking to a woman who taught at Hampton High. He'd forgotten her name, but remembered a yearbook photo Kick showed him. The bartender said he would be more than happy to point out a person that fit the description Ray gave him. Ray knew the bartender would go to work for him; leaving generous tips saw to that.

Several minutes later, the bartender got Ray's attention and motioned toward a woman sitting at the bar. Ray slid into the seat next her. Her mouth was full of pizza. Perfect timing.

"Hi, I'm Ray Krouse. You talked to my publicist, Kick Jetton."

The woman mumbled something as she nodded. Ray held up two fingers at the bartender, pointing at the woman and himself. As the bartender set the drinks in front of them, the woman was finally able to introduce herself.

"Hi, I'm Josie Kreps," she said, wiping her hands with a drink napkin. "You're the writer researching the unsolved murders of that Lentz woman and the Brice girl."

"Just the Brice murder," Ray said. He wondered if there was something more than a casual association between the two crimes. He'd have to get Kick to do a little research on the Lentz case, but not until he closed the books on Trudie Brice.

Josie Kreps was nice looking in a slightly disheveled, wholesome way. The kind of young woman who's easily taken advantage of because of her circumstances — low pay, long hours. She liked coming to the Aftermath because it meant she wouldn't have to cook, plus she could always count on one of the local men to buy a drink.

Ray raised his glass to hers, then went into small talk about how teachers had so much responsibility with so little pay. Experience told him this would lead to another drink and open up the conversation to what he was really looking for. Teachers are a discreet lot, Ray had discovered. More private than lawyers and doctors, in his opinion. He didn't want to do anything that might cause Josie Kreps to clam up.

"Was Cleve Hauser involved in the ICE Program?" Ray asked.

"We didn't have that program back then," Josie said.

"It came later."

Josie said that she thought Cleve left his teaching position at Hampton High in the fall after the little girl's murder. She was quick to explain that he left in good repute, and she added, had an offer of more money. "A sales job," she said.

Josie told Ray that the day of the murder, Cleve had been attending an elementary school Christmas program. It was on a Thursday afternoon. "He was heading home when he saw the fire at the Brice's," she said.

"He left work right after the program?" Ray asked.

"Oh, the day of the program is always a half day. He could have left at noon if he wanted to," Josie said.

"And nobody would have noticed?" Ray asked.

"The Christmas program is pretty wild," Josie said.

Ray thought she said this in the manner of somebody who had almost never been to a city and seen real wildness, and who maybe would like to, some time.

"So you're certain he was still teaching at the time?" Ray asked.

"Positive," she said. "My husband's an attorney, and he's from Hampton — home grown. He knows everybody. He had a theory that the murder shook up the whole town. People moved away, they changed jobs, etc. He has a lot of theories. He studied psychology in college."

"Do you think that he'd be open to discussing the Brice murder?" Ray said.

"You kidding? Garrett loves these types of things... murder mysteries, that is," she said. "That's what got him into law. He's nosy ... or should I say inquisitive."

Ray handed her a business card. "Give Kick a call," Ray said. "You and your husband are welcome to come out to my lake house. I'd like to show you something you'll both find interesting. Kick will rustle up some hors d'oeuvres and I'll fix you folks one of my favorite drinks."

Josie sat looking at the card in one hand, as she reached for another slice of pizza. Ray tossed a ten-dollar bill up on the bar and walked out.

Kick was worried about falling behind, becoming disorganized with all Ray's interviews. She came into the office on Sunday and spent time with her notes, Xeroxes, and a three-hole punch getting her data in order. She wanted to be prepared when the week began.

First thing on Monday morning, she called the Hampton Trailer Park manager's office. A woman picked up. The connection was a little scratchy and for a moment, Kick was afraid that somehow the trailer park had some kind of phone installation that gave the park a party-line effect. Kick told her she was looking for a tenant named Tammy Lemel who used to live in the trailer court. Kick said that she worked for a writer who was researching the 1986 murder of a little girl in Hampton. Tammy was a friend of the family, Kick said, and, though a lot of time had passed, the author wanted to express his condolences. The woman, it turned out, was a secretary who lived nearby. She said she had heard about the murder, but she only moved to Hampton the year after it happened. She gave Kick the trailer number where the current trailer park manager and his girlfriend lived.

"You can probably catch them both home now," the woman said.

Ray drove up and down the small gravel road that separated the variety of trailers — some newer doublewides and others that looked like they'd been around since before television.

"You know, Kick, when I was a kid, I thought it would be fun to live in a trailer," Ray said.

"Me too," Kick said.

"I knew a couple of playmates of mine that lived in trailers," Ray said.

"And?" Kick said.

"And, here we are," Ray said, pointing to one of the older trailers in the park.

They got out of the truck and walked up. Ray gave the door a couple of hard knocks. A middle-aged woman wearing a muu-muu with rollers in her fire-truck red hair came to the door.

"I'm Ray Krouse. This is Kick Jetton," Ray said. "We were told that the park manager might know where we can find a woman named Tammy Lemel."

It was an exceptionally hot day, so the scent of B.O. came immediately.

"Who is that," a gruff voice yelled out in the background.

"It's a couple of folks looking for Tammy Lemel,

Bubba," the redhead said.

"Shut the f'ing door, and get your ass back in here," Bubba said.

Ray stepped back and gave Kick a nudge on the shoulder, pushing her toward the door.

"We have a check for her," Kick said.

The woman turned in the doorway. "They have some money for Tammy," she called out.

"Take it and shut that damn door," Bubba said.

The woman's mouth opened to let out a scream just as a fat, hairy arm yanked her back. The door banged shut.

Kick turned to Ray and threw up her hands. Ray took her by her arm.

"Looks like you got the door slammed in your face," Ray said. He winked at her.

"Very funny, Boss," Kick said as she wrinkled her nose and stuck her tongue out at him.

That afternoon Dina Schwin called Ray again. Dina had had some time to think about their first conversation. Dina told him the last time she spoke with Trudie was on Wednesday night after supper. They talked about asking their parents if they could stay together if they were still sick on Thursday. As it turned out, Dina was well enough to return to school on Thursday. She was looking for-ward to being in the Christmas music program that day. Trudie still had a fever and didn't feel up to returning to school. They had both stayed home alone sick on Monday,

Tuesday, and Wednesday.

"I know I originally told you the program was on Friday, but it wasn't, I checked," Dina said. "Trudie died the day of the program, on Thursday."

Dina said the kids at school thought their classmate died around the time the Christmas concert began which would have been around two o'clock. Ray asked Dina why Trudie and she wanted to stay with one another. If it was anyone's idea, it would have been Trudie's. She was somewhat of a scaredy-cat, Dina explained.

Dina talked on for several minutes remembering her childhood. She tried to block out that day that ended Trudie's life, and changed hers.

Ray had the distinct feeling that his questions had opened a can of worms for Dina — bad memories and deeply hidden feelings. Included amongst these was a strong sense of survivor guilt. Somewhere deep down, Dina believed that if she had stayed home sick just one more day, her friend Trudie would still be alive.

She told Ray that at her house they never used to lock their doors and, as an eleven-year-old back then, she might have even let a stranger in. Ray knew it was so because Dina's father, Nick, had said the same thing about leaving his house open. Her father said Ray probably couldn't see leaving his house or car unlocked because he was from the city. But country folks were different, he said.

Dina reaffirmed to Ray that the rules for Trudie were stricter. "Trudie always knew to lock up the house whenever she was alone," Dina said.

Ray found a way to end the conversation. His heart went out to this poor young woman, but he knew that the only thing he could do was to provide closure. Once the murderer was finally identified, maybe people wouldn't be so filled with suspicion, blame, and self-doubt.

"You'd think they've learned to be more suspicious," Kick said.

"I bet with all the meth heads and poachers roaming around, most everyone is locking up their goods these days," Ray said. "They sure should."

"Did Dina mention Trudie's dog?" Kick asked.

"Yes, that dog was definitely Trudie's protector. Dina said she had a scar to prove it, the dog bit her on her leg. Dina said she and Trudie were rough-housing the day it happened," Ray said.

"I started calling on some of the retired Sheriff's deputies," Kick said. "Somebody must remember something more than what the newspapers said."

"Any luck?" Ray asked.

"Bad luck," Kick said. "It seems the word has pretty much spread for them not to talk to you or me about the Brice case."

"Spread from where do you think?"

"From the top down," Kick said.

"You'd think that the Sheriff would want to co-operate with me, or anyone else for that matter, on a cold-case murder," Ray said. "It's been over twenty years and the killer is still out there."

Was it false pride? No money to investigate? Pigheadedness? Competition for the credit for solving the case? Or, Ray wondered, was there a cover-up? Or a combination of things?

After lunch a few days later Kick called Reverend Storm's office. Ray listened.

"Gone until tomorrow?" Kick said. She asked to whom she was speaking. It was Emily, the Pastor's wife. Kick gave Ray the thumbs up. He took out his car keys and headed toward the door.

"Ray was planning to ask you a few questions ... Okay," Kick said. "You'll be there yourself." Ray was already in the car by the time Kick hung up the phone.

Ray drove over to Riverside and parked at a meter across from the library. There was a pretty good little coffee shop called The Cup and Saucer that drew in a group of bookworms. Apparently, Emily Storm, the wife of the Reverend Brett Storm, liked going there to get away from church business, and to read; that's where she wanted to meet.

Ray got coffee at the counter and looked around. Emily waved him over to a small table stuck in the corner. She looked more like a perfume clerk than a preacher's wife.

Emily told him she babysat Trudie at the parsonage up until the time she and Reverend Storm left Hampton in July, 1986.

Emily said that Ronda Jo and Stan were very protective of Trudie, almost over-protective. She didn't see Trudie as spoiled, but rather as a shy and, at times, a spunky little girl. Emily was surprised that Trudie was left all by herself for four days while Ronda Jo went to work.

At the funeral service, Ronda Jo told Emily that she wished Emily had been babysitting Trudie that Thursday. Emily said she wished Ronda Jo hadn't told her that, it only made her feel uncomfortable.

Just the way Dina felt guilty, Ray thought. The whole community taking on responsibility for the sins of the murderer.

Emily talked about Ronda Jo having a troubled childhood. Ronda Jo wasn't a complainer but the two became close enough to share confidences. Ronda Jo's mother was an alcoholic and her father was a womanizer.

Emily envisioned that, on the day of the murder, Trudie had gone upstairs, looking for a change of clothes when the killer came in on her. Emily thought it was odd that Trudie's dog wouldn't have gone after the attacker. She paused as she remembered the dog's name: "Tuffy," she blurted out. Emily then said the killer had to be someone the Brices knew. Tuffy would never let a stranger in the house. Emily was very firm on this point. Many people find dog habits more reliable than people habits, Ray thought to himself. Kick and Emily seemed to agree on this well-known quality.

Emily said she heard the rumors about who might have murdered Trudie — Ronda Jo's druggie brother,

Trudie's own father, Stan, Tammy Lemel's boyfriend, who everyone kept referring to as "the Englishman." She didn't go for any of the more far-fetched candidates.

Basically, Emily just backed up her husband's story. She confirmed that the Brices moved in with Reverend Hummock and his wife, Helen, after the murder, months after the Storms had left Hampton. She said she believed Ronda Jo and Stan stayed with the Hummocks for at least a month — Emily hesitated, then added, While they figured out how to resume their life.

Ray sensed there was something that Emily wasn't telling him, though. Something of importance. Then it came.

"There is one more thing," she said. "But I'm not sure that I should say...."

Ray moved forward in his chair. He reminded her that his one and only interest was in finding Trudie's killer. Emily finally said she'd had a few conversations with Ronda Jo after Trudie's death. Ronda Jo had confided in her that the reason she moved out of the parsonage was because Reverend Hummock became attracted to her.

Ray surmised that Emily was reluctant with this piece of information since Ray had told her at the outset of their conversation that he would keep no secrets that might be of significance in solving the murder. She probably opened up to him because he clearly seemed to be a kind man with a sense of justice.

Emily told Ray how she had prayed for Trudie over

the years and said now she would pray that Ray could finally make things right.

As Ray drove back from Riverside, though it was only a week before Labor Day, it felt hot as July. There should have been swarms of insects but they were fewer in number. There was more than the usual amount of road kill. Ray wasn't sure he believed in global warming, but something strange was certainly going on with the weather.

He parked and went inside. Kick had new information.

"Boss, I finally stumbled on a phone number for the Hummocks," Kick said. "Reverend Billy Jack Hummock is now affiliated with a Baptist Church in Georgia. His wife, Helen, told me they've been there for six years."

"So, he left Indiana and the Methodist Church," Ray said.

"I just spoke to him a few minutes ago," Kick said.

"What did he say?" Ray asked.

"I'm going to have to call him back," Kick said. "He gave me his cell phone number and told me wait fifteen minutes, he wanted to take the call at the church — not at his house."

"How convenient," Ray said.

Kick looked at the clock and made the call. She handed the phone to Ray.

Ray told Reverend Hummock that he was a writer investigating the Trudie Brice murder. Ray reassured the

Reverend several times that he was in no way connected with the police, nor did he believe Reverend Hummock was implicated in any way. Except, of course, as a friend of the family.

Reverend Hummock found Ray easy to talk with. He said Ronda Jo and Stan had been on the Board of Directors at the church and they had become good friends of the Hummocks. Reverend Hummock mentioned that he and his wife had dinner at the Brices' many times. He said he occasionally visited the Brice house by himself. They were a lovely family. Ray felt there was something too pat about Reverend Hummock's description. He wondered if it was true that the Brices had served on the church board. It would explain the friendship, but it really didn't square with the picture of the Brices that had emerged in Ray's head. He was learning about how they had behaved in a stressful time, of course, but the Brices seemed too emotional to be the kind of people who are asked to serve on the boards of churches. He made a note on a post-it asking Kick if she could get a look into the church records.

Reverend Hummock remembered that the week of the murder, his wife was sick with the flu that was going around Hampton. Hummock, who hadn't caught the bug, had gone Christmas shopping in Ashbrook the day of the murder. The Reverend said that he was questioned by the Sheriff's Department and presented them with receipts that showed both date and time, which cleared him. He also told Ray that he believed that the detective who questioned him — a man named Lou Skipper — was a drunk.

He's answering questions I never asked, Ray thought. Never a good sign. Ray thought it best to follow his list of questions with Reverend Hummock since he seemed curious and had already started sidestepping.

Point blank, Ray asked the Reverend how he knew about the bruises on Trudie's body. Reverend Hummock was surprised by Ray's question. Ray told the Reverend that Ted Morrow overheard him tell Ronda Jo not to pick up Trudie from the casket in the church. The visitors would have seen her black and blue body. The Reverend said that Ronda Jo had been at the autopsy and shared a lot of information with him, including details of Trudie's bruises. Reverend Hummock made it clear that he was just reminding Ronda Jo about Trudie's condition. He wasn't telling her something she didn't already know. If Ronda Jo were to lift Trudie, the strangulation marks would show. Ray assured the Reverend he understood. He thought that Reverend Hummock had acted in the Brice family's best interests.

From all the information he'd gathered over the past few months, Ray guessed that Trudie died around one-thirty. Ray took a stab in the dark and asked if that time was consistent with what Ronda Jo told the Reverend. Hummock confirmed that was the right time, according to Ronda Jo.

Almost as an afterthought, Reverend Hummock mentioned that Trudie was raped post-mortem. He must have assumed that Ray already knew this; it verified what Ray had suspected about the rape. It was, in fact, what he had told Dorothy Johnson when he was trying to get her attention. The post-mortem part was new information, however, Ray betrayed no surprise. Even Kick, who was listening in, didn't realize that Hummock had dropped a bombshell. Ray's instincts told him that Reverend Hummock was holding back more; he knew more than he let on. Still, Ray didn't press him. He thought the Reverend might offer to unfold the story without being asked. He wanted the Reverend to think of him as a friend, not an interrogator.

In time, it seemed that Reverend Hummock was more interested in what Ray knew about him than what, if anything new, was known about the murder. Ray couldn't be sure whether Hummock had something to hide or whether he was just exhibiting clerical vanity.

Without shifting gears, Ray now began boring in on Hummock. Ray shared with the Reverend that many of the locals suspected him of having had an affair with Ronda Jo. Ray went on to say that the Reverend should consider him a friend, for Ray was the one who cleared the Reverend's name of being a suspect in Trudie's murder.

When Ray mentioned about his being attracted to Ronda Jo, the Reverend denied it. He wanted to know who told Ray that. Ray said it was Emily Storm. It was information that could have backfired. Ray certainly didn't want to compromise Emily, but he also knew he had boxed Hummock in. Now the Reverend couldn't lie, or get angry and hang up without making himself look suspicious. The news would be all over town. As the new pastor in a conservative congregation, Hummock definitely did not need any of the gossip following him from Hampton.

Ray went into details. He asked the Reverend about the rock that Ronda Jo was said to have thrown through her picture window while at the fire. Reverend Hummock said it wasn't a rock, rather it was an old wagon wheel that sat in the Brices' front yard. He was standing next to her when this happened, and remembered it distinctly because he was surprised she could pick up, let alone throw, such a heavy object.

Afterwards, Kick checked the newspaper photos of the house. Of course it wasn't clear exactly when the pictures were taken. In one or two you could make out a broken window. The wagon wheels sat upright in the front yard. Kick thought you'd have to have superhuman strength to pull one of those out of the ground and throw it. "Why would Reverend Hummock make something like that up?" she asked Ray.

"The clergy are kind of like politicians," Ray said. "They exaggerate."

Ray asked Reverend Hummock about Trudie's behavior, in general. The Reverend confirmed that Trudie was a good girl. He told of how she would run up the aisle at church and hug him. Sometimes she would run up to him singing the hymn, "Great is thy faithfulness." He said that now, whenever he heard that song, it made him cry.

Reverend Hummock affirmed that Ronda Jo and Stan lived in the parsonage with him and his wife for approximately a month after the murder. He said Ronda Jo gave him and Helen their china, saying she would never be able to eat off the dishes again. "We in turn gave them to charity," he said.

"When Trudie was sick, did Ronda Jo ask someone to stop by and check on her from time to time?" Ray asked.

Reverend Hummock said he didn't know for sure. His recollection was that Ronda Jo didn't have lunch with Trudie the day of the murder, and then he inferred that Ronda Jo told him she hadn't. The Reverend added that his wife thought the police said that water was still running in the bathtub when the firemen arrived. Ray changed the subject as the Reverend began waffling.

Reverend Hummock went on to say that, about two or three weeks after the murder, when Ronda Jo and Stan had moved in with them, late one night he and Helen woke up to noises from downstairs. They went down to see what was going on. Ronda Jo was in the kitchen with a butcher knife in her hand. She cried out that she couldn't live without her little Trudie. Reverend Hummock took the knife from Ronda Jo's hand, and then he and Helen sat with Ronda Jo on the kitchen floor, hugging and consoling her. It had been a tough moment but the Spirit was with them that night.

After about a month, the Brices moved to a house caddy-corner from the church. And though the Brices were nearby, the Hummocks lost contact with them.

Ronda Jo and Stan stopped coming to church. In time, both families moved out of Hampton, though Reverend Hummock couldn't recall who moved away first.

Reverend Hummock said he didn't know much about the two children the Brices adopted after their daughter's death.

Reverend Hummock said the church congregation had always been "behind" the Brices. He also had done everything he could to help.

Ray once knew a priest who told him that once you'd gone through a tragedy with somebody, you never really forget, rather you only regret that you couldn't have done more for them. Ray knew that this was true for people, in general. It's called life experience, Ray thought to himself.

"Did anybody think you were doing too much?" Ray asked. "You were all pretty good friends before the tragedy, right?"

"I worked very hard in those days," Reverend Hummock told Ray. "I was young and I was trying to save the world." He admitted that maybe he ministered to Ronda Jo unwisely but what did a young pastor know? Ray asked him to explain.

Reverend Hummock thought that Ronda Jo got tired of talking to the Sheriff about the details of the murder, so he told her she had to start putting all this behind her. He said he told her nothing could bring Trudie back, that she was in God's hands. Reverend Hummock paused then said, "Maybe I gave her wrong advice," and repeated he was young at the time.

When Ronda Jo told Reverend Hummock that the Sheriff told her Trudie had been raped post-mortem, the Reverend told Ray he thought the Sheriff might have said that to spare her feelings. Ronda Jo had asked if her daughter had much pain before she died. Ray didn't see how any kind of detailed information about the rape would comfort the Brices. People say strange things in moments of tragedy, he thought.

Reverend Hummock said the killer started the fire in the middle of Stan and Ronda Jo's bed in the master bedroom. Everybody agreed about that.

Ray had first believed it was going to be a struggle to keep Reverend Hummock on the line. Now, in fact, he couldn't make him stop from repeating himself. Ray shifted the phone to his other ear and changed the subject. Reverend Hummock couldn't remember the old vacant house across the street. He would ask his wife about it. He was surprised when Ray told him that the Brice house was built by and lived in by Ray's great-great-grandparents. Reverend Hummock felt he was a good judge of character, but he couldn't get a handle on Ray.

"At times, God works in mysterious ways," Reverend Hummock said.

Ray laid out for the Reverend his theory about the house across the street. Ray thought that, from time to time, the killer hid there, peeping out the window. Maybe he was possessive or jealous. Maybe he saw Reverend

Hummock giving Ronda Jo an innocent hug, or saying good night to Trudie who had just been tucked in for the night. Just maybe this sort of thing gave the peeper a reason to get enraged. Who knows, it was all conjecture on Ray's part. One thing Ray did know was that voyeurism was a broad subject. The Reverend became defensive, but Ray pressed on. Interestingly, the sense of guilt felt by Dina and Emily didn't seem to have touched Reverend Hummock. Maybe ministers were more successful at controlling such feelings.

Ray reminded the Reverend that sometimes men and women flirt when they are in their youth.

"As a minister that definitely wouldn't be my case," Reverend Hummock said.

Ray asked him if he'd ever read the book, *The Scarlet Letter.*

"No," the Reverend said.

"When you have time, read it," Ray said.

Reverend Hummock repeated that he did not find Ronda Jo attractive. He also believed that Ronda Jo and Stan had no idea who murdered their daughter, though he heard the Brices say that it might have been an Englishman.

Kick made notes of Ray's end of the conversation with Reverend Hummock. She could usually pick up on what the person on the other end of the line was saying by Ray's comments. It was something Ray had taught her to do. He told her if you listen very carefully to what people are saying, you can fill in the blanks. Ray laughed when he told her how good friends could end each other's sentences at times.

This conversation might have gone on longer except that the battery on Reverend Hummock's cell phone ran out of juice and the voices began to cut out. The Reverend agreed to talk later.

When the conversation was finally over, Ray set the phone back in its cradle. He rubbed both ears with the heels of his hands and then shook his head. He felt as if his ears had silted up and he had to clear out all that verbiage. "At times the Reverend sounded like he was delivering a sermon, not just talking on the phone," Ray said.

Kick nodded.

"Kick, I get the feeling that Reverend Hummock isn't telling all he knows," Ray said.

"If he told all he knew, he'd be the exception to the 'clergy rule,'" she said. "I do think it's strange that he wanted to take your call on his cell phone at the church. And why did he change his church affiliation?"

"He told me his wife was Baptist," Ray said. "But I don't believe that's the real reason he changed denominations."

"Sorry, I remember you repeating that on the phone," Kick said. "You think he was just putting distance between himself and the murder?"

"It didn't work," Ray said.

"I'd sure like to catch Helen home alone," Kick said.

"It's too soon," Ray said. "You'd spook Hummock. And besides, I want to keep all lines open with him for now."

Later in the afternoon, Kick had to go out for a dentist's appointment. When she came back, she was surprised Ray's car was still parked by the curb. Inside, Ray was in his office, staring at what Kick always called Ray's "Wall of Fame." On it were hung his degree in Clinical Psychology from the University of Chicago, his certificate as a Life Fellow of the American Psychotherapy Association, and his Distinguished Corporate Community Service Award from Purdue University.

Years after he finished school, he finally took the advice of a college professor and took up writing. All of his various professions, combined with a lot of his business experience, had served him well. In Ray's mind, studying people, analyzing situations, and figuring things out made it possible for him to take what was complex and break it down into something simple. Simple enough to be understood. Ray believed that, in the long run, it was an appreciation of the simple things, or common sense, that carried most people through life.

What troubled him were the times when people acted contrary to common sense.

He had trouble getting it to sink in that Ronda Jo didn't want to know who it was that tried to revive her daughter — in her case, the only natural daughter she and her husband would ever have.

The local papers didn't mention, let alone name, the passerby but the Keysville newspaper did. Ray had since interviewed dozens of folks in Penn County who knew the passerby by name. For Ronda Jo not to know the name was beyond the pale. Everyone Ray talked to agreed with him on this.

Ray leaned back in his chair, propping his feet up on the desk. "Ronda Jo said she didn't need to know who killed her daughter. She said *they* know," Ray reiterated.

"What's that supposed to mean?" Kick said.

"You tell me," Ray said.

"At first, Reverend Hummock said that Ronda Jo didn't have any idea who killed Trudie. Then later he said she thought the Englishman did it," Kick said.

"Two contradictions in one conversation," Ray said. "If someone brought your lost dog back home, wouldn't you want to know who it was?"

"Yes, I'd want to know who it was that returned anything of mine," Kick said.

"She said that her daughter's murder wasn't any of my business," Ray said.

"You've got to forget about the case for a while," Kick said. "Let's go fishing."

The lake was calm. Ray sat up front in the bass boat, watching for floating logs and stumps. He took a deep breath, smelling the scents coming off the lake and the shore. Ray's stomach growled as the smell of bacon hit his nostrils. Someone was having breakfast.

Kick lowered the throttle on the outboard motor. Gas fumes camouflaged the aromas.

"Want to troll or hit the banks?" Kick asked.

"Neither, take me to the falls. We'll plug for the bass in the rocks," Ray said.

"How should I rig you up?" Kick said.

"Spin bait," Ray said.

"I'm going with a rubber worm," Kick said. "Texas rigged."

"Spin bait," Ray repeated.

"Dollar on first fish," Kick said.

"Another dollar on biggest," Ray said.

"I got one," Kick said.

Ray watched as she played the fish, running it into the fishing net. Ray pressed his thumb down on its lower lip, held it up for her to see, then carefully worked the barb out and released it.

"You know, Kick, if Ronda Jo would talk to me, I know I could get her to come to closure. Her anger and grief must give her great pain," Ray said.

"She's hiding something, something scandalous," Kick said. "Too defamatory for her to bear."

"That's her problem. There's nothing so shocking that folks wouldn't forgive her," Ray said. "It might take time, but they'd forgive her. After all, the death of a child is something every one would understand."

"Especially a mother," Kick said.

"Yes," Ray said.

Ray raised the anchor.

"You owe me two bucks," Kick said.

"Better owing than never paying," Ray laughed.

"I'm going to type up your notes after we get back to

the house so you can read over them," Kick said.

"I'm going to smoke a cigar and fish off the pier," Ray said.

Ray came in a few hours later as Kick was finishing entering her notes on the laptop.

"I forgot to tell you," Ray said. "I talked to a defense attorney about Detective Skipper not being sure if he could discuss an open murder case. He assured me that there's no statute, and no rule of law that would prevent a retired officer from talking about the case. Skipper became nothing more than a witness when he retired."

"No exceptions?" Kick asked.

"With the law, there always is. He could be stopped from talking if he were a key witness in a current investigation, if the judge had issued a gag rule, but that's pretty much it," Ray said.

"Makes sense to me. Just because he used to be the Sheriff doesn't mean he can issue a traffic ticket now that he's retired," Kick said.

"That would be some kind of chaos, wouldn't it?" Ray said.

"Ex-officers performing arrests? Oh my," said Kick, making a silent whistling sound.

"If you ask me, Kick, Detective Lou Skipper is hiding something," Ray said. "Reverend Hummock said he believed the detective was a tippler."

"I think he's hiding a number of things," Kick said. "Some of which pertain to Trudie Brice, some of which don't."

Things were quiet then for a while. Back at the company office, Ray went into his own office with Kick's notes and clippings and kept to himself for most of the day. In the afternoon, he came to the door to bring Kick up to date. "I called Reverend Storm this morning. I thought that maybe his wife might remember something else that would help us," Ray said.

"Does he know you talked to her?" Kick asked.

"I guess," Ray said. "Why?"

"What were you after?" Kick asked.

"I asked him if Ronda Jo was an attractive woman back then. He said, 'I didn't find her to be.' I laughed and said, 'Okay, Reverend, who've you been talking to.' He didn't sound like himself. He said Reverend Hummock e-mailed him, wanting to know why Emily told me what Ronda Jo said — that Hummock was attracted to her. Reverend Storm said that Hummock was concerned about his reputation."

"Maybe he should have been a little more concerned about that when he lived in Hampton," Kick said.

"I told Storm that Hummock ought to be thanking me. After all, plenty of people in Hampton thought that he had something to do with the murder and that's why he left town so quickly," Ray said. "It would be better for him if people just think he left because he was fooling around."

"Maybe Reverend Storm was upset that you gave his wife away," Kick said.

"Too bad. You know I told Emily that I'd use her

name, same as I tell everyone. There's been way too much secrecy in this case from the get go," Ray said.

"Maybe the Reverend is concerned about the brotherhood," Kick said.

"They're not in the same denomination," Ray said.

"I mean the brotherhood of pastors," Kick said.

"I don't really care about his personal affairs. I'm only concerned about finding Trudie's killer," Ray said. "I wonder why Hummock is covering his tracks, because that's what he seems to be doing. Damage control. Before I hung up with him, he wanted to know if I had Ronda Jo's telephone number."

"What did you tell him?" Kick asked.

"I told him no," Ray said.

"You know you do have it, don't you," Kick said.

"I didn't remember," Ray said.

Kick tracked down a retired captain from the Penn County Sheriff's Department. He wasn't much help — he just recalled newspaper stories and gossip like everybody else. He remembered helping search the area in a helicopter, flying over nearby fields, looking for the missing telephone. So there were two search parties, Ray thought, this one and the one on the ground by Les and the Chief of Police. According to the retired captain, nothing of interest was ever found. He told Kick it would be a good thing if the Brice case could be solved. It had turned people suspicious. Among other concerns, they were afraid they might still have a murderer living amongst them.

A week later, Kick received a voice mail message from the retired captain saying that he'd done some checking but since the case was still open, he couldn't provide her with any further information. His message ended wishing Kick and Ray the best of luck.

"That was kind of encouraging, seems to me," Kick said. "Maybe he was sending a signal we should keep digging."

"Someone got to him, maybe the Sheriff or the Prosecutor," Ray said.

"Good ol' boys at what they do," Kick said.

Ray walked away, thinking about the next move.

The more he thought about it, the more Ray decided that the captain was teasing him or putting him in his shoes. The captain seemed to be suggesting that he knew something but that Ray couldn't get it out of him. Or, Kick suggested, maybe he'd been told to keep quiet by someone higher up. It didn't really matter because Ray was too determined to buy into his story totally. Trudie Brice deserved it and so did those who loved her. So, indeed, did the whole community. The local people had been wounded by the crime and they needed to be healed.

Ray decided to do an end around. For the moment, he'd learned as much as he could by trying to find out what the local citizens knew. Now, he had to find more people who had been directly involved. He had to get into the records.

"You really think they'll help?" Kick asked him.

Ray knew the value of primary sources — unless they had been faked or doctored.

Ray and Kick drew up a list of insiders who might have information. Sheriff Wiersma was one....

They struck gold right away. Kick called Ron Sellars, the former Penn County Coroner, who confirmed that a forensic pathologist in West Bend had performed a private autopsy on Trudie. He said the autopsy report would not be available to Ray. Kick continued the conversation and Sellars finally admitted that the Coroner's report was public record and could be requested through the current Penn County Coroner. At least three of Ray's questions would be answered once the report was received — when, where, and what. The who and why still needed to be figured out.

"Did Sellars give you a hard time?" Ray asked.

"Not at all," Kick said. "He even told me we could use his name when we made the request for the records."

"Kick, we need to continue on the same course that we started, discount all rumors that have nothing to do with the murder and eliminate any and all suspects who have an ironclad alibi. We need to keep gathering information on the key suspect," Ray said.

"What about Hummock?" Kick asked. She didn't trust the man.

"He says he was shopping in Ashbrook," Ray said.

"Do you believe him?" Kick asked.

"He's not a stupid man. His credit card records could be checked," Ray said.

"I wouldn't be surprised if he's lying," Kick said.

"To protect Ronda Jo?" Ray asked.

"No, to protect his own righteous self," Kick said.

"Not much doubt there was something going on between him and Ronda Jo. But what?"

"Okay, I guess that eliminates Reverend Hummock," Kick said. "As a suspect ..." she mumbled.

"Only as a suspect. I still believe he's got more information," Ray said.

Kick continued down the list of insiders. She tracked down a former Penn County patrolman. It turned out he was working in Champaign at the time of the Brice murder. He told Kick he didn't become a deputy in Penn County until 1988.

The only thing he'd heard about the Brice case was that a little girl drowned in a bathtub. He recalled that there had been a string of unsolved homicides in and around Penn County about the same time.

Kick told Ray the patrolman would have been a good one to interview, since he was now an attorney living outside the county.

"He wanted to help, but he knew nothing about the murder," Kick said.

"Calling on him was a waste of time then?" Ray said.

"Not really, he said one of the investigating detectives, Dick Fowler, was someone we should call on," Kick said.

"Why?" Ray asked.

"He said Fowler seemed like he lived with that case on his mind for a long time," Kick said.

"Add him to the list," Ray said.

Kick went to work calling other retired deputies and anyone else who might have attended the Christmas program at Hampton School the day Trudie died. She was looking for someone who might know the identities of the two law officers the passerby claimed he had been talking with just minutes before discovering the fire at the Brice home. The papers had mentioned them but never identified them. By now, Ray was beginning to wonder if these two unidentified law officers were something akin to a child's imaginary little friends.

She checked with a few local officers without much success. Finally, she got Wayne Dumas on the phone, the man Reverend Storm mentioned. He was a former patrolman with the Penn County Sheriff's Department back in 1986. Dumas told Kick he was off duty the day of the murder, but that he and his wife had attended the Christmas program at the Hampton School. He and his wife had been members of the Hampton Methodist Church. They knew the Brices, as well as Reverend Brett Storm and Reverend Billy Jack Hummock.

Dumas said he did not know who the two unidentified Penn County patrolmen were that the newspaper mentioned. Clearly they were officers who hadn't been at the Christmas program, because if they were, chances are good they would have said, Hello, Dumas told her. But he couldn't remember who all had been in the audience and who had not. "It's twenty years ago," Dumas said. "You'd have a hard time remembering who *was* there. You want me to tell you who *wasn't* there?" Dumas thought the question answered itself.

Kick asked Dumas if he remembered seeing Cleve Hauser at the program. He said he hadn't. "No one saw him," Dumas said.

Kick asked him if he was hazy about who was in the audience, how he knew that. Dumas remembered that one of Hauser's children was in the school musical. There had been a little incident. Dumas's wife had asked Mrs. Hauser where her "better half" was. Mrs. Hauser shrugged her shoulders and didn't answer. Dumas's wife made a comment to him that she thought it was rude of Mrs. Hauser; otherwise he wouldn't have remembered that Cleve hadn't been there.

Dumas told Kick that he believed Ray was wrong in thinking that the case could be solved. He told Kick that the person of primary interest at the time went back to Great Britain and was now deceased. Kick asked Dumas how he knew this. Dumas bragged about being an insider who heard bits and pieces of information while working at the Sheriff's Department back then. He was proud that he had a good memory. Kick thought that if Dumas said he was an insider, he was probably kidding himself. And how could he not know the Englishman's name, but know that he had died?

Kick wrote to the Indiana State Fire Marshall requesting any available records pertaining to the investigation of the Brice fire. The Chief of Investigations didn't send records. Criminal investigative reports were not public record and any more detail would require a proper subpoena. The chief did write a little summary from what he looked up in the file. He said that the conclusion of the officers who examined the scene was that the fire was determined to be malicious in origin. It had been started on a mattress in a bedroom with a sloped ceiling.

Kick put the letter in her binder and let out a sigh. She'd hoped to get more information. She'd come to another dead end.

"Don't worry about that letter, Kick," Ray said. "It just backs up what we suspected. The eyewitnesses, or at least people who were on the scene, have already given us enough to know it was arson. In fact, I have a feeling the fire was started with a log from the wood burning stove. Only we don't know exactly when it was started."

"How long does it take for a mattress to burn?" Kick asked. It was the kind of thing Ray often had an answer to. This time he didn't. But he knew how to find out. "I want you to check when mattresses first became fire retardant," he said.

"That's going to take some time, plus I'll need the manufacturer's name," Kick said.

"I don't think so, fast fingers. Your computer will have all the information we need," Ray said.

Kick Googled mattresses.

Kick went over her notes, checking to see if all the calls she was supposed to make were made. She made a second list of all the voice mail calls that hadn't been returned. She was just about to scratch Josie and Garrett Kreps off her list when Ray walked into her office.

"What's the story on that Josie lady and her attorney husband, what's his name?" Ray said.

"I've left several messages and never got a call back," Kick said.

"Maybe she was talking out of turn when she accepted my invitation for her and her husband to come out to the lake house," Ray said.

"I think you're right. She told me she wanted to get together after a couple weeks. They're well into the school year now," Kick said.

"I'll say this, our time wasn't totally wasted," Ray said. "She told us the Christmas play was on Thursday, not Friday. Dina Schwin had gotten it wrong the first time. Now we need to find someone who actually remembers seeing Cleve there. Wayne Dumas says Hauser absolutely was not."

"Josie didn't?" Kick asked.

"Nope," Ray said. "Here's what I think. Teachers meet in the school lounge, drink coffee, smoke cigarettes, and gossip — mostly about each other. I think Josie and her husband didn't want to get involved with what we're doing. It's too controversial; plus the fact that her husband has a law practice in town. When he found out that we weren't playing some kind of crime-solving board game, so to speak, but that I had factual information on who the killer was, he bailed."

"Attorneys do like cases that are iffy, ones that can go either way," Kick said.

"Do I detect a little sarcasm?" Ray said.

"The Kreps are scratched," Kick replied.

Chapter 5

The letter to the Fire Marshall turned out not to have been a dead end after all. Indiana State Police Cold Case Detective Tim Fields told Kick he got her name from the Penn County Prosecutor.

Kick cupped her hand over the telephone receiver. "Boss, a detective from the Indiana State Police is on the phone," she said. "He heard you were working on the Brice case."

"How'd he know?" Ray asked.

"He talked to somebody," Kick said.

"You take it," Ray said.

"No, he wants to speak to you," Kick said.

Detective Fields said he was going to be receiving a

written request from the Penn County Prosecutor to review copies of the Sheriff Department's case file. The Detective indicated that he already received a verbal request to give a read on the Brice murder.

"Why did you call me about this?" Ray asked. It didn't entirely make sense.

Fields had to admit that they didn't know how much good information the authorities had. Pure and simple, he wanted to find out what Ray knew.

Ray briefed Detective Fields on his research. He pointed out the inconsistencies in the stories that had been reported about the events of the day Trudie Brice was murdered. He agreed to send the detective a copy of his map. Detective Fields wanted to see all of Ray's records. Ray agreed to meet with Detective Fields once Fields had an opportunity to review the case files. Ray wanted his word that they would share each other's files. After the lake house interview with Sheriff Wiersma, give and take was what Ray was looking for, not just take.

Detective Fields was curious why Ray was conducting this investigation. Ray told him the truth — that he felt Trudie wanted it. He mentioned that people around Hampton still wondered about it.

Detective Fields assumed that Ray thought the murderer was still living in the community. He told Ray if that was so he thought it strange that the killer hadn't killed again in the past twenty years. Ray thought it strange that Fields would say such a thing. He wondered if the Detective was trying to draw him out. Ray reminded the

Detective of the other unsolved murders in Penn County.

"Maybe the killer did them too," Ray said. "It's difficult to get into the mind of a psychopath."

They agreed to talk later. Ray hung up the phone and turned to Kick.

"Now there's a lie that caught up with the Sheriff," Ray said.

"What's that?" Kick asked.

"If the State Police were originally asked to participate in the Brice murder case, they'd already have copies of the files," Ray said.

"You kind of knew that already," Kick said.

"Now I know for sure," Ray said.

Ray's poking around had caught the attention of the authorities. That afternoon, Ray went to work sharing the good news of his phone call from the Cold Case Detective with a few of the locals, the first being Ted Morrow. Ted was impressed. If Ray was negotiating with the State Police, being called into the case as a partner gave Ray credibility. Ted said he would pass along the information to the breakfast crowd in Hampton. It was just what Ray was hoping he would do. This was better than being deputized by Sheriff Wiersma. Ray thought it would encourage more people to talk with to him.

Ted then told Ray that he had previously overheard Cleve Hauser at one of the marts in town bragging about all the people he had killed in Vietnam while on a tour of duty in the Army.

Ray asked who Cleve was telling the story to. Ted said he didn't know the couple. Ray didn't press the issue.

The bar at the Winners' Circle was filled two deep with people on every stool and standing room only behind them. Most of the regulars were either talking too low or too loud to hear any particular conversation. Off to the side sat the cigarette-scarred piano. The piano man's fingers tickled the keyboard, filling the room with soft jazz. The back wall was lined with leather appointed booths, from which every area could be seen. It usually took a fifty to the maitre d' to dine or drink in the lounge. The hungry and the hurried preferred either of the two large dining rooms. Word was that the owner always kept one booth reserved for Ray. Nobody asked why.

Though Ray loved the country, the city was his home.

"You know, Kick, the Sheriff was a bit pretentious," Ray said.

"He seemed friendly," Kick said. "Though maybe a little bit stuck on himself."

"He treated me like an outsider," Ray said. "He thought he could get away with lying to me."

"You are an outsider," Kick said.

"Not really," Ray said. "We're lodge brothers."

"From different lodges," Kick said. "Besides, didn't you say every fraternity has both its good and bad members?"

"Forget it," Ray said.

"No, go on," Kick motioned with her hand.

Ray tossed down a glass of golden-hued rye and

rattled the melting ice cubes. Kick waited.

"The Sheriff lied about the State Police cold case detectives. They were never invited in on the Brice murder," Ray said.

Kick bit on a jagged cuticle.

"Do you have anything to say?" Ray asked.

"We've been over this before," Kick said.

"That's what I do, go over and over, again and again," Ray said.

"Okay then, he probably also lied about the FBI checking the evidence and reading the case files," Kick said. "No wonder the Feds never answered my letter to them."

"There's your answer," Ray said. "They had no knowledge of the case. The FBI that I know doesn't look for work."

Kick's eyes narrowed. She thought that her letter had triggered everything that had followed, including the call from Detective Fields.

"Hold on, Kick, let me think," Ray said.

Kick sat back and watched the piano man mouth the lyrics as his fingers floated across the ivory.

The next day, Ray contacted Reverend Hummock about his e-mail message to Reverend Storm. Ray told Reverend Hummock he thought it unusual that the Reverend would keep track of and inquire about Ray's investigation after all his years away from Indiana. Reverend Hummock told Ray he was still unhappy about what Emily Storm claimed

Ronda Jo said about him. According to the Reverend, either Ronda Jo or Emily lied. After all, he was still a minister and had a reputation that needed to be upheld. Ray assured him it was only girl-talk between the two and that Emily was only trying to be helpful. Kick listened as Ray spoke. She choked on Ray's girl-talk remark. Ray handed her a bottle of water and motioned her to zip up.

Ray asked a couple of questions that he knew would get the Reverend going. It didn't take long before Hummock was reviewing the whole case.

Reverend Hummock reiterated to Ray that he was certain Ronda Jo didn't have lunch at home the day Trudie was murdered. He remembered Ronda Jo saying that she just dropped by to check on Trudie and make sure the wood burning stove was filled up with enough wood. Reverend Hummock also confirmed the Brice's telephone was on the kitchen wall.

When asked about the dog, Reverend Hummock confirmed that it was Trudie's guardian and when it wasn't following her, it would lay by her side.

Ray told Reverend Hummock that he was still searching for Tammy Lemel. And he'd heard some things about the Englishman's whereabouts that he wanted to verify. Ray had a feeling that the Reverend either knew where Tammy was or was withholding information until he could get in touch with Ronda Jo to find out what was going on.

Strangely enough, the mention of Tammy Lemel stopped the usually talkative Reverend. He apologized, saying he had to take another call.

"Is he going to get back with you?" Kick asked.

"I'm not holding my breath," Ray said. "I think I hit a nerve."

"I called Wayne Dumas again," Kick said. "He didn't know who the passerby was. He also didn't know that Reverend Hummock was once a suspect. And get this, when I told him you were going to be working with the Indiana State Police, he boasted that he was the reason the State Police called you in the first place. He told a lieutenant detective from the Sheriff's Department that you were snooping around, trying to get information and he thought they should know. I told him it was no secret."

"Scratch him off your call list. He knows nothing about the case and he's just kissing up to feel important and get a couple of 'good boys,'" Ray said.

"Do you think it was Detective Skipper who told the Prosecutor about you?" Kick asked.

"I have no idea. He said he was going to talk to the Prosecutor and that's still fine with me. As long as the case moves forward, I'm not going to concern myself with things I have no control over," Ray said. "Anyway, I'm not in the secrets-keeping business. If there were fewer secrets around here, things would be a whole lot healthier."

"Just the same, if it was Detective Skipper who called the Prosecutor, then Detective Skipper's holding out on us, too," Kick said.

"Would that surprise you?" Ray said.

Ray took Kick out to lunch. They sat in a booth near the window. It would not have been Ray's first choice. He preferred privacy. Kick preferred sunlight.

"I called Martha Mann," Kick said. "She sent her best to you."

"Why did you call her?" Ray asked.

"Because I wanted to see if she was any relation to the Manns who currently live in the Brice house."

"Funny that never occurred to me," Ray said. "Is she?"

"No," Kick said. "But she'd like to talk to you."

Martha, or Marti, as her friends called her, was a good-looking woman with plenty of spunk and spirit. Ray and Kick first met her when Ray was looking to buy a piece of property up the road from Marti and her husband's house. At the time, Ray thought that his grandfather owned property close by, if not the Manns' property itself. Kick searched old surveys and proved Ray wrong.

That afternoon, Ray and Kick drove out to Marti Mann's house. They sat down at the kitchen table to talk. The kitchen was at the back of the house where you couldn't see the road. There was a big oak tree at the far end of the yard. The room was sunny and comfortable. Marti was a good cook and there was the scent of baking in the room. Ray took out his tiny spiral notebook and doodled, or wrote down a word or two once in a while.

Ray gave Marti a run-down of his investigation. She

remembered the Brice murder well and without being asked, blurted out the passerby's name. She thought most everyone knew it. Her neighbors were also suspicious of Hauser. Marti said a friend of hers inside the Sheriff's Department told her that Hauser was a suspect. Like Dorothy Johnson, the librarian, Marti thought Hauser was strange. Really strange.

Marti told Ray about a time she was out in her front yard trimming bushes when Cleve Hauser drove his truck by her house at a crawl. She was pretty sure he was looking at her, looking hard. It unnerved her so much that she ran back into her house and phoned her sister. Marti remembered telling her sister that if anything happened to her, it was Cleve Hauser who did it. Marti was not the kind of woman who usually gets panicky. So her reaction to Hauser was extreme for her.

On another occasion, Marti and her husband were at the American Legion in Hampton, having a couple of beers, when Cleve and his good buddy, Val White, a farmer, sat down with them. Val was his usual rattle-brained self, Marti said. Cleve was silent, so quiet it was eerie, she added. Marti said Cleve was a good-looking man back then.

Ray wanted to know what Marti could tell him about Detective Skipper. She said it was common knowledge that Detective Lou Skipper was a drinker, one of those kind of controlled drinkers who knows how to stay out of trouble. Whenever there was a police or a fire department party at the Legion, Detective Skipper would offer people a ride home so they'd be safe — a standing joke amongst the townsfolk since Detective Skipper was usually plastered at such functions. Detective Skipper and Hauser used to share their war stories at the Legion. It was one of the few things Cleve would open up about. Ray didn't need anyone to tell him that, he was a veteran himself and sometimes it was good therapy just to talk. He also knew that there were guys who could significantly exaggerate, if not outright invent, their wartime experiences. Ray could usually spot them pretty quickly. He wondered if Cleve was one of those yarn spinners.

While Marti talked, she went to the counter and got down a hand-painted china plate. She set out some fresh cookies from a jar she kept next to the canisters of flour and sugar — big oatmeal cookies. She arranged them in a circle with one in the center and set them down on the table.

Ray told Marti he was looking for a friend of Ronda Jo's, Tammy Lemel. The name didn't ring a bell. Marti mentioned that her friend, Pauline Graygo, a horse trainer and the owner of a shop in Hampton called Standard Saddle, might be able to help. Pauline was about the same age as Ronda Jo, Marti thought, they might have had friends in common. Marti said she would have Pauline contact Ray.

Marti said she and her husband lived in Hampton for over thirty years. She indicated that many folks thought the old bunch at the Sheriff's Department were like Keystone Cops. They were more amusing than helpful and it was a good thing that most of the time they had no major crimes to deal with. It was pretty appalling to see how they'd mishandled Trudie's murder. She knew one of the other detectives on the case, Dick Fowler. He came to her house six months after the murder, questioning her husband about where he'd been that day. Marti said she knew Detective Fowler was just doing his job, but it angered her that it took him six months to get around to it. Never mind the fact that her husband was the last man on the planet any person with good sense would question.

When they got back to the office, Ray tore a page out of his notebook and set it down on Kick's desk.

"Here, I jotted these names down," Ray said. "Pauline Graygo and Agnes Mann."

Kick was surprised when she saw the second name. "You want to talk to the woman who lives in the Brice house?"

"I think it's time to try," Ray said. "Might be good to look around, since it doesn't seem as though the police have done their job."

Chapter 6

Ray wasn't surprised to discover that Pauline Graygo was well thought of in and around Penn County. If Marti liked her, she had to be a good woman, trustworthy and honest to the core. She turned out to be a great asset. Thus far, Ray had had to rely on his own resources, dealing with the folks in the countryside. Once Pauline came aboard, Ray need only mention Pauline's name as a friend, fill people in on his investigation, then ask if they could remember anything that might bring him closer to solving Trudie's murder. Indications were that Pauline's name would help open quite a few doors.

Ray met Pauline at Standard Saddle on a Saturday. It was a pretty big operation. There was a barn that must have been able to hold a dozen horses plus an indoor ring. Pauline's daughter was giving lessons to a class of girl riders. Ray and Kick thought they'd never seen so much concentration and focus in human beings as they could see in these girls. Kick stopped to watch for a second while Pauline, apologizing for the fact that she was in work clothes, led Ray into her office and offered him a chair. Marti had called to vouch for Ray, so Pauline had made time in her schedule for him. Ray knew that running a stable was a very difficult job. He appreciated the fact that Pauline had a ready smile.

Pauline knew the passerby was Cleve Hauser. She said that Cleve was strange, the way he looked at you. She said it also wouldn't surprise her if it turned out he were the murderer. Most of the townies Ray talked to described Cleve in a negative way. In fact, there was an essentially uniform opinion about him, though he'd never been charged with anything. Ray wondered what it would be like to be held in such suspicion by a whole community.

Ray told Pauline that it would take the help of the citizens of Penn County to solve the Brice murder, especially since the Sheriff's Department appeared to be completely disinterested. For more than twenty years, they had chosen to exclude the public and to keep things "secret" with their files locked away, gathering dust. Ray often thought the evidence, if they actually had any, could get lost — that is if it weren't already contaminated.

Pauline, however, did have some new insights into

what had happened the day of the murder. She gave Ray the name of a man who she thought held a huge piece to the crime puzzle — Hugh Dixon. This was a new name to Ray and he wondered why nobody else had mentioned Dixon.

Pauline said she'd heard that Dixon spotted a car in the Brice driveway the day of the murder; but that was all Pauline knew. She couldn't remember the source. She'd heard the story right after the murder and it didn't seem important at the time. Later, as it became clear that the police were clueless about the murder, it stuck in her mind. No, she hadn't taken the story to authorities, there didn't seem to be much to it and she thought the police weren't much interested. Pauline said she'd get Dixon's phone number for Ray.

Ray mentioned to Pauline that he had hoped to get inside the Brice house. He wanted to get a picture of the layout, but he hadn't pushed the matter. He didn't know how much the owner knew about the murder. He didn't want to scare her. Pauline said she had always assumed that Agnes Mann knew — it would seem impossible for her not to hear stories, though it wasn't the sort of thing one would bring up. Pauline thought that she might be able to arrange a visit. Agnes was a client of hers. Her daughter was one of the little girls in the riding class. Pauline opened one of the drawers in her desk and pulled out an address book. She copied down Agnes Mann's number on a post-it note and handed it to Ray.

On the way back from the stable Kick asked Ray if

it was possible that they were being too hasty in zeroing in on Cleve. "Sometimes," Kick said, "a person attracts suspicion just because of rumors about them. That could certainly cause problems."

"People around here know that," Ray said. "They're like any community, they have their fair share of odd-balls. But you have to kind of admire the fact that they haven't all piled on Cleve. People in Hampton seem fair minded."

Ray tried several times to get Agnes on the phone without success. Tuesday afternoon, however, she called him back. She seemed pleasant enough but jittery, as if she thought she might be in some kind of trouble. Ray tried to reassure her. He didn't believe you could scare information out of people. Anyway he wasn't entirely sure Agnes had any information. As subtle as he could, he asked her if she knew "the history of the house." She said she did. She said she hadn't known at first and wished someone had told her.

Agnes gave Ray a general description of the layout of both floors. She confirmed Ray's belief that there was a wall phone in the kitchen. He asked a few questions about when she and her family moved in, fishing for information.

Abruptly she asked Ray for his opinion on something she'd been concerned about. "Do you believe in spirits?" she asked Ray.

"What kind of spirits," Ray said.

"You know, friendly spirits, hostile spirits, ones who have been wronged," Agnes said.

"Like ghosts?" Ray said.

"A little bit like ghosts," she said. "People misunderstand about ghosts. They make them into something silly. I mean spirits," she said again.

"I do," Ray said. "I believe in them."

She asked Ray if he thought Trudie's spirit was still in the house. Ray was caught a little off guard though the question didn't seem foolish. He said that he didn't think Trudie would haunt the place, in general. But he said Trudie just might be there for him if he were to visit the house.

Agnes said she always thought the master bedroom upstairs was where something awful took place. That certainly fit with Ray's theory.

He didn't put any pressure on her but at the end of the conversation, Agnes invited Ray and Kick to come into her home. She set up a time she was sure that the kids would be gone so they wouldn't be hounding her with questions or eavesdropping.

"I don't want them to have nightmares," Agnes said.

Whenever Ray called or met with someone referred to him by Pauline, he called Pauline and filled her in. He found that they usually called Pauline back afterwards. The next morning, Pauline said Agnes called to tell her she'd invited Ray to visit. Agnes was generally a very private woman so the invitation had not been a sure thing. Agnes told Pauline she thought Ray was sincere. She didn't quite say, though she probably thought it, that Ray might be someone who had a lot of knowledge and would be happy to share it.

At first, Pauline's other lead didn't appear to be so helpful. The day Kick called Hugh Dixon to set up a meeting with Ray, Hugh told her that Ray was "opening a can of worms" getting himself involved. Hugh said he always thought the whole Brice thing was "shady" as far as the police investigation went. Nevertheless, he was willing to talk. Ray got on the phone to set up a place and time. He was happy to meet Hugh anywhere. Hugh said he'd come to Ray's office. Ray again offered to meet somewhere more convenient, but Hugh wanted to come to the office.

He arrived that same afternoon. He'd come straight from work. Apparently Hugh tinkered with cars. Around his fingernails and the ends of his fingers there was grease ground deep into his skin. Once Hugh took a seat, he fidgeted. He was a big man and well worn, but his easy manner came out as the conversation drew on between Ray and him.

In his younger days, Hugh was one of Hampton's "bad boys," and somewhat of a ladies' man. His smile widened as he shared some of his old yarns with Ray and Kick.

Hugh wasn't ashamed of the fact that he wasn't school smart. He said he didn't have much use for authority figures. He thought most officials were on a power trip at other folks' expense. Not surprisingly, Hugh lacked formal education. He said when he was sixteen, his high school counselor told him he ought to consider quitting school and getting a job. He took the counselor's advice and dropped out. Hugh was blessed with common sense and street smarts, and he was a definite people person. Ray listened while Kick asked questions about some of the people Hugh talked about.

On the day of the murder, Hugh said he was driving home from work. He remembered slowing down when he noticed a green 1970's Old Cutlass with primed fenders parked in the driveway of the Brices. He knew it wasn't Stan Brice's, because Hugh went to school with Stan and he knew Stan wasn't "into that shit," he said. Hugh said Stan was one of the high-school "dorks," and not one to be driving a hopped-up car.

Hugh had left his bartending job at Harry's Place around lunchtime, so it was between noon and one o'clock that he saw the Olds Cutlass. After the murder, Hugh said he reported spotting the car to the Penn County Sheriff's Department. He said no one ever questioned him about the car and Hugh never saw it again, that is until 1991, five years after the murder.

He remembered working later than usual at Harry's Place. Around four in the morning, he was driving home when he spotted the same green Olds parked near the Hampton fire station. Hugh paid attention to cars and there was no mistaking this one for the one he'd seen before. Hugh said he got excited and drove all over town, searching for a police officer. He eventually found Officer

Spencer Logan who was driving up and down the streets, his radio tuned to an all-night country-music station.

Hugh reminded Logan of the conversation they'd had at the time of Trudie's death, when he saw the car parked in the Brice's driveway. Officer Logan remembered the incident, but, not surprisingly, was reluctant to send out an all points bulletin only because Hugh saw a car on the street that he'd recognized from five years earlier. Hugh said it was probably lucky for him that Officer Logan didn't ask him to take a breathalyzer test. Nevertheless, the next day the officer checked the car out. When Hugh went by the station, Officer Logan told Hugh that Mitch Wiersma owned the Olds Cutlass. He'd owned it for years. It was then that Hugh recalled selling Mitch a replacement engine for a Cutlass five or six years earlier.

"Wiersma?" Ray asked.

"Yep," Hugh said. "Sheriff Chip Wiersma's nephew."

In a roundabout way, Hugh hinted to Ray that Hampton people weren't always who they appeared to be. Whether he knew something he wasn't letting on, or suspicious of something he couldn't get a handle on, Hugh suggested there were many possibilities about what went on the day of the murder. Hugh said he was told that a guy named Springer was the one who doubled back to resuscitate Trudie. Hugh had verified the name by talking to "Shine" Nutt just before he showed up at Ray's place. Shine was one of the locals who seemed to conduct most of his business, whatever it was, in the local bars. His name had come up once or twice before and probably would again, Ray thought.

Like many of the people Ray spoke with, Hugh knew Trudie had been strangled with a cord. Many also expressed their anger about the murder, and the fact that it had never been solved or even officially acknowledged. It all sifted down into a real distrust of the local police. Hugh described Detective Skipper as a prick and his partner, Fowler, as a "Yes, sir" and "No, sir" man. Hugh knew more of the local goings-on than most of the folks around Penn County, a trait of most all bartenders.

As the conversation came to a conclusion, Hugh confided to Ray that he knew the details of Oldsmobile's final demise. He swore Ray and Kick to secrecy about the automobile's final resting place. Word was the car had been crushed at a Hampton scrap yard and hauled away on a flatbed truck somewhere out of the county. Hugh thought the story about what happened to the car was pretty significant. He had a very bad feeling about that particular car.

Both Kick and Ray had noticed that, genial as he was, Hugh spoke about the details of Trudie's murder with a lot of passion. Kick wasn't quite sure where that came from but Ray had a pretty good idea and he was right. Toward the end of the conversation, Hugh nearly broke down when he told them he thought that he might have made a difference if he had stopped at the Brice home that dreary December day in 1986 to check out the vehicle in the driveway. The unresolved murder had made a lot of people feel personally responsible. Many members of the community seemed to want to shoulder some of the blame because they believed that the crime shouldn't have taken place, that it was in their power, somehow, to have stopped it.

"You ever hear anything about a Guatemalan or an Englishman?" Ray asked.

"Never heard about the Guatemalan," Hugh said. "But the Englishmen were only interested in riding motor-cycles when they were here."

Ray looked over at Kick. She picked up his cue. Reverend Storm had only mentioned one Englishman. Now there were more?

After he drove off, Hugh called back from his cell phone and gave Kick the name of a colleague of Cleve Hauser's, a teacher named Gordon Wiggs. As an after-thought, he also told Kick that he remembered that Ronda Jo didn't have lunch with Trudie the day of the murder. He couldn't say how he knew that. He just knew.

"I talked to Nick Schwin," Ray told Kick the next morning. He'd been holed up in his office for a couple of hours and Kick had wondered what he was up to.

"You called him?" she asked.

"He called me," Ray said. "He said that he'd been thinking back. He thought it would be a lot harder to remember, but he took my suggestion and focused on some of the main people who investigated the murder."

"Seems like with such a big event you'd remember everything," Kick said.

"People do a lot of forgetting sometimes," Ray said. "Saves their sanity. Some memories are too painful."

Kick remembered Nick had had a pretty clear memory of events the first time Ray talked to him. She was surprised that he'd dug up more. She thought that maybe because of his daughter's friendship with Trudie, Nick felt particularly motivated to help Ray in his investigation.

"He said it might be of no importance whatsoever but in a small town like Hampton there weren't hardly any places that a person could go to get away on their own," Ray said. "It got him thinking that he would run into Detectives Skipper and Fowler from time to time, especially Fowler, since he was a neighbor. He figured the subject of the murder investigation would come up. He wanted to know what their thinking was but didn't think he'd get any information out of them if he asked straightforwardly."

"So he never brought it up?" Kick said.

"No, but they didn't either," Ray said. "He said neither of the detectives ever asked him about what he saw or heard about the Brice girl's murder. Nick thought it was strange since everyone knew his daughter was one of Trudie's best friends. He wondered why the police weren't trying harder to solve the case."

"So did you pick up anything else from what he said?" Kick asked.

"Yes. For a man who can remember that his family didn't lock their doors and would let a stranger in, don't you think it's strange that something as big as a murder in a small town *would* be a popular topic of conversation? Especially between a fireman and a detective who were on the scene at the same time," Ray said. "Nick's an observant and thoughtful guy, why wouldn't you question him? Nick said he could understand that during all the confusion at the time of the murder, the detectives might overlook interviewing the firemen, but after giving it some serious thought, he said it would really be a stretch for the Sheriff's Department *not* to talk to him about the murder over the last twenty-something years."

"He's right, you know," Kick said. "Does he have a theory why not?"

Ray just shook his head.

Ray was back in his office, going over again the photocopies from the newspapers that had been piling up. He'd paid little or no attention to the phone that had rung several times in the past couple of hours. After one such call, Kick stepped into the doorway. "Pauline spoke to Gordon Wiggs and he wants to meet with you," Kick said.

Apparently, Hugh Dixon had also talked to Pauline after his conversation with Ray. He told Pauline he'd given Gordon's name to Ray and she'd made a call. Pauline was continuing to be a valuable ally. Even more than that, Ray thought, his investigation was having a kind of ripple effect throughout the community. This was a good thing in itself.

"You know, Kick," Ray said, "I'd be more than happy to drop Cleve Hauser as the key suspect if the Sheriff could explain to me why Cleve put himself in a crime scene. Why'd he boast that to the Keysville paper? So far, every one of the professionals on site told me that he wasn't around."

"Apparently, you got Nick Schwin thinking," Kick said. "Anyway, Pauline told me that Gordon is very personable and a good friend of hers. She said he wants to tell you about a recent conversation he had with Cleve Hauser, something about how Cleve was once a suspect in the Brice girl's murder, but said he wasn't anymore."

"They're both teachers at Bloom?" Ray asked.

"Yes," Kick said.

"I wonder what makes Cleve feel he's exonerated?" Ray asked, "when there hasn't been any official interest in the case for years. He wasn't accused in the first place."

"Also, it seems as though Detective Skipper is lying low, he's not returning my calls," Kick said.

"I have a feeling he knows something and he ain't telling," Ray said.

"You mean something other than what's in the case files?" Kick asked.

"I'm not so sure everything went into the files. Detective Skipper and Hauser were both Vietnam vets and more than likely they had a few beers together at the American Legion from time to time," Ray said. "Another thing that crosses my mind is some of the main characters in this murder case have either died or moved out of the state."

"That happens all the time," Kick said.

"Not with Hoosiers. Seventy-seven percent of us who are born in Indiana stay," Ray said.

"That's a high number," Kick said.

"I think it would be even higher amongst individuals who served our state in some capacity," Ray said.

"You talking about Detective Skipper?" Kick asked.

"He was the Sheriff of Penn County for eight years after his detective stint," Ray said. "Then all of a sudden he moves his family to Florida, leaving all his friends behind."

"Kinda like that Kay at the museum,... Kay Ledbetter. She said she was good friends with Cleve, until you showed her how he couldn't have done what he said he did. Then all of a sudden she not only wasn't that good of a friend, but didn't know him that well," Kick said.

"Kay Ledbetter's just covering herself," Ray said. "I'm not talking about good or bad friends, but individuals who grew up together, remained in the same neighborhood, fought a war, came back, then took up where they left off — drinking beer and chasing women. It's hard for them to leave. Pulling up roots isn't natural and it hurts. They have to have very good reasons. Indiana gets a pretty strong hold on you. You never get that out of your system."

Ray turned his truck into Willow Grove Cemetery and stopped at Trudie's gravesite. He stared at the heart shaped stone, then pulled out his cell phone.

"Kick, go ahead and set up a meeting with Gordon Wiggs," Ray said.

Gordon Wiggs pulled into the drive of Ray's lake house in a late-model Cadillac. He got out of the car and walked to the front door. Once inside, Gordon declined a cup of coffee or even water. He sat on the edge of the couch, glancing at the map that Ray had laid out on the coffee table. He was a thin man with a cowlick. He looked like a teacher.

Gordon ducked the conversation Ray was trying to start. He began relaying a story about how his daughter's husband had recently passed away at thirty-three years old. He spoke of the incompetence of Penn County paramedics, the Penn County Sheriff's Department, and the County Coroner to save the young man. Then, for a while, he talked about his Harley Davidson.

When Gordon finished talking about the Harley, he brought up the subject of his recent divorce. Ray decided to try harder to focus the interview. He pushed the map closer to Gordon. Ray pointed to the map and began explaining, in detail, the time frames.

Gordon's attention went from the map to a conversation he remembered having with Cleve Hauser a few years back in his office at Bloom High School. They were reminiscing about a long, on-going murder investigation in a town not far away. Then the subject of other unsolved murders in the area popped up. Gordon said when the Brice murder was mentioned, Cleve bragged that the Penn County Sheriff's Department had him as a suspect in it. Gordon said he asked Cleve, Well, did you do it? Gordon said he was just jerking Cleve's chain. Cleve was a man with not enough excitement in his life and he was capable of exaggeration. Cleve didn't answer and walked out of Gordon's office. Gordon was surprised he took offense.

Gordon described Cleve as an "old maid" — the type with a lot of time on his hands. "He always wants to talk, talk, talk," Gordon said. He also described Cleve as a con-guy, using the example that Cleve could sell a neighbor a tractor that he knew would blow its engine within the next six months and think nothing of it.

Talk in the teacher's lounge from time to time was that the teachers kept their fingers crossed that Cleve would go bug someone else. According to Gordon, Cleve was a person who liked to eavesdrop on anyone's conversation so he could be "in the know" of all the gossip and rumors.

Gordon said that Cleve quit Hampton school because Cleve said he needed more money and more freedom. "That's why Cleve resigned and went to work at a feed and seed company as a sales rep about a year before the Brice girl's murder," Gordon said. "It allowed him to roam the countryside." It also gave Cleve bragging rights about his new job, no longer having to work long hours for short wages as a teacher. "Those who can, do," Cleve said one night within Gordon's hearing. "Those who can't, teach." This attitude did not win Cleve friends amongst his former colleagues.

The sales job didn't work out. The story goes that Cleve was getting pressure by his competition and decided to go back to a teaching job — this time at Bloom High School. According to Gordon, Cleve did just enough to get by at Bloom. Cleve was also a teaching aide in Bloom High's farm husbandry program. "Just the right job for a lazy teacher," Gordon said. He wasn't any more popular amongst students than he was with faculty. One of the kids started calling him "WAS." The other kids picked it up. The principal finally called a few of them into the office and told them to cut it out. That didn't change the students' feelings, though.

As Gordon warmed up, he got more emotionally involved. Ray felt that there was a lot of bad feeling bottled up inside Gordon. Probably some of it right now could be attributed to his ex-wife, or the fact that he was getting old and still struggling to make a living. But Gordon also had a lot of resentment about various acquaintances. Kick offered Gordon a glass of water again and he accepted.

Gordon said Cleve recently attended the funeral of a man who was also a Vietnam veteran. Gordon inquired about what had happened to the man. Cleve just shrugged his shoulders and said, "He was just like the rest of us Nam vets, his head filled with bad stuff from the war." Gordon said it was pretty much the same comment Cleve made about another friend, a veteran, who committed suicide a year earlier. Cleve was happy to share with you the most minute details of his own inconveniences and misfortunes, but when it came to the sufferings of others, he was unmoved.

In the back of his mind, Ray remained puzzled. All

versions of Cleve he had received could be summarized, as Kick said, by the moniker "weird as shit" that Kick had come up with, although the stories didn't fit together. Some, especially men, said Cleve was a talker at times. The women found him withdrawn and eccentric. Maybe Cleve was different in different sorts of company.

Ray thought Gordon might be able to give him some hard evidence, not just of what Cleve seemed like, but of what he was capable of doing. For example, could he commit arson?

Gordon said that being an Agriculture teacher, Cleve would know how to mix gasoline and diesel fuel to start certain types of fires — slow burners or flare-ups. He'd even given Gordon some advice on brush burning. Gordon said Cleve told him about how he would sit in his basement, stoking his wood burning furnace while drinking cherry mash and whiskey.

Gordon mentioned how Cleve could, at times, make sense when he spoke, while at other times Cleve would ramble on. Sometimes Cleve would say nothing even if spoken to. This matched Dorothy Johnson's story.

Gordon said that it wouldn't blow his mind if he were to find out that Hauser had murdered the little Brice girl. Ray asked why. Gordon said Cleve seemed so flippant about death. After the death of Gordon's young son-in-law, Cleve told Gordon, "Your daughter's young, she'll land another one."

Cleve also shrugged off the recent death of a farmer and cut off Gordon's comments at the farmer's funeral.

According to Gordon, Cleve was a very detached man.

This struck Ray as odd. It seemed to him that most people, suspecting a local citizen of a heinous crime would do something about it — talk to the police, start a petition. If nothing else, they'd keep their distance, stop treating the suspected murderer as a friend. Gordon and many others had tolerated Cleve, despite his eccentricities, though he had every right and reason to think ill him.

Pauline called Ray to give him some of the scuttlebutt going around town. She said that Cleve Hauser had recently paid a visit to a retired farmer's home, a friend of hers. Cleve asked him if anything new was going on in town. Cleve wanted to know the local gossip.

The farmer was surprised to see Cleve since he hadn't heard from him in five or six years. He knew Cleve had been around, but they hadn't crossed paths. Why would Cleve be looking for information as if he'd been away? The farmer had no idea what Cleve was getting at, then, out of the blue, Cleve told him that he sees his granddaughter, a junior, at Bloom High School. Cleve seemed to know a lot about the girl. He admired the way she looked and talked. He wondered if she had a boyfriend. The farmer felt uneasy about the conversation because Cleve never once mentioned the farmer's grandson who went to the same school.

The farmer felt helpless, as if he didn't know what to do. But if Cleve laid one finger on his granddaughter, he would be looking down the business end of the farmer's double-barrel shotgun.

The farmer remembered a hunting incident involving a friend of his who was hunting with his son. Cleve ran them off his property with his shotgun. The farmer's friend told him that Cleve threatened to shoot them, but Cleve's buddy, Val White, intervened.

The farmer was uncomfortable enough about Cleve's visit that he called his daughter, a teacher's aide at Bloom, and told her to keep an eye on the granddaughter.

The farmer suspected, as many folks in the community were now convinced, that Cleve had something to do with Trudie's murder.

Pauline also told Ray that she had talked to Ronda Jo's sister-in-law, Trudie's aunt. The sister-in-law told Pauline that Ray was the answer to her prayers.

"I gave her your private phone number," Pauline said. "For some reason, she wouldn't give hers out."

Ray thought it best to wait for the sister-in-law to call him. Maybe she could add another piece to the puzzle — she *was* family.

Ray and Kick drove over to Agnes Mann's residence — the old Brice place. It looked as though no one was home, the driveway was empty and there were no lights on inside.

"You sure you got the right day?" Ray asked.

"I'm sure. Let's come back in an hour," Kick said.

When they dropped back by the Manns', no one answered the door, although there was now a car parked in the driveway. Ray decided that he and Kick should head back to the office.

They had gone a couple of miles down the road when Ray's cell phone rang. Kick was driving so Ray took the call. He didn't say much. When he hung up, she glanced at him.

"That was Agnes's husband. He said he and Agnes had to run some errands. That's why they weren't home," Ray said.

"So are we going back another day?" Kick asked.

"He said he decided he didn't want to get involved, what with Agnes being pregnant and having the other five children to worry about. He said things were going good for them and he didn't want to upset anything," Ray said.

"He's scared," Kick said.

"He thanked me when I told him I understood," Ray said.

"What do you think he's scared about?" Kick asked.

A few days later, Ray went out to the lake house to start closing things up. He'd had new Pella windows installed and he hoped that would keep the place warmer in the winter and cooler in the summer. The installation had gone better than expected. There were blinds in between the thermopane windows, enabling Ray to throw out the sun-faded hanging curtains. The contractor told Ray to make a list if anything concerned him. So far, the list was blank.

While he was there, his cell phone rang. Ray had left it inside and didn't hear the call come in. Before he got into the car to leave, he returned the call.

When he went back into the office, Kick was there. He was eager to tell her what he'd found out.

"Pauline contacted a Keith Hartsock," Ray said. "Keith lives a few towns over. He once owned the Brice house. He and his wife lived there for six months, then divorced and went their separate ways. She said Keith was going to give me a call. I want to know more about that wall phone in the kitchen."

"Now you can find out about the inside of the house," Kick said. She was glad that Agnes's husband wasn't going to have the power to veto their investigation.

When Keith called Ray, late that afternoon, he was more than willing to offer what help he could. Keith said he moved away from Hampton some time ago. He was also once a Hampton police officer himself, though not at the time of the Brice murder. Keith accused most of the Hampton cops of being crooked as hell back then.

Keith knew the first paramedic on the crime scene, Joe Fletcher. Ray jotted down the name.

Keith said he replaced the phone in the kitchen himself, though the original backboard was still in place. He also wallpapered the kitchen, redid the kitchen floor, installed a new window at the back of the house and remodeled the entire downstairs bathroom. The old tub, toilet, and vanity were disposed of. Keith said he kept some photos of the inside of the house, as it was when the

Brices lived there. He promised to mail them to Ray.

Keith said the first family to move into the Brice home after the murder had kids that used to say that Trudie's ghost pinched their butts whenever they misbehaved.

Ray found out what he wanted to know about the phone. It was as he thought.

Chapter 7

Ray sometimes felt he was repeating things to people, but he didn't get frustrated. Every new call from an earlier contact, every name that came back around, turned up some new bit of evidence.

Kick heard the phone ring in Ray's office and a few minutes passed. Then he came to the door to let her in on his conversation.

"Junebug called," Ray said. "He heard that the detective from the Indiana State Police contacted us."

"Good to know the line of communication is still working," Kick said.

"Yeah, he also said he heard I was still stirring up the

shit in Penn County," Ray laughed.

Junebug was actually pretty cooperative. He might have been expected to be more competitive. For a long time, people in town, like Del for example, had considered him the expert on the Brice case. Now Ray was becoming the expert. Junebug still liked to think of himself as the go-to guy when it came to the Brice case. If he was going to relinquish his reputation for insider knowledge, he decided he'd have to start working with Ray.

"Did he remember seeing that paramedic at the murder scene?" Kick asked.

"No. Junebug knows him, but thought Joe must have arrived later," Ray said. "Running into Junebug was a lucky break."

"Not luck, serendipity," Kick reminded Ray.

Ray nodded.

It was only a day or so later that Junebug's call paid off. The phone rang and Kick handed it to Ray, whispering, "Fletcher, the paramedic."

Ray was glad Fletcher had called so quickly. Fletcher's name hadn't come up until Ray talked to Keith. He could be pretty important.

Joe Fletcher said he thought the first law officer on the scene was Bud Lackey, Hampton's Chief of Police. Since the murder took place outside the city limits, Joe knew the Penn County Sheriff's Department would eventually take charge.

Fletcher arrived around 3:45 p.m. He remembered

the time because he was supposed to take his youngest son deer hunting that day and the high school's final bell was at 3:30 p.m.

Joe spoke as a corpsman. He seemed like the kind of man who wanted to be sure he'd been understood completely. He said by the time he arrived, someone had already taken Trudie out of the bathtub and laid her body outside the bathroom along the kitchen wall. Her head faced west and she was on her right side, Joe said. He was absolutely sure of that. He paused for a moment, then said he remembered that someone had thrown an orange colored throw rug over her nude body.

Joe then described Trudie's condition. He said her skin was pale blue and her eyes were already bulging. Her tongue stuck out of her mouth and had already begun to discolor. As routine, he pressed on her neck arteries. He knew he'd feel nothing and he didn't. Trudie's body had the stiffness of death. Joe choked up then continued on. He said he didn't try to revive her because of her condition. Vomit was still foaming out of her mouth from the strangulation. The cord marks were deep. Joe said he knew she had been murdered even before he did the medical procedures.

Joe had been a medic in Vietnam, so death was no stranger to him. However, he wasn't used to having to treat children who'd been the victims of violent crime. He'd gone to war to protect kids at home like his own kids. Joe let out a deep breath and concluded by saying that Trudie was a sweet girl and he hoped Ray could get this crime solved, something that was long overdue. Joe was another person, Ray thought, who'd been wounded by the murder, who still hadn't come to terms with it.

Things were quiet for a few days. Ray was going over Kick's notebooks, lists of names, newspaper clippings, transcripts. Sometimes he wished he could bring along a tape recorder when he talked with people but he knew that almost everyone is intimidated when they know they're being recorded. They clam right up.

Going over the notes, Ray was noticing a pattern. People he talked to face-to-face could generally be pretty cooperative. Getting information from public officials, on the other hand, could be tricky. Individuals who held any public office were usually unwilling to forward documents. They first had to try to figure out why the requester wanted them in the first place — even if they were told the reason up front. They were very reluctant to supply the answers to exactly those questions Ray needed to have answered.

Unlike many people who bang their heads against doors that won't open, Ray realized that it was in the nature of public officials to be evasive and also protective because of possible legal entanglements; but of most concern was their job security. Requesting the Coroner's reports from the time of Trudie's murder proved Ray's beliefs correct.

He stood in the doorway looking at an item in one of Kick's notes.

"When did you first contact the Coroner, Kick?" Ray asked.

"I mailed him a formal request back in August," Kick said.

"What did you say in your letter?" Ray asked.

She turned her chair to face him. "I said you were a writer investigating a cold case murder," Kick said. "And I told him that you believed it could be solved. He agreed, so I don't get why he's not sending the stuff."

"How long has it been since you've heard from him, or have you?" Ray asked.

"He called back once, but it's been nearly five weeks now," Kick said. "I've left a few voice messages since then."

"Both Ted Morrow and Pauline Graygo mentioned to me that he had a heart attack," Ray said.

"That's been a while back," Kick said. "He's recovered and been back on the job for some time now."

"How do you know?"

"I made friends with his secretary," Kick said. "She's pretty chatty."

"Well then he's stonewalling," Ray said. "Write the proper authorities downstate. Maybe they can help."

"I've already got an e-mail ready to go to the State Coroner's Association," Kick said.

One week after Kick had written the Coroners' organization, she received an envelope in the mail from the Penn County Coroner. She opened the thick packet and pulled out the cover letter, then walked into Ray's office holding it out for him to see.

"Did he send everything that we were entitled to?" Ray asked.

"More," Kick said. "Apparently he didn't read the law. It looks like he included some copies of photographs."

"He didn't have to send those," Ray said. "We got lucky."

Kick read the cover letter to herself. "Plus he made some snide remark about me contacting his state agency not being a good way to receive assistance from his office."

"Seems like it was the only way," Ray said as Kick handed him the packet.

"His excuse was that he wasn't aware of the location of the file when he originally told me he'd have it for me in a week," Kick said.

"Right," Ray said, thumbing through the papers.

"He must have forgot I called him at least six times," Kick said.

Ray smiled. "Go ahead and be snippy all you want," he said. "He did what we wanted.... And then some," he added.

Next morning, Pauline called Ray for an update and to check if everything was going well with the people she put Ray in touch with. Ray filled her in, then asked her if she would contact Bud Lackey since he hadn't returned any of Kick's phone calls. Ray told her he was still waiting for

Ronda Jo's sister-in-law to call. Pauline said she'd get on the case. She was a woman of her word and a persuasive one. She got results, like Kick.

When the sister-in-law eventually called, Ray took nearly two hours filling her in on his findings. He was careful to stay with all the facts, since he wanted to gain her confidence. In time, as they talked, she began to open up.

The sister-in-law recalled Ronda Jo telling her and her husband that the Sheriff's Department had Trudie's fingernail clippings as part of their evidence.

"You mean they took them at the house?" Ray asked.

"No," she said. Her voice started getting a little thick. "They clipped them themselves at the Coroner's office." She imagined the police assumed that Trudie had scratched the person who killed her. The sister-in-law thought if they had the murderer's DNA, a match could be made.

Ray detected resentment from her when she commented that she would have never left her children home alone. She mentioned to Ray that Trudie had gotten an obscene phone call that day, just before she was murdered. Somebody who had just breathed over the phone. Trudie did the right thing, she called Ronda Jo, but Ronda Jo didn't take the whole thing seriously. "She told the newspaper about the call," she said. "It didn't even embarrass her that she'd been neglectful." Everything Ronda Jo had done really upset her. She said that Ronda Jo was the one who wore the pants in the Brice household, not her husband, Stan. She said Stan would have hell to pay if he even thought of calling Ray without Ronda Jo's knowledge. Ray wondered if this was a signal from the sister-in-law that Ray should call Stan. He didn't think she was being coy, he just thought she'd accidentally let something slip that gave him an idea. Maybe Ray couldn't get Stan to talk directly, but maybe he could use Stan as an intermediary.

When Ray asked about Ronda Jo being pretty when she was younger, she said that her sister-in-law was too mean to be pretty, then added Ronda Jo was flirtatious back then. Ray occasionally heard her husband mumbling in the background. He wondered if he was feeding her things to say.

The sister-in-law said she'd tell Ronda Jo that she talked with Ray. Ray almost told her it probably wasn't a good idea, but he thought, what difference would it make? He knew if she talked to Ronda Jo, Ronda Jo would be angry; and if she didn't, and Ronda Jo found out later, Ronda Jo would still be mad. Apparently, Ronda Jo pretty much controlled the whole family.

Ray was looking forward to getting some hard facts and instead all he got was the jealousy and resentment of a sister-in-law.

When he hung up, Ray shook his head. "Talk about a lose-lose situation," he said. "She told me Trudie got an obscene phone call the day she was murdered. She said Ronda Jo let the whole thing slide."

"Wow," Kick said. "That's a new one."

"She could be making it up. She's not a big fan of her Ronda Jo's." Ray shook his head again, as if to clear out the cobwebs. "You want to have a drink with me, Kick?"

"Not right now," Kick said.

"Then fix me a double," Ray said.

Hugh Dixon, like Pauline, kept in close contact with Ray, reporting back any information he thought might help. Ray thought that even just investigating the crime, showing concern and compassion for the murdered child, was having a good effect. It seemed to make Hugh feel that though he didn't save the girl's life twenty years ago, he could do something now. Hugh called Ray to tell him that he dropped in on Mitch Wiersma's ex-wife. She remembered the Olds Cutlass; the car was hers. It was originally black and white, then her father painted it green for her. Mitch did body work on the car, one of those ongoing projects that he never got completed. She hated the fading primer on one fender. She was glad that Mitch never got the car finished. She wouldn't have wanted to be seen in it.

Hugh told the ex that back in 1991, he spotted the Olds parked near the Penn County Fairgrounds. She told him that made sense to her since she and Mitch lived close by. The ex remembered that Mitch took the car to a junkyard himself, though she couldn't say where or when because Mitch didn't share a lot of information with her. The ex accused Mitch of being violent and told Hugh that she'd "washed her hands of him." He was glad and somewhat surprised that she told him as much as she did.

Hugh wanted to know if Ray knew whatever happened to Trudie's dog. Ray told him that, according to the newspaper article from 1986, the passerby let the dog out of the Brice house when he returned to the scene. But based on what Emily Storm told Kick, Ronda Jo had sent Emily some photographs of the dog, Tuffy, sometime after the murder, so the dog was still around. Ray wanted to know what Hugh was getting at. Hugh thought the dog would have bitten a stranger, for sure, a thing most every dog owner would know, Ray figured.

Ray felt there was something of importance with talk of the dog popping up in the investigation so many times. Ray would think about Tuffy from time to time, trying to fit him into the puzzle.

Hugh also mentioned that his best friend was a fireman on the scene back then. The friend gave him a call. Hugh tried to sound casual, tried to downplay how much he was interested, but the friend read his mind right away. Hugh didn't care. He had nothing to hide and he wanted to do the right thing. The friend told Hugh that he didn't see Cleve Hauser anywhere on the Brice premises. The friend also said that he got along with Cleve, but said Cleve's "weird as hell."

Looks like Kick got that right, Ray thought to himself.

Hugh asked Ray if he could tell other people about Ray's investigation of Trudie's murder. Ray told Hugh to tell anyone he wanted. Maybe Hugh, with his wide circle of acquaintances, could flush out information that had been kept under wraps for more than two decades. He was a bartender after all, and people talk to bartenders.

Ray told Kick that Hugh could be a good resource — maybe as good as Pauline.

"What's that old saying?" Kick asked. "In vino veritas."

"Well, if there's truth in wine," Ray said, "Imagine what you'll find in a bottle of Wild Turkey."

"How's this distance?" Ray said, holding up a shooting target.

"Move it back a little further," Kick said.

Ray tacked it up on a dead tree.

"Is it one of those bulls eyes that turns colors when you hit it?" Kick asked.

"It is, but what do you care? Last time we target practiced, you hit the barn door," Ray said.

"Did not. You did," Kick said. "It's your turn, Boss, but let me know before you shoot so I can put my earplugs in."

"I can't hear you," Ray said, pointing to his earplugs.

"I don't want to hear a lot of bad language if you should happen to miss," Kick said. It was a pretty useless remark; he couldn't hear a thing.

Kick stuffed the plugs into her ears as Ray pulled the trigger.

"You didn't hit the bulls eye once," Kick said.

"Sure I did. I shot through the shots you made," Ray said.

Afterwards, Ray wiped down the weapons, slid them into their cases and put them in the back of the truck.

Ray was feeling adventurous. He thought it might be worth trying to get something out of Mitch Wiersma and wanted to know if Kick thought this was worth pursuing.

"Junebug said if we were to run into Mitch at the tavern, he'd probably talk with us," Kick said.

"We'd have to catch him early," Ray said, making the motion of downing a shot.

"Be serious," Kick said.

"I think one of the reasons Mitch won't step forward is because his uncle's the sheriff," Ray said.

"Maybe he's protecting Ronda Jo," Kick said.

"No, I don't think so. He's the same as Reverend Hummock, looking out for himself," Ray said.

"I guess chivalry's dead," Kick said.

"Something will eventually break," Ray said.

"What are you doing?" Kick asked.

"Picking up the spent cartridges so we can get back to town," Ray said.

"What's the hurry?" Kick said.

"The bars should be filling up. It's almost five," Ray said. "We'll have a couple of drinks and snoop around."

"You hoping we'll stumble into Mitch?" Kick asked.

"From what people say, maybe he'll stumble into us," Ray said.

But they didn't find him.

Ray was having breakfast with Del in the local diner. Ray wasn't a big breakfast eater, but he liked seeing Del, and their conversations were a way for Ray to get information out. They were finishing their refills of coffee when Bud Lackey's name came up.

Ray eventually made contact with Lackey later that day. He was evasive when Ray mentioned the Brice murder. "That was over twenty years ago," Lackey told Ray.

Though Ray thought the conversation was going nowhere, he asked Lackey a few questions anyway.

Lackey confirmed he was the Hampton Chief of Police at the time of the murder. Lackey said he didn't remember if he arrived at the murder scene before, or after, the Sheriff's Department. He said one of his police officers was at the house ahead of him, though he couldn't remember who it was.

Lackey said he couldn't recall who took Trudie out of the bathtub; he never went into the Brice house. He said it was his "boys" who put up the crime tape. Lackey told Ray he didn't know who the passerby was. "Hell, I can't remember yesterday," Lackey laughed.

Lackey seemed anxious to get off the phone. Not any more anxious than Ray. At least they agreed on something.

When Ray got back to the office, he shut the door harder than usual.

"Kick, don't call Lackey again. He still has a job with the city, one of the so-called bigwigs in Hampton," Ray said. "And he has a convenient case of forgetfulness."

Ray was restless. After he dithered a while, he asked Kick if she was busy.

"I've got this stack of handwritten notes," she said. "I was hoping to finish typing them up."

"I was thinking I might drive out to Pauline's," Ray said. "Isn't Thursday a quiet day for her?"

"Probably as quiet as any other," Kick said. "Why don't you go. Take her a present or something. She's sure been a help."

When Ray got to the stable, Pauline was gone. There was a young woman there, currying her horse. She said Pauline was picking up some meds from the vet and would be right back. Ray wandered around, admiring the horses. It was pretty amazing, he thought, that for his grandfather and many generations before him, a horse wasn't a luxury but an absolute necessity. Even as a child, he remembered seeing lots of horses as he rode in the back of his parents' car, driving through the country. Now they were a much rarer sight.

Pauline came back after a few minutes. She shook Ray's hand as her usual welcoming smile formed. She motioned for Ray to sit down. Ray could see she had saddles ready to soap and bridles to hang up. He took a seat in her office and talked for a few minutes. When he emerged, he walked past the girl who had finished grooming her animal. He barely nodded at her and she thought he looked pretty unhappy.

When Ray walked in the door, it was clear to Kick that the visit hadn't been encouraging.

"You can strike Ronda Jo's sister-in-law from your list," Ray said.

"Why?" Kick asked.

"She told Pauline this morning that she held back some things because she was afraid to tell me," Ray said. "I think she made up things too. Like Ronda Jo ignoring the obscene phone call. Who could tell what someone would do in a situation like that?"

"I don't understand these people," Kick said.

"Well don't feel too bad, because Pauline said if Ronda Jo's sister-in-law had any useful information, she'd tell everyone," Ray said.

"In other words, she's bragging that she told you nothing — even though she has nothing to tell?" Kick said.

"Something like that," Ray said.

"Did Pauline say anything else?" Kick asked.

"She gave me another name to follow-up on," Ray said. "A man who worked with Ronda Jo at the hardware store."

Kick pulled the note from Ray's hand. It read:

Contact Alvin Keen

~ Ray

A few days later, Kick was finally able to find Alvin Keen. It wasn't that he was in hiding, or that he had moved away. He lived near the center of town in a house that he rented. Alvin was just one of those modest, quiet, unremarkable people who doesn't get noticed. Ray thought he recognized Alvin, but he wasn't sure. If he had seen him before, he certainly didn't know his name.

Keen was retired from Sauers' Hardware Store. His work had required knowing stock and inventory, so Alvin had developed a good memory. He remembered Ronda Jo leaving for lunch at noon the day of the murder. She told him she was going home to look in on Trudie and check the wood burning stove. Alvin remembered asking if Trudie was afraid to be alone and Ronda Jo said no, she just wanted to make sure the girl's fever hadn't come back. According to Alvin, Ronda Jo had an hour for lunch, like everyone else.

"When Ronda Jo came back from lunch, do you remember her getting a phone call from Trudie?" Ray asked.

Alvin said he wasn't aware of Ronda Jo getting a phone call from Trudie about the breather's phone call. Ray mentioned it to him, though the only report about it was in the newspaper article, and the newspapers seemed to have relied on a lot of hearsay. Alvin thought it was strange that Ronda Jo would get such a call and never mention it to him. "That wouldn't be like her," Alvin said. "She shared most personal things."

Alvin said he drove down to the Brice's house somewhere between 3:15 p.m. and 3:20 p.m., after he'd heard about the fire. He wanted to make sure everything was all right. When he got there, it was pretty clear that things were not all right. Ronda Jo was already there, standing in the front yard. When Alvin walked up, Ronda Jo beat on his chest, accusing Alvin of starting the fire. "Hold on, Ronda Jo, I've been working with you all day," Alvin told her. Alvin remembered thinking Ronda Jo's lost it. Alvin said Ronda Jo returned to the hardware store around 3:30 p.m., stayed there another half hour, then left. She was angry and upset. Ray guessed that Alvin didn't have a whole lot of experience with what people say or do during a crisis. Alvin, he was pretty sure though, had Ronda Jo's concern in mind.

"Was she a good mom?" Ray asked.

Alvin thought that over a second or two. "She sure liked to think so," Alvin said.

Alvin knew Cleve Hauser; he was a regular customer at Sauers'. Both he and Ronda Jo had the occasion to talk to Cleve, helping him find whatever he was looking for, that sort of thing. Ronda Jo was a clerk, while Alvin mainly worked back in the storeroom. "She knew him better than I did," Alvin said. Alvin didn't have much to tell Ray. What he did have, he shared.

The days were getting shorter now and it was getting cold. Ray and Kick went out to the lake house. Ray double-checked to make sure that all of the taps were dripping so that the pipes wouldn't freeze. Ray lit a fire. Kick fixed up something for dinner. Afterwards, Ray sat on the couch and looked at the blaze in the fireplace. The fire upstairs at the Brice house continued to bother him. Why would somebody do something that would draw attention like that? What evidence would he hope to destroy? And if the killer had a plan to burn the house when he came in, why hadn't he started a better fire? Ray rubbed his chin. "You know, Kick, a burning piece of wood tossed on a mattress would definitely cause a slow burning fire."

"I already checked on the Internet to verify the year that fire retardant mattresses came out," Kick said. "It was after 1986. We should be surprised it didn't burn faster."

"Depends on the size of the piece of wood. Depends on how determined the arsonist was," Ray said. He looked into the fire a while longer. "Jeanne Shackley told me that no one from the Sheriff's Department stopped by their home until two or three days after the fire. Both her and her husband thought that was strange since Cleve was on their doorstep."

"Mrs. Shackley told me that Cleve Hauser was at her door somewhere around three o'clock. Now she says she didn't see him go back to the Brice house, but remembered Cleve telling her, 'No one's home at the Brices, I'm going back.' She wondered why Cleve was out of school early that day," Kick said.

"Does that make sense to you?" Ray asked. "Cleve saying, 'I'm going back to the house because no one's there?' If no one was there why would he risk hurting himself by going back? Why not just wait for the Fire Department?"

Kick continued. "The Shackleys said they still think the person who killed Trudie hung out in the old place across the street, looking out the front window, watching the comings and goings at the Brices' house. I don't think they ever suspected Cleve."

"That teaching job of Cleve's still bothers me," Ray said. "We can't prove Cleve wasn't working at the school at the time of the murder, nor can we prove he was out at the time. Who would remember that far back, with no records?"

"The Christmas program was that Thursday," Kick said.

"It's still a long shot as to who saw him, or didn't see him there," Ray said. "It don't make sense that retired law officers and county officials are told not to give out any information on a twenty-something-year-old murder case that has been dormant. Even the local newspaper hasn't shown any interest. The only new articles were written back in January 1987 and then only a couple, none since."

Ray had Kick contact an editor from a major newspaper, *The West Bend Press,* to tell them about Ray's investigation. The editor told Kick he'd be in touch. He never called back. All the experience Ray and Kick had with newspapers showed that they operated less efficiently than people realized. This editor, though, seemed genuinely interested. There must be a reason that Ray's story didn't make it to the newspaper, Kick thought. Maybe it was just as well.

Chapter 8

Ray decided it was time to call the Brices one last time. For close to two years now, Ray had been working on finding Trudie's killer.

"Try to get Stan on the phone, instead of Ronda Jo. I remember last time him saying that he wanted to see the police files. It was as if Ronda Jo had seen them but he hadn't," Ray said. "From what Ronda Jo's sister-in-law said about who wears the pants in that family, I'd bet he's in the dark about a lot of what happened."

"Strange," Kick mumbled as she dialed the Brice residence.

A man answered. Kick introduced herself and

reminded Stan who Ray was. She said that Ray had continued doing what he set out to do — he'd made some discoveries and come to some tentative conclusions about Trudie's death. She said that Ray wanted to share the information with Ronda Jo and him. Ray was ready to tell them who the only remaining suspect was, the person Ray believed committed the crime. Kick assured Stan that all he and Ronda Jo had to do was listen. They could ask all the questions they wanted. Ray didn't want to go any further with this until Trudie's parents were brought into it. Some decisions had to be made about whether and how to go to the authorities. Kick ended by giving Stan Ray's website and phone number. Stan listened to what Kick had to say, then said he would have to ask Ronda Jo first. He promised he'd get back to them once he told his wife.

"He told me he was going to put me on speaker phone when he wrote down the contact information," Kick said.

"And I'm sure Ronda Jo was in the background listening," Ray said. "The chances of us meeting with the Brices are slim to none."

"Why don't you think she wants to know?" Kick asked.

"I have mixed feelings on that. That's the part of this whole case that baffles me the most," Ray said.

Time went by and there was no call back from the Brices. One afternoon Pauline surprised Ray and Kick by coming by. She was in town, she said, picking up some packages and thought she'd look in on them. She admired the office and accepted Kick's offer of a hot chocolate. Ray shared his bewilderment that Ronda Jo didn't call back. He couldn't get rid of the feeling that there was something wrong with that.

Pauline told Ray that, as a mother herself, she thought it was unusual that Ronda Jo hadn't been more cooperative. Maybe Ronda Jo was involved somehow, she said. Ray thought Pauline was trying to be helpful in her own way. He thought there was plenty wrong with Ronda Jo but he didn't think she'd killed her own daughter. Ray explained to Pauline that Ronda Jo wasn't part of the actual murder, nor did she set the house on fire. He was pretty sure that, for some reason, she was hiding something that must be of major importance to her.

Everything pointed to the possibility that she had an affair of some sorts with Cleve Hauser, Reverend Hummock, and even possibly Mitch Wiersma. That kind of news would be scathing in a small town. All three were covering up something. Ray thought about how he caught Ronda Jo and Reverend Hummock lying. And why hadn't Mitch stepped forward to explain his Olds Cutlass being seen in the Brice driveway that day?

Mitch's uncle, Sheriff Chip Wiersma, told Ted Morrow that Ray was "barking up the wrong tree." What was the Sheriff covering up? He saw the map himself; the time frames were fact, not assumptions. Or maybe he was tripping Ray up so he would take another direction with his investigation.

Ray knew that the Brices, or at least Ronda Jo, had talked to the Sheriff about him. Ronda Jo slipped when she told Ray, You can't see the files without my approval.

When Reverend Hummock told Ronda Jo right after Trudie's death that she had talked to the Sheriff's Department enough, was he thinking about what was good for Ronda Jo or what was good for his own reputation? After all, he did admit that he probably gave Ronda Jo faulty advice. His excuse was that he was a young minister back then. Ray thought the preacher knew exactly what he was doing — covering his own butt.

Then there was Mitch Wiersma. He had friends and family trying to keep him out of the limelight. Sometimes folks get a strange idea in their head that they have to protect their family's name. Ray thought this notion was one that royalty probably adopted, maybe even before the castles and dragons. Ray had a difficult time with the Wiersma family name. The family's lineage was known only within a thirty-mile radius at most. Still, though he was a major local figure, Mitch Wiersma wouldn't step forward and explain what he knew. He was an ex-cop. His uncle and dad were both policemen. The big fish in a small pond syndrome, Ray thought. Or maybe he just thought he could get away with his illicit relationship.

It was rumored that Mitch Wiersma had an eye for the women — that and other hearsay had been repeated by his ex-wife for whatever it was worth. So Mitch was a second "involved party," Ray told Pauline.

"And number three is Cleve Hauser?" Pauline said.

"Looks like it," Ray said. "Of course I can't prove that yet. It's all circumstantial."

"Well," Pauline said as she sat back and sighed, "Ronda Jo sure knew how to pick 'em."

Since the local newspaper never returned Kick's telephone calls, Ray decided to have Kick go ahead and set up a meeting at the lake house with an out-of-town newspaper reporter, a lady friend of Pauline's.

Pauline assured Ray that the reporter had a theory about Trudie's murder, but the reporter wanted to share it with Ray herself. Pauline said she'd only met the reporter recently when she was doing a story on the ethanol controversy, a plant some of the locals in the county wanted, but others opposed.

Seeing as it had been over three weeks since Ray talked to Indiana State Police Detective Tim Fields, Kick decided to call the Penn County Prosecutor, Rudy Fisher, to see where things stood.

Fisher told Kick that his office never asked the Indiana State Police to do a read of the Brice case. Instead, he told Kick that he asked the State Police to do a read on another unsolved murder that happened around the same time, in the same area. Kick didn't believe him. She knew Fields was very clear about the message he received from the Penn County Prosecutor. He was being asked to investigate the Brice case; there was no way to confuse it with another murder.

Kick asked Fisher if he thought that Fields would make up such a thing about the Brice case. Fisher told her, "You wouldn't think so." Was Fisher trying to confuse the issue at hand? Kick thought. She tried to pin him down by telling him that Fields had originally requested Ray's map that showed the passerby's actions after he saw the flames shooting out the roof. Kick sent the map to Fields. Fisher asked her if the map had anything to do with a Mr. Lacey and his travels around Hampton.

"I'm not familiar with that name, but would this Mr. Lacey be an Englishman?" Kick asked.

Fisher laughed and said, Yes. You know of him?

"Not unless he was the passerby," Kick said. It was pretty clear by now that if a new possibility was offered for consideration, it was likely to be an Englishman.

Kick invited herself into Ray's office and sat down. She sighed. "An awful lot of stories flying around. Seems like all of a sudden everybody is trying to avoid being implicated."

"He mention any names?" Ray asked.

"There was someone he called a 'Mr. Lacey,'" Kick said.

"Maybe there's a mistake," Ray said. "Sounds like Detective Fields was confused. Could he have been talking about the Chief Prosecutor at the time of Trudie's murder, when he told us about the request?"

"It doesn't matter. Fisher worked for the Chief Prosecutor as an assistant back in 1986," Kick said. "He was in a position to sort things out. He just didn't want to tell us the truth."

Ben Shackley called Ray. He had a few things he wanted to talk over, he said. Ray was encouraged whenever folks in town took an interest in helping on the Brice murder. He knew the locals were not only left out of the original investigation, but they had been lied to. They might not have had hard evidence, but they felt that they had been misled and that didn't sit well with them.

Ray had barely finished mulling over his thought when he pulled up to Ben's in his truck less than fifteen minutes after the call. Ben was already out waiting on the porch. He was lacing up his boots when Ray walked up.

Ben told Ray that it was Detective Fowler who stopped by their house to ask Mrs. Shackley about her call in to the fire department. The Detective also took her statement in reference to her conversation with Cleve Hauser that day. Ben had respected his wife's unwilling-ness to talk, but he felt now that he was honor bound to tell Ray the whole truth. He repeated what he'd told Ray and Kick earlier, that the detectives hadn't come by until three days after the murder, and that they hadn't asked anything about Cleve.

Ben remembered telling Detective Fowler about the old house that sat on the property he was farming across from the Brices. He told Detective Fowler how the curtain in the front window had been deliberately pulled back and tucked into the windowsill by someone who had evidently been using the place as a look-out. The intruder set an old wooden chair at the window, apparently to peep across the street at the Brice house, Ben said.

Ray asked Ben if there was anything on the floor — empty beer cans, cigarette butts, candy wrappers. Ben shook his head. "You should have been on the case back then," he said. Whether or not it was true, Ben seemed to feel that he'd been part of a "conspiracy of silence." Even if he didn't have a lot of new information for Ray, he wanted to be sure that he'd told everything he knew — whatever the Mrs. thought.

Ray told Ben that he was right in his thinking about the old house across the street. If it were kids, they always left their signs — a smiley face, or a swastika drawn somewhere, coke or beer cans. And, of course, usually something would be broken, mostly windows. Ray felt that whoever had been spying on the Brice house was likely Trudie's killer. Ben told Ray the house was easy to get into — the door hinges were made out of leather.

Ben said he repeated the information he'd given Detective Fowler to Detective Skipper when Skipper finally showed up days later. Detective Skipper told Ben that Detective Fowler never shared any of Ben's information with him. Ben said he even gave the Sheriff himself the same information at a later date. None of the three lawmen ever got back to him. He suspected the three men had never pooled their information. Ben had the feeling that Ray wouldn't drop the whole matter the way the authorities had.

182

What interested Ray was that the three might not have been talking to one another. The pit bulls, apparently, hadn't been hunting in unison.

Ray knew that professional jealousy was hard to overcome. Many times law officers argued over who should get credit for the collar, since arrests had a lot to do with promotions. Competition on a police force didn't end at the target range and sometimes the victim ended up the loser in many a botched investigation.

Ray gave Ben a summary of what the passerby said he did when he returned to the Brice house after reporting the fire to Mrs. Shackley. Ben seemed confused. He thought that the passerby should have taken the girl's body outside the burning house even if he hadn't been successful in reviving her. Ray assured Ben that this was just one of the many problems with the passerby's story.

Ray reminded Ben that the day after the murder, the newspaper printed a statement, by the then Chief Prosecutor, quoting the passerby's account of what he said he did. In the same article, the Chief Prosecutor confirmed that the passerby was definitely not a suspect. Ray figured this statement alone threw most everyone who read the story off the passerby's tail. Although, since the Chief Prosecutor and the newspaper didn't mention the passerby's name, the fact that he was being exonerated didn't have a whole lot of practical effect. Ray didn't mention that Cleve Hauser had been identified as the passerby in the Keysville newspaper.

Ben's tone of voice changed when he again told Ray

that Cleve Hauser was not only a friend of his, but had also been a colleague of his at Hampton High back then. Even the breath of suspicion pained Ben. Ray suspected that this friendship, as much as anything else, had made Ben less inclined to reveal everything he knew. Ray pointed out to Ben that he wasn't calling Cleve the killer, but that as things were playing out, Cleve was not only the key suspect, but also the only suspect. "I don't want to argue with you. I only want to find the person who murdered Trudie," Ray said. "And I do think the old house played a major part in the murder."

Ben told Ray that it was hard for him to believe that Cleve would do something like this.

Ray offered that maybe his research would clear Cleve once and for all.

Ray opened the truck door and then turned and held out his hand. Ben responded with a hardy handshake.

Ray had put the truck into gear when Ben signaled him to stop. "There's one thing I should tell you, I guess," he said.

Ray could tell that Ben had been holding something back. And now he couldn't any more.

"I walked over to the vacant house one afternoon ... it must have been a day or two after Trudie ... you know. Fowler and one of the others were looking at something I guess they found outside the house. It had a little bit of mud on it. They didn't know I was there and so I got a look. It was one of those old lunch buckets with the round top. It was black."

"You sure they didn't bring it themselves?" Ray asked.

"It had a name stenciled on it. It said, 'C. Hauser.'"

Ray thought about that for a second. "Did they know that you saw it?"

"Oh yeah," Ben said. "They said they were sure there was some reasonable explanation. I told them I was a friend of Cleve's and didn't want to cause trouble. They told me if that was true I'd keep my mouth shut."

"I guess you did," Ray said.

"You won't tell anybody you heard it from me ..."

Ray reached out the window and shook Ben's hand again.

As he drove off, Ray thought accepting the murder of little Trudie Brice by one of their own, especially a school-teacher, left a bad taste in their mouths. They choked on it. For some, it was impossible to swallow.

Kick set up the meeting at the lake house with the reporter from *The Keysville Press*. Pauline came too. Kick gave the reporter detailed directions but the reporter got a map from Google that took her miles out of her way, so she breezed in almost an hour late. She took a seat on the couch and flounced a little. She seemed to enjoy atten-tion, an unusual quality in a reporter.

Ray set a bottle of wine on the coffee table and poured a glass. The reporter took a sip. She then lit up what would become a chain of cigarettes. She told the group that the former Green County Sheriff visited Trudie's grave every

Memorial Day to set out flowers.

She then spun a yarn about a rape case she covered that had nothing to do with the Brice murder. She gossiped about old skeletons that lay dormant in various people's closets. She said that she was good friends with a Keysville police officer, an Indiana State Police captain, as well as the former Green County Sheriff. "Talk to him," she said. "Don't hesitate to use my name."

She promised Ray that she would see about requesting copies of the Brice case files from Penn County and bragged that she would obtain radio logs from the day of Trudie's murder. She said that, by law, officials would have to give them to her. She pretty much made clear her opinion that she could open doors that were barred to more ordinary mortals.

By now more than half an hour had passed. Pauline looked about as uncomfortable as it was possible to look. The reporter made a note also to talk to several law enforcement officers who were friends of hers. She said that when her boss got back from vacation, she would get him to sign off on a series of stories about Ray's efforts to solve the murder. All of her promises were made only after Mister Cork Top was pulled from a second bottle of wine. Pauline followed Kick into the kitchen to help bring out some snacks. She told Kick she didn't really know the reporter very well, she had no idea she got this way. Kick assured her that the reporter's behavior wouldn't change their opinion of Pauline one bit. Pauline had been a valuable ally. Kick said she thought it would be okay if

Pauline went home early. Pauline said she felt she should stay in case the woman couldn't drive.

Two-and-a-half hours and another bottle of wine later, Ray poured the reporter out of his lake house. She turned down Pauline's offer to spend a night on her couch. The three of them watched the reporter back her car out of the driveway and head up the road, driving down the center of it. They were all pretty sure she would make it home all right.

"She probably has experience with this kind of altered state," Ray said.

Weeks later, Ray and Kick sat eating lunch. Ray offered Kick a glass of wine, which she refused. It reminded Kick of the evening at the lake house.

"It's been nearly a month and not a word from the reporter," Kick said.

"At least a couple of good things came out of talking with her," Ray said.

"One is she's not coming back," Kick said. "At least not by invitation."

"First of all, we verified that the Keysville newspaper was the only paper that mentioned the passerby's name, and it helped you set up a meeting for me with that retired Sheriff of Green County," Ray said.

"The Sheriff didn't seem like he knew her," Kick said.

Ray sat in Harry's Place, swirling an ice cube with his

finger in a glass of Canadian rye. His eyes roamed up and down the bar, studying the telltale signs of the century-old tavern — bar nicks, bar stains, cracked glass on the liquor cabinet doors.

The jukebox blared. Every so often a person would cup their ear, or lean toward the person next to them to talk. You didn't see it happen often because Harry's wasn't the sort of place people came to for conversation. Pool balls banged against one another on the large pool table that sat toward the back part of the bar.

As a young man, Ray remembered the spittoons that were attached every so often to the bar's brass foot rail. The rail was still there, the brass cuspidors were gone. Ray couldn't help but notice that the men were spitting in their empty beer bottles. He made sure he pointed it out to Kick. She scowled. She would be the first to acknowl-edge that many people acted like animals, but she didn't like to be reminded.

Ray felt a tap on his shoulder. A tall man with yellow-ish-gray hair and stubble to match was standing behind him.

He mumbled his name, then added he used to be the Sheriff of Green County over twenty years ago. "You're Ray Krouse, the writer?" the man asked.

Ray held out his hand, then motioned for the Sheriff to take a seat across from him. Ray thanked him for taking the time to meet. The Sheriff tipped his Stetson and told Ray to call him Boyd, the way everyone else did. Ray could see that this Sheriff was one who wore a white hat.

"I hear you had a pow-wow with Keysville's finest journalist," the Sheriff said.

"We met a few weeks ago," Ray said.

"Well that's a once-in-a-lifetime experience, isn't it?"

Ray and Kick both smiled.

The Sheriff told Ray that the extent of his involvement in the Brice case was going door-to-door at the request of Penn County's Sheriff and checking out the alibi of "an Englishman" who'd come to Keysville on a job interview the day of the murder. The Sheriff referred to Trudie's death and a couple of others in Penn County that were considered unsolved homicides.

As he sipped on his whiskey, Ray filled the old Sheriff in on what he knew, following his rule of sharing what information he had, then letting the other person have their say. Ray told him how Penn County's so-called "pit bull detectives" missed the passerby's cover-up on the murder scene.

"Sounds like the pit bulls had no bite to them," the Sheriff laughed.

Ray saw the concern in the old Sheriff's mannerisms, so Ray told him how, at first, he thought he stumbled on this murder case through serendipity. "Eventually, divine intervention took over," Ray said.

Ray realized he was revealing something about himself that he talked about rarely. He had a feeling in his gut that the Sheriff would understand. Ray trusted his instincts on this. "I call Trudie Angel-puss," Ray said. It was a term of endearment, of course, but the "angel" part was something Ray meant pretty literally.

The Sheriff smiled. One good story deserved another, so the Sheriff offered that every once in a while, he would visit Trudie's grave and place flowers on it. He lowered his voice as he told Ray that every lawman had one or two cases that stayed with them forever. One of his was a case in which a mother beat her child to death, a case the Sheriff solved. The other case was Trudie's. That case had no closure. Until it did, he thought, it would be impossible to forget.

Over an hour into their conversation, the Sheriff told Ray that he'd given him ninety percent more information than he ever knew about the Brice case. He said Penn County law officers were very closed-mouthed about the case and didn't share any information. The Sheriff mentioned that the present Penn County Sheriff, Chip Wiersma, used to be a good guy when he was a patrolman.

"He's not the man he used to be," the Sheriff said. "Politics will do that to a person."

Ray thought that the particular Wiersma tendency toward self-importance, to thinking of themselves as local royalty, also played a part in Chip's moral and spiritual decline.

The Sheriff asked Ray if Ray minded him talking to Junebug Davenport about the case. Ray downed the rest of his drink.

"Help yourself," Ray said. He turned to Kick and gave her a big smile.

Sheriff Boyd had said that there were many aspects of this case that had not become public. He had heard all kinds of rumors but he also felt that there were so many holes in the story that nothing could be taken for granted.

The next day, both Ray and Kick sat down separately and tried to make lists of things they had assumed, or might have accepted, without corroboration, things that needed to be double-checked. Kick called Ron Sellars again, the Coroner at the time of Trudie's murder. She wanted to be sure she'd heard everything she could about the physical evidence at the scene.

At first, the Coroner wasn't much help. Sellars didn't know who removed Trudie from the bathtub. Kick reminded him that his notes named Penn County Deputy Patrolman Mickey Wayland as the first county lawman to arrive at the murder scene. Sellars said that it could have been the deputy that removed her body, but he wasn't sure because the Coroner's Office was usually the last to be called to the scene.

Kick wanted to know if the "foamy material" named in the autopsy report was still seeping out of the dead girl's mouth. Sellars couldn't remember.

When Kick asked the approximate time of her death, Sellars said that the Coroner usually didn't get involved in trying to determine the time of death. He said it was too "tricky-sticky" guesswork. Kick knew better. No good coroner would critically accept the estimated time of death provided by a police officer. Even forensic technicians were suspect; after all, they were on the payroll of the police departments.

However, Sellars was helpful about some other things. The last he heard, Mickey Wayland, the first Sheriff's Deputy on the scene, was now living in Clayport. Sellars went on to say that he was still good friends with retired Detective Lou Skipper, and that he had visited him in Florida. Kick shared that she tried several times to contact Detective Skipper, to no avail. Sellars pointed out that Lou could be difficult. If he didn't want to talk, or even if he gave a reason why he didn't want to talk, it might not make sense to anyone but Lou. That was just how he was, according to Sellars. He seemed to believe that a personal idiosyncrasy was enough excuse not to cooperate with a murder investigation.

Sellars assured Kick that Detective Skipper and his partner, Fowler, did not get along at all. He said they eventually opposed each other in a Sheriff's race. Sellars added that he believed the lawmen had trouble figuring things out, even with the tips and other information from the community.

Kick was fundamentally glad to have gotten the Coroner to share what he knew; but what she had learned from him, unfortunately, was that many of the people whose names had come up in the case were unreliable.

"Sellars said they didn't always communicate with each other," Kick told Ray.

Ray nodded. "We've heard that more than once,"

he said.

Ray shuffled through a pile of papers that were spread across his desk. Ray's office seemed disorganized but he knew where everything was and Kick resisted the impulse to tell the cleaning woman to tidy up the room.

When he found the sheet of paper he was looking for, Ray turned to Kick. "Kick, did Sellars mention that his son, Warren, was his assistant at the time of Trudie's murder?" Ray asked. "In this report it says he was a Deputy Coroner."

"Yes and he said that his boy was only a teenager when he took those photographs of the murder scene. He didn't say Warren had a title though," Kick said.

"Nepotism," Ray said. "Remind me where Warren is now."

"Warren is presently a lieutenant detective on the Penn County Sheriff's Department," Kick said.

"Well that takes care of trying to get any information from him," Ray said. One consistent pattern in this case was that once people became public officials, they stopped talking.

"Correct," Kick grinned. "Sellars asked me if I knew what 'turf wars' meant. When I said I did, he laughed. I know he was talking about the various divisions and personnel rifts within the Penn County Sheriff's Department."

"So the door's still open with Sellars for future contact?" Ray asked.

"Definitely," Kick said. Though she wasn't really sure what her next questions would be.

Chapter 9

Kick spotted Marti Mann putting out some Halloween decorations in her front yard. Marti waved Kick over. Halloween is a big holiday in these counties and it's not just for kids. Since she'd gotten involved in the case, by conversations with Ray and Kick, Marti had been keeping her ears open. Stories, rumors, and passing remarks had been circulating around Hampton for decades, Marti realized, and she had treated them as white noise. She guessed that most other local people had also treated the stories with willful forgetfulness.

Marti wished to remain anonymous when she told Kick that a friend of hers heard that the first patrolman on the scene, Mickey Wayland, was managing a bar in

Clayport. Marti didn't know how fresh this information was. Marti also said that a person who might know exactly where to find him would be a friend of his who was presently a Penn County Sheriff's deputy.

When Kick returned to the lake house, Ray was out on the pier fishing. She grabbed a chair and began filling him in on her conversation with Marti.

"I thanked Marti, but told her at the present I wouldn't be contacting any active lawmen on the Penn County Sheriff's Department," Kick said.

"Did you explain why?" Ray said.

"I didn't go into it. I thought she'd understand that the department has been ignoring the case, if not burying it for the last twenty-something years. Marti's been around for a long time. She knows what's up," Kick said.

"Just call some taverns in Clayport, Kick. Someone will talk," Ray said.

"By the way, I asked Marti who the high school kid was that gave Cleve Hauser that nickname all the students used," Kick said.

"She tell you?" Ray asked.

"No, but Pauline did. It was Marti's son," Kick said.

A day later, on a cold, bright afternoon, Ray decided to drive out to Pauline's stable. He was tired. He hadn't slept well again last night. He woke up regularly now, night after night, at the same time, and when he woke up it was hard for him to go back to sleep. He could have accused himself of being obsessed. Sitting at the kitchen table, drinking water, hoping to get sleepy again, he ran through again and again what he knew about Trudie's murder. But he wasn't obsessing. He felt as though he was simply acting responsible, simply doing the kind of thing any human ought to do — trying to make the world a better place.

Along the road to Pauline's, the color on the maples was better than last year — it was the wettest fall in a long while. On one or two farms where there must have been kids, there were sheets with bucket shapes for heads hanging by nooses from the trees. There was fake cobwebbing stretched between the pillars on the porches. And on or next to fence posts, you could see the occasional jack-o'-lantern. If there was a freeze tonight, as predicted, they'd be soft and rotten and collapsing in the morning — which would make them even scarier.

Pauline took a break when Ray arrived. She invited him into her office and put a kettle on a hotplate to make some tea. She told Ray that just that morning, she'd spoken with retired Detective Fowler's wife. As soon as Pauline mentioned Ray's name, Mrs. Fowler told her, "We know all about him from the current officers on Penn County Sheriff's Department."

"All about him" was a phrase just dripping with innuendo, Pauline surmised.

"You don't think they'd try to stop me do you?" Ray asked.

Pauline told Ray she was surprised at how defensive Mrs. Fowler was; she assured Pauline that her husband wouldn't be talking with Ray. Pauline asked her if Ray could contact her husband. Mrs. Fowler said he could, but repeated it wouldn't do any good. Her and her husband had put all that Sheriff's business behind them. She told Pauline, "If I were you, I wouldn't get involved in this."

"That sound like a threat to you?" Ray asked.

"It sounds like some kind of bullying," Pauline said. "It sounds like she might, you know, snub me at the bake sale or something."

"Sounds like sour grapes," Ray said. "It's all about Detective Fowler losing the Penn County Sheriff's election, and who knows what else."

"I don't think they'd try to stop you legally," Pauline said. "Though I bet they wish they could scare you off."

"So far what they're doing mostly is wearing me down," Ray said.

Pauline stopped to pour the hot water into two cups, each with a tea bag. This was the only time she'd ever seen Ray admit to frustration or fatigue.

"Can I ask you something?" Ray asked.

"I haven't found a way to stop you yet," Pauline said, flashing him a little grin.

"Do you believe in spirits?" Ray asked. He'd never talked to anybody about this, really, except for Kick.

Pauline could tell that this was not an idle question. "Well, I'm a country person, Ray," she answered. "I watch the seasons, I hang out with horses.... Of course I believe in spirits."

Ray told her that shortly after taking on the murder investigation, he would all of a sudden awaken out of a deep sleep, only to find the numbers 11:11 displayed on the digital clock on his bedside table.

"Ummm," Pauline said, blowing on the hot tea in her cup.

"You know about 1111?" Ray asked. "It's in the Kabala."

"I've heard of it. I couldn't explain it to you," she said.

Ray told her that he'd studied a little Jewish mysticism. He knew that in Kabala, the numbers 1111 played an important spiritual role. The time 11:11, it was believed, was when spirits or guardians would appear — some people called them spirit guardians or midwayers ...

"Or lightworkers," Pauline said.

It would have been the next word out of Ray's mouth. He knew now that Pauline was a good person to share this with. "Lightworkers," he echoed. "It's all the same idea."

Pauline was impressed with how much Ray knew and by Ray's seriousness. She agreed that the numbers 11:11 on the clock must mean something.

"Did you become interested in spiritual things because of your reading?" Pauline asked. "Most people don't go to the city to explore their spirituality."

"I always had an interest. Maybe I have an ESP gene. Really," he said. "I learned about that side of life ... from Trudie."

When Kick found out from Ray that Pauline had talked with Mrs. Fowler, she was curious about what had been said. She had come to accept Pauline as her friend and felt that whatever Pauline said would be helpful, as well as truthful.

"I told Pauline that you talked to Wayne Dumas, that retired deputy with that chickenshit job of putting ankle monitors on Sheriff's prisoners," Ray said.

Ray had asked Kick to come for a ride with him in the country. She didn't know the destination, but it was a nice day and she liked looking out the window at the farmland.

"Did you tell her how he tattled on us to his lieutenant, and the Indiana State Police?" Kick asked.

"Pauline was right when she said Dumas was known as a person who couldn't be trusted, and she's never heard Mrs. Fowler be so hostile," Ray said. "I told her a story about a young woman from New York City who was raped, then beaten to death while residents of her apartment complex watched from their windows. Not one person called the police."

"I read about that case," Kick said. "The girl's name was Kitty something...."

"Right," Ray said. "Maybe it's sort of similar with law enforcement here. Maybe it's something about avoiding court. It might have been different if the victim was one of their loved ones."

"That's a terrible thought," Kick said.

"Or maybe it's just self-interest. The Penn County officials are just too prideful to admit that they botched up the Brice case," Ray said.

"Or, like you said, it could be a cover-up," Kick said. "Sheriff Wiersma couldn't prove you wrong, so he chooses to poor mouth you. Shame on them all."

"It would be so simple for the Sheriff to ask for Hauser's DNA. The locals ask me why he doesn't. I wish I knew what to tell them," Ray said.

"And to think some of the officials still pin the blame of Trudie's murder on an Englishman," Kick said.

"Hell, they're not even sure which Englishman to blame," Ray said.

They drove for a while in silence. Then Kick said, "What kind of a job would that be? — putting shackles on prisoners?"

"Beats me," Ray said. "Doesn't seem like there'd be much to it."

"It couldn't take more than a few minutes. Maybe then he has to track them electronically. There must be some way he justifies a full salary," Kick said.

"I don't know, Kick. I'm not caught up with cutting-edge police procedures. I just drive around and look for answers."

Ray turned down a country road that ran between two fields down toward a stream. At the end of the road was a little fishing cabin so hidden away in a stand of cottonwoods that nobody would know it was there. There was a late-model car in the driveway.

"Where are we?" Kick asked.

"This is a little place Ted Morrow keeps as a getaway spot," Ray said.

He opened the door and got out. Kick followed him.

Ted Morrow invited them in. He offered Ray a cup of coffee, which Ray was happy to take. "Just one," Ray kidded. "I'm driving." Ted filled the mug almost to the top.

Ted told Ray that he'd seen Ronda Jo and Stan at a coffee shop and they turned their backs on him. Ray believed that they were trying to distance themselves from Ted since he was the one who put Ray in touch with Ronda Jo originally. Ted was almost sorrowful. Kick called him "Godfather," but he was a tenderhearted god-father. Ronda Jo and Stan weren't particularly friends of his, but Ted and his wife liked to think they were friends with everybody in town. Doris's family had been selling gifts downtown for decades. Ted had embalmed the relatives of many of them. A snub by any of the locals was a big deal to the Morrows.

Ray knew that it was time to back off talking about the case to Ted. Ray also knew, in the end, that Ted would still be somebody he could share a good tale with. He hoped that Ted wouldn't lose any more friends than he might have already.

As they drove back up the road, Ray told Kick he wanted to set up a meeting of a few of the locals who had been helping him work the Brice murder case. Ray had already seen some folks drop out. He understood the workings of a small, close-knit community, but went out of his way to show his gratitude to those who had helped. Ray knew there were folks with political interests who, for one reason or another, wanted to see Ray give up. But Ray knew the best way to keep the investigation going was to keep the public interested and involved.

And then, all of a sudden, they got a break. Kick got a call on her cell phone as she pulled into a fast food parking lot. She turned off the radio and parked, forgetting to turn off the engine. The caller was a woman who claimed to be a good friend of Roger Lawford, one of the Englishmen who had visited Hampton. Roger lived in an apartment above Harry's Place whenever he was in town. It wasn't clear exactly who she'd gotten the story from, but the caller had heard that Ray's investigation had people talking again about an Englishman who might be involved in the crime. "Involved" was the word the woman on the phone used. She avoided the word "murder."

The woman said that Roger didn't know the Brice family and she believed that Roger wasn't even in the United States when Trudie was killed. She knew that Roger came back to Hampton in 1987, a year after the murder, in order to attend a wedding of a couple he met while he was in the States some time back in the early 1980's.

As Ray had learned from Hugh Dixon, there was more than one Englishman. Some local people probably got them mixed up. Roger and another Brit, named Willy, originally came to Hampton to buy collectible motorcycles and ship them back to England then sell them throughout Europe. It seemed implausible that the Indiana countryside was full of Englishmen riding around buying old bikes, but that's how it was.

The woman said that Roger's friend, Willy, met an American bike enthusiast at a motorcycle show in London. The American told Willy there were some antique cycles throughout the countryside back in the States. The Brits were told that farmers hardly ever sold their equipment; it mostly sat around and became obsolete or eventually rusted out.

Various people in Hampton confirmed that Roger was the leader of the group of Englishmen who came and went. The woman on the phone, Roger's friend, said when the Englishmen weren't chasing down antique motorcycles throughout the Midwest, they spent their free time at the local tavern. The locals weren't all that friendly. They referred to the Brits as "the aliens" and made fun of the way they talked. A lot of the people thought their accent suggested that they were effeminate. The woman on the phone had met them at the bar and they had become friendly. She thought the Englishmen were more polite and more sophisticated than the usual crowd. She also said she wasn't sure if Roger Lawford was still alive. She'd heard rumors not so many years ago. When the woman hung up, Kick didn't really have much more information than before, but the woman seemed relieved. It was like Ray said, just talking to people helped heal the fear and shame a lot of local people had.

Kick turned the radio on again, backed out of the parking place, and entered the drive-through line.

Ray visited Hugh Dixon at the hospital to see how he was feeling. Hugh had been there a day and a half. Like most people in the hospital, Hugh looked worse after having been admitted than he did before. He had gotten an infection in his toe that had become gangrenous. "The doc said my gangrene toe would fall off on its own," Hugh said.

"You'll have to get new shoes," Ray said, knowing that Hugh liked gallows humor.

Hugh had a lot of time on his hands. There was a TV in his room, but Hugh associated television with being in the bar.

"The doc also told me to lay off the booze," Hugh said.

Hugh hated reading, always had. He and Ray got talking about the Brice case.

Hugh said he knew Roger Lawford. Several years ago, he and Roger drove to California together to visit Roger's aunt. They'd knocked down their fair share of black and tans together. Hugh assured Ray that two friends wouldn't drive thousands of miles together and not know what each other was about. Hugh didn't believe that Roger had anything to do with Trudie's murder. Hugh mentioned that Roger was small, maybe 120 pounds, the size of a jockey.

Word had gotten around, maybe because Hugh asked

so many questions over the bar, that he and Ray were having conversations. Ray wondered whether this was causing Hugh to lose friends or business. He didn't want another situation like Ted's, where his people were ostracized for cooperating. It would tear up the social fabric of the town. It could also hurt Ray's investigation.

Another one of Hugh's friends told Hugh that when he was fighting the fire at the Brice house, it was Bud Lackey, the Chief of Police in Hampton, who was the first policeman on the scene. That agreed with what Ray had been told by Junebug. Hugh's friend also said it was Lackey who took Trudie out of the bathtub and covered her with a throw rug. His friend even remembered the color of the rug. Ray had been told the rug was orange and Hugh's friend said the same thing. The friend had been standing right outside the bathroom door when Lackey came out with the body. The girl's hair was limp, hanging down and dripping. Her arms were stiff and swollen. If what the friend said was correct, then the ex-Chief of Police lied to Ray. Lackey said he never entered the Brice house. He said he didn't know who brought the girl out of the bathtub. The lie bothered Ray. Any ordinary person would remember going into a burning house and finding a dead girl. No ordinary person would have kept secret the fact he'd had the dead girl in his arms. It was the kind of memory that would stamp itself on a person for life. The kind of story you'd want to tell, to get it off your chest, if nothing else. Ray also remembered Lackey telling him that his boys taped off the crime scene. Ray, as well as everybody else, knew the crime scene was inside the house.

Ray confided in Hugh that many of the people closest to the crime — you could say many of the people who should have been most interested and most helpful to Ray — seemed to want to avoid the issue.

Hugh said he thought it was strange that Ronda Jo didn't want to talk to Ray, but he knew that she was secretive about it. Someone told him that she had never ever visited the grave. Hugh didn't know how anyone would know that. He imagined it was some friend of Ronda Jo's who said so, or it was someone who was just being spiteful. Out of curiosity, Hugh asked the groundskeeper when he dropped in the bar for a cold one if there were ever any flowers on the grave. The old man told Hugh there were. He confirmed Ray's observation that the gravesite was well kept. The groundskeeper knew that Boyd, the old Sheriff of Green County, visited the grave sometimes — he'd seen him there himself. He'd seen others there, too. Ray imagined it was probably because a few never really got over the murder of the innocent young girl. It made them feel good, taking flowers to the grave, pulling up weeds, tending it; as was the case with Sheriff Boyd, the story stayed with them. Ray told Hugh that the only reason Ronda Jo probably talked to him in the first place was to find out just how much Ray knew. She had to have known who the passerby was. For some secret reason of hers, she wanted to deny knowing the passerby.

A nurse came in to check Hugh's temperature. She

plumped up his pillow, said something encouraging, then moved to the next bed.

Ray said he didn't know a mother who wouldn't want to know the name of the person who tried to save her child. Half the countryside was suspicious about Cleve Hauser; yet another half knew he was the passerby. More interesting was that no one ever spoke of him as the hero. It was just too unbelievable that Ronda Jo didn't want to know the answers. Ray knew it was against the psychological thinking of a mother.

Ray awoke to a noise in the bathroom. It sounded like something falling. He rolled over and looked at the clock. It said 11:11, just as it always did. He got up and went to see what the noise was. There was a tin soap dish that had fallen from the counter. He had probably left it too close to the edge. The dish was old and beat up. He held on to it for sentimental reasons. His cat, Murray, had treated it as a toy, knocking it off on the floor and then pushing it around with his nose. Ray put the soap dish back where it belonged. He splashed water on his face and went back to bed, hoping against hope he could fall asleep.

The next day, Pauline called Ray at his office about the meeting Kick had set up at Ray's lake house. She thought that there were some things that could be taken off the table. She mentioned that she'd spoken to a friend who was a special agent with the Indiana State Police.

Pauline's friend told her that some of the Indiana State Troopers said the Brice murder was still unsolved. This contradicted all those who continued to charge that Trudie's killer was an Englishman. The little Englishman, Roger, had been a pretty unlikely suspect. According to his friend who called Kick, Roger Lawford hadn't been in the country at the time. And though Sheriff Boyd said his department made inquiries about an English visitor at the request of the Penn County Sheriff, they'd turned up nothing. Penn County officials must have accepted the story that the Englishman had gone to Keysville the day of the murder. If the case was still open, the Englishman couldn't be a suspect.

Pauline assumed Ray knew about this and was curious why Ray was tracking Roger Lawford. Ray told Pauline that he would pursue any and all individuals that either, by suspicion, or rumor, were tied in any fashion to the murder, even if it meant tracking someone down in England. Ray said he wanted to eliminate named suspects only if they had an ironclad alibi at the time of the murder. As the investigation moved on, Ray was more determined than ever to solve Trudie's murder, not for justice to be served, or to write a book, but for a greater purpose.

Hugh Dixon called Ray back from his hospital bed.

He told Ray that lying alone in the hospital gave him time to think back. He said he was positive that he was passing the Brice home between noon and one o'clock when he saw the Olds Cutlass in the driveway the day of the murder.

He said he was bartending at Harry's Place and got off around noon the day of the murder. Hugh said he was working a split shift that day so he had to be back to the bar by four o'clock. The thing that jarred his memory was that he had to get a brake job done on his car before he returned to work. No one would still have receipts but he was positive that it had been that day.

Then Hugh told Ray about another conversation he had with his friend, Shine. After Hugh's conversation with Ray at the lake house and seeing Ray's map, Hugh remembered that Shine told him that a man named Springer relayed a story about his brother-in-law. Originally, Hugh thought he understood Shine to say that Springer was the passerby who told him he tried to resuscitate Trudie, but then Hugh remembered it wasn't Springer at all; rather it was Springer's *brother-in-law* who told Springer that he tried to revive Trudie.

Ray felt goose bumps on his arms. He asked Hugh to hang on a minute and called to Kick. She'd done a check of records — births, marriages, deaths, and so forth, a few weeks earlier. He asked her to bring him the list. He looked at Kick's notes and his memory was right. Ray put the phone back to his ear and told Hugh that Cleve Hauser's wife's maiden name was Springer. The phone went silent.

Ray waited for Hugh to come to his own conclusion. Finally Hugh spoke. "My God, it's Hauser that

Springer was talking about back then."

Ray now knew that he and Hugh were on the same track. Ray wanted to know how well Hugh knew Springer.

"Not good enough to have a chicken dinner with him," Hugh said, though he was comfortable enough to ask him a few questions, if that was what Ray wanted.

Bud Lackey's name also popped up during Hugh and Ray's conversation. Hugh remembered that it was Lackey who told him that Trudie was strangled with a telephone cord. This agreed with what Nick Schwin had heard and what Les Dupont had said.

Hugh said he still couldn't remember the person who told him that Ronda Jo didn't have lunch with Trudie that day, but said it would eventually cross his mind.

"It doesn't matter, Hugh," Ray said. "Somebody brought her lunch."

"They find something?" Hugh asked.

"In her stomach. Onions, mushrooms, tomato sauce, dough ..."

"Pizza," Hugh said.

"Maybe Ronda Jo went by there after all," Ray said. "She didn't stay though."

Hugh ended the call by saying that a couple of friends had been up to see him and that one of them, Gordon Wiggs, was trying to say it was someone else who committed the murder, not Cleve Hauser. "He's full of shit," Hugh said. "He's pulling our chains."

Ray told Hugh that he'd come by and see him again

as soon as he had a free moment. Hugh said that he hoped to be back on his feet long before Ray made time to take a breather.

After Ray hung up, he thought about his conversation with Gordon Wiggs. "Kick, that Gordon Wiggs is too into himself. I don't trust him," Ray said.

The next morning's mail brought the pictures Keith had promised of the interior of the Brice house. Ray and Kick sat down in his office and went through the pictures quickly. Things had been cleaned up and furniture was gone but you certainly got the idea of the house. The design broke things up into a lot of little rooms. Ray thought it would have made him claustrophobic. Aside from peeling wallpaper, there was nothing remarkable one way or another about the kitchen. The bathroom off of the kitchen was an add-on. The house, Ray thought, probably had originally been built without indoor plumbing, like a lot older houses hereabouts.

He took the pictures back from Kick and got a marker out of his desk drawer. One by one he went through them, drawing arrows, circling items and areas of interest. Kick studied the photos carefully. When they were done, Kick tucked them into the envelope they came in and put them in the safe.

Ray finally had a few people over at his lake house. The group Kick jokingly referred to as his "posse." For all the support Ray offered them, not much new evidence turned up. After the last guest left, he and Kick compared notes.

"Did you hear any new information, Kick?" Ray asked.

"Mostly they talked about things that we heard before," Kick said.

They had also invited a few people who hadn't been cooperative, just to see if they would show up.

"Who was a no show?" Ray asked.

"Mrs. Fowler called Pauline and said that she and her husband didn't want anything to do with the Brice case," Kick said.

"Seems like he didn't do much when he was assigned to the Brice case," Ray said. "Why start now?" He thought about it for a few seconds. "Maybe he doesn't want anybody to know how bad this case was botched."

Ray had tried to jog the group's memories, but hadn't had much luck.

"Val White, Hauser's buddy, was trying to eavesdrop on Pauline and her friend while they were having lunch at the American Legion. She said he mumbled something dumb," Kick said.

"There's not much we can do with that information," Ray said. "Maybe that's why she didn't tell us before."

"I wonder why they just didn't ask Val if he would be willing to talk with you," Kick said.

"It's hard for the locals to confront one another," Ray said.

"I'll call him myself," Kick said.

Ray had made a couple calls to England to try to find the whereabouts of the Englishmen. A few days after the lake house meeting, Ray received a telephone call from England; it was Roger Lawford's friend, Willy. Willy said he was a pallbearer at Roger's funeral in September, 2004. Roger had died, fittingly enough, in a motorcycle accident. Willy said he was the one who got Roger to come to the States with him. Willy and Roger traveled to Canada in 1987 and arrived in Indianapolis in 1988. He wasn't sure that Roger was even in the country in 1986. Willy said he'd ask Roger's mother if she had kept Roger's passport so he could find out. If he could lay his hands on it, he promised that he would send Ray copies of it to verify the dates.

Willy didn't know anything about the 1986 murder. He didn't even know the Brice name. Willy said it sounded convenient that the Penn County Sheriff's Department was trying to pin the murder on a "bloke" who wasn't even in the country at the time.

Willy said that Roger's mother was still distraught over her son's passing. Ray assured Willy that he would personally clear Roger's good name. Willy was grateful.

Willy asked Ray if he would send some pictures of Hampton as it was now. Willy said he had fond memories of the good times and he was sorry to hear about the little girl who was murdered. "I'll have you take some pictures for Willy this weekend, Kick," Ray said. "I know what he's talking about, the Brits were swell to me every time I visited their country. I spent a good deal of time in London and around the countryside. I like our British cousins."

Kick's calls to Clayport paid off. Word had gotten around and former Penn County Sheriff's Deputy Mickey Wayland called Ray at his office. He verified that he was the first county officer on the murder scene. When he arrived, the only officials at the house were the firefighters. Mickey said he picked up the emergency call on his squad car's two-way radio. He estimated his arrival at the Brices' at 3:30 p.m. He said Junebug had already blocked the door to the bathroom, though he recalled seeing Trudie laying face up in the water-filled bathtub.

Mickey confirmed that the fire had been set on a bed in the master bedroom, in the middle of the mattress. He said he stayed on the scene until after 4:30 p.m.; it was getting dark outside. He waited for Penn County detectives Skipper and Fowler to arrive. He knew one of them, if not both, would be assigned to the murder case since the crime took place in the Penn County Sheriff's Department's jurisdiction.

Ray told Mickey that the paramedic said that when he arrived, Trudie's body had already been taken out of the bathtub and covered. Mickey said he saw Hampton Chief of Police Bud Lackey in the house and was pretty sure Lackey was the one who removed her from the bathtub.

Kick had been standing in the doorway, trying to track the conversation. When Ray got off the phone, he gave her a quizzical look.

"I filled Mickey in on our investigation," Ray said.

"What did he have to say?" Kick asked.

"He said Sheriff Wiersma is a slo-mo," Ray said.

"I guess he knows him, after all the Sheriff refers to himself as a bumpkin," Kick said.

"Any luck finding Sherry Marshall?" Ray asked.

Kick had been talking with Dina, Trudie's other girlhood friend, pretty regularly, trying to track Sherry down. "Working on it," Kick said.

"Spencer Logan?" Ray asked. Not long after Logan had helped Hugh figure out who owned the car parked in the Brice driveway — Mitch Wiersma's car, as it turned out — he'd moved away.

"Working on it," Kick said.

Ray had told Kick that it was hard to pull up roots and leave Indiana. They were certainly finding exceptions to the rule. A lot of people whose names they were turning up had packed their bags and gone.

Ray phoned Reverend Hummock again. The Reverend's wife, Helen, answered her husband's cell phone. She added that he left his cell phone home to be charged. The Reverend wasn't home. Ray knew it was a perfect time to get Helen's take on a couple things since he knew the Reverend hadn't been completely truthful with him.

Ray reiterated to Helen that he never thought her husband was a suspect in the little girl's murder, but he knew the Reverend was a friend and confidant of the Brice family. Helen mentioned Reverend Storm also knew the Brices. Ray decided it was best not to get started talking about the Storms, especially after what Emily Storm said.

Helen said her husband was out of town Christmas shopping the day of the murder. Ray said the Reverend already told him that he was in West Bend.

Helen corrected Ray. She said Ashbrook was where her husband went Christmas shopping, not West Bend. She said she was sure of that because she was home, sick in bed with the flu.

When Ray asked about the Englishman, Helen repeated, "What Englishman?" then said, "Oh, the Reverend just walked in the door." Ray figured her husband was home, since he heard whispering in the background.

The Reverend told Ray he knew an Englishman named Peter Lacey and that he thought that Lacey once lived in a trailer court near the high school with Tammy Lemel. Ray heard Helen tell the Reverend, "You know about Peter and Tammy, dear. You married them."

Ray heard Reverend Hummock cup his hand over the phone. When he came back on the line, he told Ray he had forgotten about performing the Laceys' wedding ceremony. The Reverend turned away from the phone and thanked his wife for reminding him. Ray was finding out that the Reverend was no amateur when it came to lying. He supposed it was second nature to him.

"You may have to go back to the county offices," Ray said to Kick. "Peter Lacey and Tammy Lemel were married in the Methodist Church by Reverend Hummock in September, 1986."

"Lacey is an Englishman's name," Kick said.

Ray gave her a thumbs up.

"They were married just a few months before the murder," Kick whispered.

"The Reverend thought Peter and Tammy had a child together, but their marriage didn't last long, about four months, then Lacey went back to England," Ray said.

"Is Lacey still alive?" Kick asked.

Ray shrugged his shoulders. "I didn't have Lacey's name when I talked with Willy, so I didn't ask about him."

"You don't think this is a real possibility do you?" Kick asked.

"I think we're going to have to take it seriously. Reverend Hummock says that Tammy told Ronda Jo that she thought Lacey killed Trudie. Later on, Ronda Jo told Reverend Hummock that she didn't think the police investigated the Englishman well enough. She was talking about Peter Lacey, not Roger Lawford."

"So the Reverend gets a second-hand report about a murder suspect and he doesn't go to the police? It's not like he'd be violating clerical privilege. None of this is making sense," Kick said.

"I think that's what everybody wants," Ray said, "to spread confusion. I'll tell you one thing for sure, both Reverend Hummock and Ronda Jo haven't been truthful."

"You can toss the Prosecutor in with them," Kick said.

"It makes sense if you piece it together. When the Prosecutor asked you if my map traced Mr. Lacey's travels, we thought he was being sarcastic and making fun of Roger Lawford by referring to him as 'Mr. Lacey,'" Ray said.

"Right," Kick said. "As if his name was spelled L-A-C-Y, like he was prissy or something."

"But he was just calling him by his real name," Ray said.

"One small oversight and the Englishmen are confused by folks. There were two Englishmen that lived in Hampton at the same time — one was Lacey, the other was Lawford. It's confusing," Kick said. "How come no one ever came right out and said there was more than one Englishman in town?"

"I don't think a lot of the residents put it together, mainly because they usually referred to them as 'the Englishmen,' not by their proper names. Even the retired Sheriff's deputies you talked to have the two Englishmen mixed up. The Sheriff might think of himself as a bumpkin, but now I'm thinking he's just trying to be clever," Ray said.

Kick rolled her eyes.

"People don't always turn out to be what they really are," Ray said. "Well, Kick, we've already tracked down and eliminated Roger Lawford, now let's get to work on Peter Lacey."

That same evening, Ray and Kick stopped in at Harry's Place. Hugh Dixon was out of the hospital, just like he said he'd be, and on his feet — minus one big toe — behind the bar, pouring drinks. When Ray asked, Hugh told him that he remembered Peter Lacey. He said that Lacey wasn't one of the motorcycle bunch from England. He also thought Lacey was still alive and living in England.

Hugh pointed over to a couple of men shooting pool. He said the one with a beard was a cousin of Ronda Jo's husband. This cousin had told Hugh earlier that he thought Ronda Jo killed Trudie because she was depressed.

Ray knew that he had to guard against being tired and impatient. It did seem as though the more he tried to narrow things down to a single suspect, the more hypothetical murderers got added to his list. The cousin told Hugh that Ronda Jo was flirtatious back then. He said she used to cut his hair and that she kept coming on to him. He said he told her he wasn't a hound dog and quit having her cut his hair.

One of the problems with the cousin's theory was that Trudie had been raped by a male.

Hugh circled his temple with his index finger. Ray downed a shot of whiskey and slapped Hugh on the back. "Keep your ears open," Ray said.

Ray called Pauline, just to check in, and got her daughter on the phone. Her mom had already filled her in on Ray's investigation. Pauline's daughter was a couple years ahead of Trudie in grammar school.

He told Kick about the call. "She wants to help," he said.

Pauline's daughter said that Sherry Marshall, one of the four musketeers, moved away from Hampton in 1987. Kick knew that all too well. She and Dina Schwin had been trying to track Sherry down for months. The daughter offered her take on the murder. She said that Trudie may have found out about an affair her mother was having with Cleve Hauser and threatened to tell her dad, so Hauser decided to kill her.

Ray had thanked Pauline's daughter without responding to what she said. He told Kick, though, that he thought the daughter had good instincts. "The daughter's take on the crime theory is getting close to some of the thoughts that run through my mind," Ray said. "It's one of the oldest acts of jealousy — the love triangle. Ronda Jo, Cleve Hauser, and Reverend Hummock, then it's possible that Mitch Wiersma entered the picture at a later date."

"Wouldn't that be a love square?" Kick said.

"Get serious, I'm trying to tell you something, Kick," Ray said. "Reverend Hummock hasn't been forthright. He told me that Ronda Jo had no idea who killed her daughter. Though later on, he mentioned that Ronda Jo suspected the Englishman, Peter Lacey."

Was Ronda Jo lying? Ray thought.

Ray continued. "He also said he didn't know who the

passerby was, which makes sense if Ronda Jo, who knows Cleve, was trying to conceal his identity from Hummock. She wouldn't want one lover to know about the other. But why would Ronda Jo take Reverend Hummock into her confidence about the gory details of her daughter's murder, and not share with him the name of the individual who reported the fire and attempted to resuscitate her daughter? What's really absurd is Ronda Jo tells him she didn't know anything about the passerby."

Kick was concentrating hard to follow this. "I think that what you're saying is that if you take the evidence, pure and simple, things aren't so clear, but if you look at motives ..."

"If you factor in human nature, if you factor in self-interest, things have a way of sorting themselves out," Ray said. "Look at it this way, there isn't any reason on God's green earth for Emily Storm to make up a story from Ronda Jo that Reverend Hummock was attracted to her. Ronda Jo refuses talk; Cleve Hauser has remained silent over two decades, except for his meddlesome inquiries around town. Yet he was supposed to be the hero who ran into a burning house that just minutes before he decided to pass by, and reports the fire to a neighbor colleague of his. Then he tries to save a little girl he had no way of knowing was inside, and who, we now know, had already been murdered two hours previously. He sticks his nose in everyone's business around Penn County, but he don't want to know what happened after he tried to revive Trudie?"

"How much do you think Reverend Hummock knows

about what we're doing?" Kick asked.

"The Reverend knows plenty. He's a gossip, remember? But he doesn't want to add any information to a two-year investigation and help catch the killer," Ray said. "By the same token, Mitch won't step forward and explain his car being in the driveway. Since he used to be a detective himself, it seems he would at least contribute to our investigation."

"Maybe he thinks it would come out that he and Ronda Jo had a relationship," Kick said.

"If Mitch made that admission, it would be easier to see why Cleve would come across the street, go crazy in the house, and kill Trudie. Mitch would be implicated," Ray said.

"Ditto Reverend Hummock, if he told the truth," Kick said.

"When Reverend Hummock talked on three different occasions, he told three different stories. It's hard to keep a lie straight. Maybe he'll come clean," Ray said. "Maybe everybody will."

Kick crossed her fingers.

Ray called Hugh. It wasn't so much that he thought Hugh had more answers, he just wanted a reality check. Hugh was at work, but on this night he had an assistant. He asked the girl to take over.

She was a pretty girl with a mostly lean body and a tan she showed off by exposing her midsection. She even had a navel ring and a tattoo that could barely be seen above her shorts when she turned around. The truth was she sold more booze than Hugh, especially as the evening wore on.

Hugh stepped out the back door with his cell phone and lit a cigarette. Ray apologized for calling him at work but there were things he simply didn't understand. Ray wanted to know why the Sheriff's Department didn't pressure Hauser and why they let the Englishman off the hook if they truly believed he was the killer. Why had the police, the press, and key people, mostly politicians, remained silent or outright lied about the circumstances surrounding Trudie's murder? The Sheriff's Department didn't want to share any information back then. Now over twenty years later, they either spun outright lies, or still wouldn't talk. Ray knew bullshit when he heard it. He paused.

"Ray," Hugh said. "You know how things are around here." Hugh said he'd been keeping his ears open and promised he'd try harder.

"You're doing great, Hugh," Ray said.

"I don't how you keep on with it Ray," Hugh said. "I really don't."

When they were finished, Hugh snapped the phone lid shut, flipped the cigarette butt into a puddle and went back inside. He washed glasses while the girl worked the bar. Business was good.

Ray hung up the phone and let out a sigh. "Those SOBs have no shame," he said.

Kick was on the phone at work talking to her sister. She didn't give the sister details but mentioned that she was helping look into a local murder case. The sister reminded Kick she'd moved to a small town to get away from city problems and Kick had to agree that life took unexpected turns. The sister reminded her that their uncle was a doctor of pathology at the University of Chicago. Maybe he could help. Kick agreed he might be a good person to talk to. He probably had never even been in their part of Indiana and could be totally objective. She called his office and left a message with the secretary. He e-mailed back a few days later and told her to send him what evidence she could.

That afternoon Kick put together the Coroner's report, the autopsy report, some police statements, and a couple of newspaper clippings. She deliberately left out the news story that mentioned the possibility of child molestation.

She'd expected she'd have to wait for weeks, but the uncle called back two days later. He asked for her by her childhood name.

"Uncle Walter?" she said.

He didn't beat around the bush. "That girl put up a brave struggle," he said.

The Doctor said the killer had to regain his strangulation grip a couple of times, as revealed by the two sets of deep marks around her neck. He felt the cuts and bruises on Trudie's arms were consistent with her hitting at her attacker, flailing her arms forward. He said that Trudie's killer approached her from the front. The location of her injuries was consistent with her being right handed and using her right hand to fend off the killer, since most were on her right arm and hand region.

He said that Trudie's head injuries were consistent with her being struck with a blunt object.

"Like a telephone receiver?" Kick asked.

"A telephone receiver would be a good guess," he said. It didn't have to have been a heavy object if the murderer used enough force.

Kick told him a phone had been taken from the house.

The Doctor said the marks around her neck were also consistent with a telephone cord being used. The marks on her bottom lip appeared to be as a result of being hit in the mouth more than once. There also were two ovoid abrasions under her neck.

"Which would mean?..."

"I'm not a forensic pathologist," the Doctor said. "But if I had to guess ... was it cold?"

"Well, you know," Kick said. "December in Indiana is never warm."

"I'd say the marks could definitely have been caused by the murderer's coat sleeve buttons," the Doctor said.

"That would mean he'd just come in from being outside for a while," Kick said.

"I'd be guessing," the Doctor said. "You can come to your own conclusions."

Kick heard a rustling that sounded like papers.

Her uncle went on. "The marks on her left knee were

scrapes, as if she fell to her knees at one point in the struggle. And the girl was molested post-mortem, anally, as demonstrated by the injuries found in her rectum."

"It's hard for me to think about what she went through," Kick said.

"I'd rather not make a judgment." Kick's uncle paused. It was as if when he had the papers in his hand he was a scientist and when he put them down, his feelings showed through.

"I can tell you this," he said. "All of her injuries point to one thing, Trudie wanted to live."

Of course, Kick offered to pay her uncle and, of course, he refused. She made a note to herself send him something on the holidays.

Ray and Kick went into the office on a Sunday. An acquaintance of Pauline's, a truck driver, wanted to talk to Ray. He was a sophomore at Hampton High School at the time of the murder. His home was a hundred miles away and he asked if he could stop by.

Ray filled him in on his investigation of the Brice murder. The truck driver told Ray that he had also been a member of the same church the Brice family attended. He said he was one of the pallbearers, all of whom were members of the church youth group, and he didn't remember seeing Cleve Hauser at Trudie's funeral.

The truck driver was adamant that Hauser left the Hampton school system in December 1985. His recollection was that another teacher took over Hauser's position as the Agriculture teacher in January of 1986.

He said he had Hauser for Ag class and stated he was pretty worthless and didn't really teach him much, even when he did show up.

The man described his former teacher as burned out on teaching and explained that quite often, Hauser would space out for long periods, just staring out the classroom window, daydreaming. Other times, he would rant. The driver could be so accurate about the date Hauser left because the new teacher had been really talented. He'd given his kids a lot of confidence; plus, the students actually started going on field trips.

Hauser went to work for the Green-Penn County Co-op after he left teaching. That new career didn't last. After Hauser left his job at the co-op, he wound up filling a vacancy at Bloom High School as their Agriculture teacher. The man had heard some other rumors about Hauser but Ray already heard them.

"There's another piece of the puzzle we've been looking for, Kick ... a big piece," Ray said. "All we need to do now is verify that Cleve Hauser left his teaching job at Hampton before Trudie's murder. If it's true, he could have been anywhere, anytime."

Kick smiled. "And to think of all the people who thought Cleve was still a teacher at the time."

"Some still do, but that'll happen when false information is repeated over and over," Ray said. "It becomes true."

"The trucker verified the student's nickname for

Hauser. They called him 'WAS.' Kids even tagged teachers when I was in school," Kick said. "Every student uses their nicknames."

"Yeah, always behind their back," Ray said. "I wonder if any teachers ever find out."

Ray read the newspapers regularly and so like everybody else, he was aware of molestation scandals in the church. Kick sent a letter of inquiry to St. Mary's Catholic School, where Cleve Hauser attended grade school. Because of the nature of the molestation of Trudie, Ray didn't discount the possibility that Cleve might have experienced a childhood trauma as a schoolboy, or even as an altar boy. Maybe there would be evidence on record. He was pretty sure it wouldn't be available, but it was worth a phone call. Some folks told Ray before that Cleve was shell-shocked from the war, but Ray was now convinced that Cleve's problem began much earlier than Vietnam. None of the people who had known Cleve longest said anything about the war changing him.

Within a couple of weeks, Kick received a reply to her letter. It said that there were no rosters of past altar servers, or the priests who were active in the school, or at the church, back in the 1950's. They were all deceased. All of the old records had been destroyed.

Ray handed the letter back to Kick. "It looks as if only Cleve Hauser himself can answer my questions," Ray said.

"Throwing records away is never a good sign," Kick said.

Ray got another break in the investigation from Trudie's best friend, Dina. Her memory was jogged during a conversation with Ray pertaining to the details of Trudie's murder.

Ray told Dina that they'd gotten an opinion by a pathologist who stated unequivocally that Trudie had been raped post-mortem.

Dina excused herself for a moment. Ray thought her voice sounded choked up. He imagined she was crying. Dina remembered that a few days after Trudie's murder, another classmate of hers, the youngest son of a Hampton police officer, told her that he overheard his dad talking to someone about Trudie's murder. His dad told the person that Trudie had been raped after she was already dead.

"How come you didn't say so?" Ray asked.

"I didn't want to think about it," Dina told him.

Ray thought back to when he was eleven years old. He decided that Kick should follow up on Dina's story about the son of the Hampton police officer. There were certain things kids didn't forget and this would be one of them.

"Dina told me that their other friend named her daughter after Trudie. These girls were tight," Ray said.

Kick drove down to the museum and pulled out a copy of a Hampton High School yearbook. She wrote down a few names and numbers and then went out into the parking lot and got into her car. She took her cell phone out of her purse.

Forty-five minutes later, she called Ray. She knew he was going to be in and out of the office and she wanted to tell what she had found. She caught him just as he was putting on his coat.

Kick had a pretty big story. "I found that classmate Dina told you about listed in the phone book, so I called. Number still works. Turns out he's the older brother of the kid from Trudie's class," Kick said. "His name's Tim Logan, Officer Spencer Logan's son."

"Is this a long story?" Ray interrupted.

"I got a lot of information, Boss."

"Did he say where you could find his little brother?" Ray asked.

"He didn't have to, he knew everything," Kick said. "And he told everything."

"Come on back to the office and tell me here," Ray said.

"I thought you were going out," Kick said.

"I'll wait," Ray said.

When Kick arrived a half hour later, she was bubbling.

"Tell me the whole thing from the beginning," Ray said. He sat back down in his desk chair.

Tim told Kick he remembered Hugh Dixon coming over to their dad's house the day of the murder. Their dad told the kids to leave the room. Tim said he and his little brother hid around the corner and listened.

Dixon told their dad that he saw a car at the Brices'

earlier in the day — a green Olds Cutlass. He said his dad told Dixon that he would pass along the information to the Sheriff's Department. Once Dixon left, Tim heard his dad tell their mother that the Olds Cutlass belonged to someone who was on the Hampton Fire Department, as well as the police department. When Tim grew up, he remembered the conversation that day. He'd been pretty shaken up by the death of Trudie. Death wasn't supposed to happen to people their age. He remembered how in the hallway of the school the next day there was a frantic buzzing and when he passed a group of girls, he heard one say that Trudie Brice was dead.

Years later, someone Tim was talking to — he couldn't even remember who — mentioned the Trudie Brice murder. Tim remembered the visit Hugh Dixon paid to their dad and he got a friend whose brother was a firefighter to check into personnel records for the Fire Department, to see if there was a name Tim might remember. The friend got his hands on a roster for the middle 1980s and copied down names. He gave the list to Tim. There was nothing really wrong with what they did, but they felt funny about it. Tim had looked down the list of names recognizing almost none, except for Mitch Wiersma. Tim knew who the Wiersmas were. Who didn't in Hampton?

Then he remembered one more thing. His father, Spencer Logan had, of course, a professional and per-sonal respect for the Wiersma family. Tim remembered his dad arguing with Hugh about what Hugh was saying. "You can't bring the Wiersmas into this," he said. Their dad was concerned how it would look for a Wiersma's car to be at the Brice house the day of the murder. The present Sheriff, Chip Wiersma, was a patrolman on the Sheriff's department when the Brice murder took place. You couldn't mess with the Wiersmas even back then.

"The brother was in school with Trudie, right?" Ray asked. "Did he know Cleve Hauser?"

"Tim said he knew Cleve, but said he didn't have him for Ag class," Kick said. "And by the time Tim was old enough to take the class, Cleve had already left and been replaced by a new instructor."

After he looked at the list from the firehouse — just a few years ago — Tim had gone over to his parents' for supper. He asked his dad if he knew anything about the old case. Spencer said he thought the murderer was a psychopath. He also thought that the murderer had been hiding in the old vacant house across the street from the Brices'. As they talked about it, his mother, who was usually pretty quiet, jumped in. She said you couldn't trust Hugh Dixon, he was a bartender, and a joker, and an unreliable witness.

"My mom didn't really know Hugh," Tim said. "But she's opposed to alcohol and in her mind even a stone sober bartender can't overcome the fact that he sells booze."

Spencer took Hugh's side. He told Tim's mom that Hugh Dixon might be a lot of things, but he'd vouch for one thing certain — Hugh Dixon was no liar, nor was he a fool.

"Good story," Ray said. "You'll want to make notes on that."

Kick reached into her purse and pulled out her notepad.

"I asked Tim to have his dad call you," Kick said.

There were plenty of ill-sorted memories and rumors about Cleve's whereabouts the day of the murder. The stories contradicted one another. Ray and Kick visited the Hampton School Superintendent's office to review the School Board minutes. Ray told the Superintendent he was trying to find out when a former teacher, Cleve Hauser, left Hampton High School. She called in her assistant who returned a few minutes later with three big leather-bound books. She set them down on a table in the waiting room. Ray stared at Kick as she flipped through the pages of one of the books.

"What would the correspondence look like?" Ray asked.

Kick turned her book sideways and pointed to a letter of resignation from another schoolteacher as an example. Ray slid one of the other books in front of him and opened it. He tapped Kick's shoulder and pointed to his book.

"This what you're looking for?" Ray asked.

Kick leaned her head back, looking up. "Thanks, Trudie."

She then pulled the book closer and read aloud:

"Members of the School Board,

Effective immediately, I wish to resign my position as

Ag teacher ... Sincerely, Cleve Hauser."

Kick looked over at Ray.

"This letter's dated August, 1985, a year and four months before the murder," Kick said. "That truck driver was right."

A couple days later, Ray was struck by a sudden impulse. He felt it was important that he and Kick go to the cemetery. They never got there.

Ray and Kick had a few miles to go to Willow Grove Cemetery when Ray pointed to the Hampton Methodist Church.

"Pull over," Ray said.

Ray knocked on the parish door of Reverend Gary Hitt and introduced himself and Kick. Reverend Hitt stepped out on the doorstep. "I got your message about the Brices, but I haven't been too successful finding the old church records," Reverend Hitt said.

Kick thought it was interesting that Reverend Hitt had even remembered the message she left. She'd called several times and gotten no response. Ray had moved on to other sources.

"I just wanted to know when Ronda Jo and Stan Brice were elected to the Church Board," Ray said.

"I'll keep looking for you," the Reverend said.

Reverend Hitt didn't ask them inside but they stood in the sun and he chatted freely. He said he was sixteen years old at the time of Trudie's murder. He remembered her attending services at the Methodist Church and said she was a good girl, and full of energy.

Then he said something casually that Ray wished he'd learned a long time ago. Reverend Hitt told them that soon after Kick's call about the Brices being on the church board, he'd gotten an e-mail from Reverend Billy Jack Hummock asking how things were going. Reverend Hitt thought that was a coincidence.

Ray looked over at Kick and raised his eyebrows. It surprised him that whenever Destiny or Grace was clearly at work, there would be a Reverend somewhere in the mix.

Reverend Hitt remarked that Cleve Hauser was a "player" with the women back then. All the kids at school knew this about him. Sometimes Hauser would come to class with scratches or bruises on his face. Rumor was either a jealous husband or boyfriend had beat up Hauser. It was yet another aspect of Hauser who, in Ray and Kick's minds, was becoming a very, very complex man.

Reverend Hitt said that Henry View, the pastor who succeeded Reverend Hummock at the Methodist Church, received a letter from Peter Lacey, Tammy's Englishman. Lacey had gone back to England and wrote wanting to know how the Brices were doing after their terrible tragedy. Reverend View gave the letter to Detective Fowler. Fowler, at the time, asked Reverend View if he found anything unusual in the letter. Reverend View told the Detective, No, it was just a letter of concern asking about the Brice family as far as he could see. It seemed to Reverend View that it strongly suggested that Lacey wasn't involved in the case in any way. Detective Fowler took the letter and told Reverend View he would file it away. He also instructed Reverend View to keep the information in the letter to himself.

Reverend Hitt said the word around town was that Detective Fowler had pretty much messed everything up on the murder case.

Ray wasn't sure what he meant.

"I think you're not supposed to mess with the evidence," the Reverend said. "People said Fowler took Trudie out of the tub, laid her on the floor and covered her with the rug. I guess they couldn't dust for fingerprints or whatever they do."

Ray said it did look as though somebody had been careless, though he wasn't sure that Detective Fowler was the only one. Ray reassured Reverend Hitt, though, that there were other ways of finding out what happened.

Reverend Hitt threw Ray a conspiratorial look. He lowered his voice a little and stepped back into the shadow of the overhang above the parish door. It all felt a little melodramatic to Ray, but often he didn't quite understand pastors. Reverend Hitt told Ray that his grandmother, who still lived near the Brice house, mentioned that Trudie's spirit appears from time to time around her house. Ray and Kick didn't know how to respond. Something about the idea of ghosts that haunted places seemed not quite to be what pastors were supposed to believe in. Reverend Hitt went on to say that his grandmother prayed, as they all did, that one day someone would finally get the person who did the awful deed.

"Sounds like our prayers are being answered," Reverend Hitt said, holding his hand out toward Ray.

Chapter 10

Ray e-mailed Willy, the same bloke that helped clear his deceased friend, Roger Lawford, of Trudie's murder.

Dear Willy,

I need your help. There is another Brit who was not part of your group of cycle enthusiasts who was in Hampton during the time of Trudie Brice's murder. His name is Peter Lacey. For years, his name has been tossed around as a suspect. Peter Lacey married a woman from Hampton named Tammy Lemel in September of 1986. They separated shortly after and finally divorced in 1987. Peter Lacey returned to England. Would you be kind enough to see if you can find the whereabouts of Peter Lacey for me?

Rumor has it that Lacey was in the States at the time of the murder and left soon after. For the life of me, I can't see why his passport wasn't pulled if he was of interest to the Sheriff's Department unless they were using him as a scapegoat, same as they used your friend Roger.

Cheerio,

Ray Krouse

Though Tim Logan had promised he'd put his father, Spencer, in touch with Ray, the call never came. Ray thought that Spencer's recurrence in the story, both times in connection with Hugh Dixon spotting the car in the Brices' driveway, was interesting but probably a coincidence. He was glad to run into Spencer Logan at one of the local watering holes. He had moved out of the county and Ray welcomed him back. Logan confirmed both his conversations with Hugh Dixon about the Olds Cutlass in 1986 and again in 1991. He also confirmed the car was Mitch Wiersma's. He told Ray he knew that the former Hampton Chief of Police, Bud Lackey, was in the Brice house and that Lackey would know who took Trudie out of the bathtub, if not himself.

However, he couldn't guarantee that Lackey would tell Ray anything useful, let alone truthful. "Lackey was one of the good ol' boys, part of Sheriff Wiersma's clique," Logan said. "You'll never get a straight answer out of him on anything."

Logan told Ray that Lackey had to know quite a bit about the case since Lackey let the Sheriff's Department use the Hampton Police Department's office as their head-quarters for at least three or four days after the murder.

Logan said Lackey eventually had to step down from his position as chief when others on the force threatened to turn him in for dummying up reports.

Ray started to slide out of the booth.

"I guess you already know about the lunch bucket," Logan said.

Ray sat back down. He signaled the bartender for a double. "You talking about the black lunch pail with Hauser's name stenciled on it?" Ray said.

"That's the one," Logan said.

"The police found it outside the old house across the street," Ray said.

"No. They found it inside," Logan said.

"Well," Ray said. He reached out and tossed a couple of bills on the waitress's tray as she passed. "You would have thought the lunch pail would get their attention."

Ray called Reverend Henry View, the pastor who received the letter from Peter Lacey. The best Reverend View could remember was that he received it some time in 1988 or 1989. He was surprised that Reverend Hitt knew the story in the first place and that he had remembered it. Reverend View, as Reverend Hitt had said, gave it to Detective Fowler. The Reverend confirmed that Fowler asked him if what the letter said meant anything to him. He told Fowler it didn't. "Lacey's letter just asked how the Brice family was getting along — nothing strange," the

Reverend said. "I was glad that he wrote. They needed support from as many people as possible then."

"Peter Lacey was a member of the same church the Brices were," Reverend View said. "I don't think a killer would write a nice letter to the members of the church if he were the little girl's killer."

Ray agreed. It was hard to believe that anyone could be so stupid.

Reverend View told Ray that Detective Fowler told him not to answer the letter and to keep its contents to himself. Fowler assured Reverend View that he would hold on to the letter.

"Looks like Reverend Hitt and Reverend View pretty much remember the same information about the letter from Peter Lacey," Ray told Kick.

Reverend View went on to tell Ray that Trudie's parents were odd from the time he first met them. He said the Brices had their adopted children write letters to Trudie and then take the letters out to the cemetery. It was creepy, the Reverend felt. He said he considered it border-line child abuse. Ray asked if the Brices' behavior became strange after their daughter's death. Reverend View said they were troubled before Trudie's murder, but after her passing, their anguish increased, especially Ronda Jo's.

Reverend View said he and Mrs. Fowler, at one time, were both school bus drivers with the Hampton school system. He told Ray that he once commented to her that he felt the Brice murder investigation had been dropped right in the middle, when things seemed to be moving along.

"Mrs. Fowler wasn't too pleased with my opinion," Reverend View said.

Ray had been out doing an errand. It was lunch time and he was hungry so he pulled over and called Kick on his cell phone. He told her to be ready, he was going to take her to lunch. It was still only November, not long before Thanksgiving, but it was already cold and there was a strong west wind.

When he pulled up to the office, Kick dashed out the door wearing her parka. She opened the door and jumped in bringing a big puff of cold air with her.

"Reverend Hitt just called," Kick said. "He finally found some of the old church records. Ronda Jo was made assistant secretary of the church board in May of 1986, and Helen Hummock made a motion to make Stan Brice a church trustee shortly after."

They headed toward the highway and pulled into a little restaurant they'd never visited but Ray had been interested in trying. The lot had several big rigs in it though they were miles from the interstate. Ray knew that if a place was popular with truckers, it must be something special. Ray ordered the shepherd's pie, good cold weather food. Kick had a bowl of minestrone.

The beginning of winter often makes people reflective. They had to get serious about survival and it was a reminder of mortality. For the last few days, Ray had been trying to figure out why his research was often disappointing.

"It isn't as though people are uninformed," Ray said. "Word gets around in the countryside."

"When they want it to," Kick said.

"Everything has to be repeated, over and over with them," Ray said. "It's not the people, it's probably me, Kick. I can't seem to stop, I owe it to Trudie. Maybe I should back off some of the folks who've been helping, you know, give them a rest."

"You've always said that Trudie was your concern," Kick said. "You're not likely to change your mind about that, Boss."

"Everyone I've talked to always says Trudie was a sweet little girl. Every once in a while someone will say she was also spunky, but most kids are full of oats," Ray said. "Especially an only child."

"I talked to Reverend Hitt's sister," Kick said.

"Anything interesting?"

"Nothing new, really. She said some of the folks liked Detective Fowler, but said that Detective Skipper was foul," Kick said. "Plus he was a big drinker."

"I knew of a lot of big drinkers in my day, but I'll say one thing, drinking and investigating don't mix too well," Ray said. "By the way, a guy named Lewis Nutt called me on the cell phone. He said he got a message from Pauline to call. I don't remember you saying anything about him."

"Someone told me he might have some radio logs. He was on the Hampton Fire Department at the time of the murder," Kick said. "Pauline knew him. She said he was a jerk. So what happened?"

"I told him I've been working on the Trudie Brice murder case for the past two years. He says to me, 'You're a little late, ain't you?' I said, 'I'm not a police officer, I'm a writer.' Then the guy says, 'Writer? Well then, I like talking to writers less than police officers.' So I hung up on him," Ray said.

"Don't you think Hugh must have let him know about you," Kick said.

"Sure I do. I just think for some reason he wanted to stick it to me," Ray said. "What's his relationship to Shine Nutt?"

"Remind me who he is," Kick said.

"Shine is the guy who'd heard direct from Cleve's own brother-in-law that Cleve had bragged he'd tried to resuscitate Trudie ..." Ray said.

"Okay, I remember now," Kick said. "Hugh talked to Shine and got the story wrong the first time."

"When a story is told too often, that happens," Ray said.

Kick shrugged. "Lewis Nutt sounds like an idiot," she said. "He had some sort of nickname though, some kind of animal."

"Yes, I think it was Weasel," Ray said.

"They say nicknames usually make a connection with the person," Kick said.

"In Weasel's case it does," Ray said.

Toward the end of the week, it turned sunny. Kick just hung up the phone as Ray walked into his office.

"Yesterday we were talking about where Cleve Hauser went after he murdered Trudie," Kick said.

Ray took off his trench coat and hung it on the coat rack. "And?" Ray said.

"I can tell you where he went after leaving the Shackleys' doorstep," Kick said.

"Home?" Ray said.

"No, to his friend's house, that Val White. I was just talking to him before you walked in," Kick said.

"Val White verified that he was with Cleve at his house?" Ray said.

"No. He told me an outrageous lie," Kick said.

"I'm waiting," Ray said.

"Okay, but let me tell you something else first," Kick said. "What you've been saying all along — that Trudie's dog played an important part in you being able to piece together the murder — is true."

"Explain it to me," Ray said.

"The dog wouldn't have left Trudie unless it recognized the man at the door ..."

"Sounds right," Ray said. "Dogs are more your specialty than mine."

"Everyone who knew about Trudie's dog, Tuffy, knew it was her protector," Kick said.

Kick explained how Tuffy had to be let out by someone the dog knew, maybe to do its "duty", but the dog was always let back in afterwards. Tuffy would have been all over anyone struggling with Trudie, growling and biting. The intruder knew that because he'd been in the Brices' house plenty of times before.

"See, once the dog was let out that day, it was never let back in," Kick said.

"And you know that because ..." Ray said.

"Because Tuffy would have never left Trudie's side. It would have laid right by the bathtub whining and guarding Trudie's body," Kick said.

Those kinds of faithful dog stories always sound like exaggerations but Ray knew some were true. "I remember a friend of mine who died and his dog wouldn't leave the man's gravesite. In fact, the dog was found dead at the site some weeks later," Ray said.

"There are plenty of stories about dogs and their loyalty to their owners," Kick said.

"The person who let Trudie's dog out was her killer," Ray said.

"There's no doubt about it," Kick said. "You remember Trudie's friend, Dina, telling us that Tuffy even bit her when her and Trudie were roughhousing."

"To tell the truth, I couldn't get that dog out of my mind. I found myself asking people that were around Trudie if they remembered her dog. Not one person didn't. And everyone would mention that the dog was Trudie's protector. Most of them didn't remember the dog's name, but just the same, they all remembered that when Trudie was around, that dog was usually by her side," Ray said.

"Enough of Tuffy," Kick said.

"Maybe for now, but I have a feeling another dog story or two will pop up again before this investigation is over," Ray said.

As December approached, Ray worked on the background. He thought that maybe the fact that this was the season, Trudie might mysteriously make someone who had held back until now step forward.

Ray finally tracked down Sherry Marshall, the other living musketeer. She had moved a few times, most recently to a town about thirty miles away, so Ray and Kick had had a hard time finding her. She didn't want to drive to Hampton and so Ray met her there in a little coffee shop in the center of town one afternoon. They sat at a table near the back though there was only one other couple there, an elderly pair in a front booth. With nothing more to do, the waitress kept filling Ray's cup with weak coffee.

As it turned out, Tammy Lemel was a half sister to Sherry's mom. Sherry had some information on Peter Lacey. She said Peter was abusive. On one occasion, he threw his stepson up against the kitchen wall. Sherry also said that she heard Lacey put out cigarettes on one of Tammy's kids.

"So much for him being a nice guy," Ray said, half to himself.

"Someone told you that?" Sherry said. "It's a lie." Like Tammy Lemel, Sherry thought Lacey was a monster.

Sherry said she got an obscene phone call after the

murder. The caller told her that he killed Trudie and then threatened to kill her if she repeated what he said. She believed it was Peter Lacey. It would have been pretty hard to fake that accent.

Once more, Ray wondered why old friends of Sherry's hadn't told him this. He was pretty sure it was something a little girl wouldn't have dreamed up on her own, and something she most likely would have shared with her friends.

Not long after Ray drove back to the office, he got a call from Sherry. Kick buzzed him in his office and he picked up. Sherry had something else for him. She said she heard that Lacey took two lie detector tests and passed, but she said the Penn County Sheriff's Department were a bunch of assholes, so what the fuck did a lie detector test mean anyway?

Sherry handed the phone to her mother. Sherry's mother told Ray that Detective Skipper came to her house the day after the lie detector test and told her family that Lacey was flying back to England. The Detective said there was no way to stop him since they didn't have any evidence to charge him with. Sherry's mom said Detective Skipper told them that Lacey was their number-one suspect. As soon as he hung up, Ray called Kick into his office and told her.

"Number one suspect? How stupid is that?" Kick said.

"Hold on, there's more," Ray said. "Sherry was also

home with the flu that day. She told me that the day of the murder, she'd been talking to Trudie on the telephone on and off all morning. Sherry remembered Trudie telling her that her mom was dropping off her lunch, so Trudie should take a bath and get dressed. Sherry said that Trudie told her to hold on, because someone was at the door. Sherry heard the knocking in the background, then the phone went dead. Afterwards, Sherry said she tried to call Trudie back but all she got was a busy signal. Sherry thought that the knock on the door was Trudie's killer. I told her it could have been anybody. Could have been Ronda Jo."

"Why would Ronda Jo knock?" Kick asked.

"Forgot her key, maybe. Lots of reasons," Ray said.

"She never told the police?" Kick asked.

"Sherry's mom said the police weren't interested in a story from a young girl, a friend of Trudie's. 'Girls make things up,' they told her."

"Nobody ever said anything about seeing Ronda Jo's car," Kick said.

"Maybe she got a ride. There was a car in the drive-way about that time," Ray said.

Kick paused for a beat. "Mitch Wiersma's green Olds." All of a sudden another piece of the puzzle was starting to fit in place.

"I told them my theory about how the murder took place since they asked me," Ray said.

"What did they have to say then?" Kick asked.

"What could they say? But then Sherry's mom said

she was standing next to Reverend Hummock at Trudie's funeral and he gave her bad vibes. She also said that Peter Lacey was crazy and did dope," Ray said.

"Are they coming to the lake house party?" Kick asked.

Ray shrugged and held out his hands. He was trying to pull together a second meeting at the lake house.

A few days later, Sherry called Ray back one more time. Kick took the call and whispered to Ray that it was Sherry. When Ray took the phone she launched to her story without any preamble. She said she had a letter with some photographs that Peter Lacey mailed from England. They were sent to a woman he was attracted to that lived next door to a relative of Sherry's. Ray didn't ask how she got her hands on them. Some things weren't worth going into.

Two of the photographs were dated the same as the letter — July, 1987. The other picture was dated January, 1993. On the reverse side of the 1993 photo, Lacey wrote:

"To my sexy friend, Laura. Lots of love."

At the bottom of the letter was Lacey's home telephone number in Great Britain. Sherry read the number to Ray and said she would send Ray copies of what she had.

Sherry asked Ray to have Kick send her copies of the class pictures of Trudie that Ray had. She said she'd lost the ones she had years ago. Sherry said she and Trudie were close, like peas in a pod. Ray told her the photos would be sent along with directions to his lake house that her mother and she were invited to.

Ray asked Kick to try again to find out where Lacey was. She came in early the next morning so her call wouldn't be received too late on account of the time difference. Kick called Lacey's number overseas. By chance, on the first call, Kick reached Peter's sister, Ruth Lacey, and explained who she was and the reason for her call. Ruth told Kick she would relay all the information to her brother, but she wasn't sure he would speak to Ray. Kick told her all Ray wanted to do was clear her brother's name from Trudie's murder. Ruth said since their mother died, her brother and she didn't see much of each other.

Driving into work, Hugh Dixon dropped by again, as on other occasions, to tell Ray he ran into "Weasel" Nutt. He hobbled into the room, his foot still hurting. Ray wondered how he could stay on his feet tending bar.

Hugh wanted to talk about Weasel. Weasel told Hugh that after Ray hung up on him, Weasel contacted the Sheriff's Department, and the County Coroner to tell them that Ray was looking for information on the Brice murder. Hugh assumed that Weasel was trying to cause trouble. He could be about as nasty as they come and he was pissed off that Ray hung up on him.

Both offices told Weasel they already knew about Ray's investigation and, according to Weasel, the Sheriff told him he didn't want anyone talking to Ray about the case. Hugh was a big supporter of Ray's investigation and when Ray ran into opposition, Hugh took it personally.

"I hope that got Weasel a couple of good boys," Ray said.

"Probably," Hugh said.

Hugh walked slowly down the steps. He blew his car horn as he pulled away.

"Now I can see why the Coroner kept lying to me about sending us copies of the Coroner's report. It's a cover-up," Kick said. "I'm glad you had me contact the down state Coroner's office on him."

Dixon had also found the firefighter who was driving the truck that Junebug Davenport was on, a guy named Shawn Harvey. Harvey told Dixon that he went up the stairway off the kitchen with his fire hose while Junebug guarded the bathroom door.

"You want me to give him a call?" Kick asked.

"Can't hurt," Ray said.

"I called Pauline this morning. So far, we have about ten people coming to the lake house," Kick said.

"That's good. Make sure we have plenty of food and drink. They've all been great help to us. I want everyone to have a good time," Ray said. "I feel it's time to let them go, I get the feeling they've had their fill of the investigation."

"Did someone say something?" Kick asked.

"No, but I can tell," Ray said. "People like Hugh and Ted are making enemies now, and they've lived here their whole lives. They're seeing a side of their neighbors that they've never seen."

"They're bound to have neighbors who see things different than them," Kick said. "That's what makes life interesting."

"Even so, that can't be good for them. You and I will push on alone," Ray said. "I'm going to start working on the first draft of my book."

"So, are we still saving Cleve Hauser for the last interview?" Kick asked.

"Yes. And isn't it's amazing that he's never tried to contact us? He's probably nervous as hell. I'll have you call him. I have a deep down feeling that he'll be more comfortable talking with you," Ray said.

Kick got another lead from Pauline, a woman from the next county, married to a lawyer. The woman used to keep a horse at Pauline's stable. The animal had to be put down and the woman was looking into buying another. Kick drove out to meet her at the stable. They stood and talked outside a stall where there was a small chestnut mare that the woman liked. Her brother, as it turned out, was married to Tammy Lemel before she married Peter Lacey. "It wasn't a marriage the family thought much of," she said. The family thought Tammy was beneath them. The woman remembered that Tammy told folks that Lacey wanted her to sell their television so he could buy a handgun.

Kick drove back to the office and told Ray the story.

"Someone who wants a gun ends up strangling his victim? I don't think so," Ray said.

"She said she was thrilled that you were working on solving Trudie's murder," Kick said.

"Did she know who the passerby was?" Ray asked.

"She said the local paper kept it a secret," Kick said.

"But she knows?" Ray asked.

"Yes, she named him," Kick said.

Ray received a telephone call from Reverend Stan Coby, a minister from the Hampton Church of the Brethren. He told Ray that he and his wife wanted to help with his investigation. Unsolicited help was such a rare thing anymore that Ray felt a little suspicious.

Ray and Kick drove over to the parish office. By the time they arrived, the Reverend's wife had left for an appointment. Ray had hoped to talk to them together. Reverend Coby showed them into his office and asked his secretary to hold all calls. Ray looked around noticing how this office looked like every other pastor's office he'd ever seen, same third-world picture of Jesus, same framed calligraphy with a favorite verse, same books, same personalized coffee mug.

Reverend Coby was a cheerful man. He told Ray that his wife, Vivian, worked with Tammy Lemel and Ronda Jo Brice at a Women's Pregnancy Care Center in Riverside around the time of the murder. The three women were very close at the time.

Reverend Coby said he and his wife recently popped into a local mart. The Reverend pointed out a woman he believed to be Ronda Jo. When he and his wife approached her, she was standoffish. Ronda Jo's demeanor shocked them. It was as if Ronda Jo wanted to avoid them.

Reverend Coby said he mentioned Tammy Lemel's name and Ronda Jo cut him off, saying she didn't want to talk about Tammy.

The Reverend told Ray that their feelings were hurt. He told Ray all he knew about the Brice murder.

Ray filled Reverend Coby in on the details of his investigation. Ray also shared the "calling" that drew him to Trudie's murder.

"God opens doors for those with compassion," Reverend Coby said. "God knows all and He's interested in the truth coming out. Therefore, God will continue to guide you."

Ray looked at his watch. Vivian hadn't returned. They agreed to talk again.

When they got back into the truck, Ray said, "At least this minister knows the works of the Holy Ghost."

"You have your doubts about Reverend Hitt, don't you?" Kick said.

"I could be wrong," Ray said.

Ruth Lacey called Ray back from England. It was a little after noon, early evening her time. She said that she passed along Ray's information to her brother, but she indicated that Peter wouldn't be calling Ray. Ruth told Ray that a serious motorcycle accident had left her brother disabled. Ruth finally admitted that she and her brother weren't close, but whether they got along or not, she didn't think her brother would harm anyone.

Ray had to accept that things weren't right between Ruth and her brother, but he didn't really think their bad relationship would have any effect on the outcome of little Trudie's murder. Cleve Hauser was the key suspect.

A day after their visit to Reverend Coby's office, Kick set up a conference call for Ray to talk with the Reverend and his wife together. Kick was prepared to piece together the whole conversation by listening to Ray, but Ray made it easy. He told her to pick up the line on another phone.

Vivian told Ray she never really heard much about Trudie's murder, other than rumors. She said her husband filled her in on all the information Ray relayed to him during their first conversation. Some of the things she remembered now made more sense to her.

Vivian remembered that before the murder, Ronda Jo was a sweet, caring mother who loved Trudie. She said that she believed Trudie got her own sweetness from Ronda Jo. Vivian told Ray that she and Ronda Jo bonded because they both had to wait so long to have a child. "Each of us was only able to have one," she said.

This was a picture of Ronda Jo very different from the one Ray had gotten from Ronda Jo's sister-in-law, who described her as anything but a "sweet" person.

Vivian said that she and her husband hadn't seen Ronda Jo for a long time until the day they ran into her at the mart. Vivian said she hardly recognized Ronda Jo, she looked as if she had aged beyond her years. She said Ronda Jo was mean and rude. Her husband, the Reverend, agreed.

Ray hung up and looked at Kick. "I was right. Tammy was pregnant when Lacey returned to England."

"He didn't want to pay child support?" Kick asked.

"Partly right. Vivian said there was a good chance that the baby wasn't even his," Ray said. "Turns out Tammy kept telling Vivian and Ronda Jo that she was worried the baby was going to be black."

Vivian said Tammy told her and Ronda Jo that she "had needs," she had to have a man.

Vivian also said Reverend Hummock was an ignorant man. Ray asked her why she thought that. She said it was because Reverend Hummock told Ronda Jo that she had an evil spirit following her, a devil that came into his home when he let the Brices move in with them after the murder.

"That sounds like something worse than ignorance to me," Kick said.

Vivian said that Tammy had been desperate enough to take out a classified ad in the newspaper seeking a Christian husband. That's how she met Peter Lacey. Because of the way they met, and the short time they knew each other — only a few months — they had a hard time finding a preacher to marry them; that is until they asked Reverend Hummock, Vivian said.

Vivian told Ray that her father called to tell her about the fire at the Brice's. Vivian thought she should call Tammy. That's when Peter Lacey answered the phone, crying and all choked up. He told Vivian that Tammy had gone over to the church to be with Ronda Jo and Reverend Hummock and that Trudie had been murdered. Vivian remembered the time was around 3:30 p.m. Vivian agreed with Ray that most everyone in Hampton knew about the fire and murder by this time, or shortly thereafter. Later on, Tammy told Vivian that her husband, Peter, said he'd gone to Keysville on a job interview.

Reverend Coby said he believed that Reverend Hummock knew more than what he let on to Ray.

The Cobys finally agreed that Ronda Jo was a loose woman. She took after her father. "She had bad childhood memories. Her mother was an alcoholic," Vivian said.

"Were the Cobys and the Brices friends?" Kick asked.

"At one time," Ray said.

Ray continued. "It's all beginning to add up. After leaving the fire, Tammy was the first person Ronda Jo called when she returned to the hardware store."

"So they were best friends," Kick said.

"I think that Tammy convinced her that Peter killed Trudie," Ray said.

"Didn't Reverend Hummock say the same thing?" Kick asked.

"He was reluctant to name names," Ray said.

Ray had Kick try to reach Reverend Hummock again. He wouldn't answer any of the calls, so finally, Ray had Kick send the Reverend an e-mail:

Hello Reverend Hummock,

I thought you'd like to know that Ray found Peter Lacey in England. If you're interested in knowing about his conversation, feel free to give Ray a call. You have his toll-free number.

"You will know the truth, and the truth will set you free." (John 8:32)

Regards,

Kick Jetton

"It's been almost two months and still no word from Hummock," Ray said. "Odd for a man who's been e-mailing some of his fellow ministers wanting to know the scuttlebutt and the goings-on in Penn County."

"Especially after all the years that have gone by with nobody hearing one word from him," Kick said.

"I'm sure we haven't heard the last of Reverend Hummock," Ray said. "I'd like to talk to him some more about Peter Lacey."

"You think he's keeping something back?" Kick asked.

"I think he's been lying from the get go," Ray said.

"The folks of Penn County have been very accommodating when they feel like it," Kick said.

"Who knows, maybe Ronda Jo, Mitch Wiersma,

Reverend Hummock, or Cleve Hauser himself will step forward and tell what was going on," Ray said.

"Don't hold your breath," Kick said.

Ray was at the strip mall getting a bad cup of coffee to go. The guy at the counter was making a new pot and Ray waited. The previous patron had left part of a newspaper on the counter. In the local news there was an article about Hauser, who had a class that was studying gun safety. Ray took the newspaper with him when he left.

When he got to the office he put the cup of hot coffee on his desk and sat down. He called one of his friends, a Conservation Officer. Ray told the Conservation Officer that if he ever saw Cleve Hauser on any of his farm property, Ray wanted him arrested for trespassing. The C.O. told Ray that he was probably overreacting and said he thought Cleve was doing something valid. Ray explained his investigation of the Brice murder, and the detailed map where Cleve Hauser put himself in the crime scene. Ray didn't trust Cleve at all.

The Conservation Officer said he didn't mean to suggest he personally liked Cleve. He told Ray a story about how he was out on patrol for poachers one night when he happened upon a parked car with its headlights off. The occupants were an older man, who turned out to be a local schoolteacher, and a young girl. Her clothes were disheveled. The officer said the teacher told him they were on a picnic.

The Conservation Officer said he reported the incident to the Sheriff's Department and the man was dismissed from his teaching job. Shortly after, the officer said Hauser inquired about his colleague's romp in the woods. Once filled in, Hauser made the comment, "So what's the big deal? She's in high school, what she was doing was her business." The Conservation Officer told Ray he knew then that Hauser lacked any moral compass. That was the kind of story Ray had heard from Pauline about Cleve's interest in her farmer friend's granddaughter. It was the kind of story that couldn't help but give one bad vibes about Hauser.

Ray told the officer he wouldn't have called him, but the article mentioned Hauser was teaching school kids about guns in local wilderness areas, and he wanted to make certain Hauser wasn't hunting on his land. Hauser might accidentally mistake him or Kick for a deer.

However much it might seem they were going in circles, Ray and Kick continued to net more information. They'd caught up with Reverend Hummock and Sherry Marshall, even Roger Lawford's friend, Willy, and Peter Lacey's sister in England. Kick had copied a list of School Board members when they were at the Superintendent's office. They recognized some of the names and a quick check of records showed that others were now deceased.

Then, Ray got a lead on a person who used to be a Hampton School Board member, Lon Coughlin. When he retired, he and his wife, Ethel, moved out of Indiana.

Kick called and found both of the Coughlins very

cooperative. Ethel repeated most of the old rumors about Peter Lacey that had been circulating the county for the past two decades. Lon, on the other hand, had some hard facts.

Lon told Ray he was in a local restaurant, Mom's Diner, the day of the murder. He remembered that Peter Lacey stopped in for coffee some time between one and two in the afternoon. He remembered Peter was dressed up, as if he were going somewhere special. Peter had on a clean, crisp, white shirt, and no tie. "He was cleaned up," Lon said. Lon wondered what the occasion was, so he asked. Lacey said he was headed for Keysville to interview for a job as a cook. This seemed to Ray to pretty definitely match what Vivian Coby said about Peter's whereabouts that afternoon.

After the murder, Lon said he told Detective Fowler about seeing Peter on his way to Keysville, ten miles out of town. Lon said no one ever followed up with him, but shortly after, word was Peter Lacey was a suspect.

Ray told Lon that two other people shared the same story that Lacey was in Keysville — one was a preacher's wife and the other was Lacey' ex-wife, Tammy Lemel.

Lon shared other stories about Hauser being a womanizer and his dark demeanor. He told Ray that he always thought that Cleve Hauser was the killer.

Kick had gone to the Green-Penn County Co-op to get a few things she needed. She was planning to do some baking and liked the freshest ingredients. The co-op was almost empty. Kick was bagging some rice when one of the employees came up to her. He was wearing an apron that was none too clean. Kick vaguely recognized him from one of the restaurants in Hampton but didn't know his name.

The employee asked if she was "that lady going around town with the man" who was involved in investigating Trudie's murder. He had heard about the Brice murder and had been told that the passerby was a one-time fellow employee of the co-op, Cleve Hauser. Someone told him that Cleve tried to revive Trudie. Around the co-op, this was pretty commonly believed. The employee told Kick that she should get in touch with a fellow who'd been Hauser's manager back in 1986. He would know more than anyone.

When she got back to the office, Kick called him. The former manager remembered the case only vaguely, but did recall seeing Cleve the day after the murder. He remembered the date because no more than a half-dozen people came shopping for several days. He said that Cleve told him that he found the Brice girl in the bathtub. "Cleve looked troubled, nervous," he said. "I never knew whether to believe him or not." It didn't seem plausible, but the manager understood that Cleve was a habitual exaggerator. The conversations with the people at the co-op seemed pretty convincing, Kick thought. Working there certainly gave Cleve much more freedom of movement, especially in the winter months when business was slower.

As she worked through her notes, Kick started to imagine the evidence not so much as pieces in a puzzle, but as streams of information. You could follow one channel only so far before there was a blockage — a lost fact, something forgotten, a lie, a liar. Kick decided to call Attorney Frank Smith, the Chief Prosecutor back in 1986. Kick wanted to know why Toner, the newspaper reporter, told Ray that everything to do with the Brice murder case had to go through Smith. They hadn't followed up on this because Smith, it was rumored, was so difficult. Ray hadn't wanted to rile Smith up so he would close off avenues of investigation. That's what had happened twenty years ago. Kick thought it was worth a shot to call him since new evidence had appeared. Ray agreed and told her to go ahead.

Even over the phone, Smith couldn't conceal his curiosity. Smith told her that he had a standing rule that he didn't want any officials commenting on any cases, because most of them didn't know what was appropriate to say. "Plus they didn't know when to stop talking," Smith said.

Kick asked if the comments Smith made to the various newspapers came from his direct knowledge of the murder, or had it come from others. Smith said he knew Cleve Hauser and he could have very well spoken to Cleve himself. Kick refreshed Smith's memory, telling him that the comments came out in the press less than twenty-four hours after the murder. Smith paused, then said he probably followed protocol and got the details from

Lead Detective Lou Skipper, either verbally or by reading Detective Skipper's investigative reports.

Then, Smith remembered the newspaper deadline was 9:30 a.m., so the information had to come from Detective Skipper direct. Smith wouldn't have had time to talk to any suspects himself. Kick reminded Smith that the newspaper said that the passerby was definitely not a suspect. Smith reaffirmed that that statement would have had to come from Detective Skipper. Smith said he hadn't been at the crime scene any time that day, or night.

Kick told him Ray found that no one was ever questioned at the scene, not any firemen, or the first Sheriff's Deputy to arrive — or any other officials, for that matter. Smith was puzzled as to why he wouldn't have picked that up from Detective Skipper's report. "If they weren't interviewed, they sure should have been," Smith said. "That's a big thing to miss. I wouldn't have had lasted long as an attorney with that type of investigative technique."

Kick wanted to know why no future newspaper articles ever mentioned that Cleve Hauser eventually became a suspect. Smith said that was hard to answer, that he didn't recall. But he was confident that he would have never speculated about any suspects to the media because he didn't want to alarm the community. Kick asked was it because Hauser was, at one time, a schoolteacher in the community? Smith said, yes.

Kick asked why the Keysville newspaper had mentioned Cleve by name when the local paper hadn't. Smith thought it was probable that Cleve himself talked to someone from Keysville. He thought that this was pretty likely.

Kick filled him in on some other pertinent details of the crime that Ray had uncovered. She told Smith that the Sheriff's Department personnel, both active and retired, had been told to remain silent on the Brice case. Smith commented that he couldn't understand why Sheriff Wiersma would take that position. "Seems like the Sheriff would welcome a guy like Ray into the cold case and use his information," Smith said.

"Even though you wanted to prevent your own people from commenting on the case," Kick said.

"Well," Smith said, "That's altogether different." Kick couldn't imagine what the difference was, but she knew she'd gotten what she was looking for out of the former Prosecutor.

Kick thanked Smith for being so honest and forward, if that was the case, she thought. Smith said he looked forward to reading Ray's novel when it came out. He laid heavy stress on the word *novel*. He seemed genuinely interested, so Kick asked him for his mailing address.

"Smith was overwhelmed by the information you've been able to gather," Kick told Ray afterward. "He was very friendly and accommodating, just the opposite of what we've been told about him."

"Refreshing for an attorney," Ray said. "Did he tell you anything?"

"Yes. He wasn't about to take the blame for the investigating detective's goofs," Kick said.

A few weeks after their initial conversation, Lon Coughlin's wife, Ethel, called back. She said she babysat Trudie and wanted to relay a story about the little girl. Kick handed the phone to Ray.

Ethel said that one morning Ronda Jo had dropped Trudie off at the Coughlin's before school. Ethel thought it strange. According to her, it was before the rooster's crow. So Trudie took a nap. When the sun came up, Ethel woke Trudie. Trudie sat down at the kitchen table for her breakfast and hurried through it. She wanted to play school with Ethel.

Trudie stood at the blackboard that hung on the kitchen wall, playing the teacher. She finally took a seat and said, "Well, class, it's the end of the day. What did you learn?"

"We learned how to dot our i's and cross our t's," Ethel said.

"Ethel, I'm a gym teacher," Trudie said. She slid out of her chair, rolling on the floor with laughter.

When Ray told her about Trudie's joke, Kick said, "That's a nice story."

Ethel remembered someone told her they had been listening to a Chicago radio station and heard that someone named Lacey had been arrested for child molesting. She admitted that was the only reason she'd ever thought Lacey had anything to do with Trudie's murder.

"You want to know what she said before she hung up?" Ray asked.

"What," Kick said.

"Thank God you came along, Ray."

"Amen," Kick said.

Ray leaned back in his chair and thought for a moment. "Someone named Lacey in a city of over three million people ..."

The next week, Ray received a detailed background report from Dewey and Associates Investigations, Ltd. Ray handed Kick the report:

TYPE OF REPORT:

Criminal History Investigation

SUBJECT:

Peter Clyde Arthur Lacey A/K/A Peter Lacey

DATE OF BIRTH:

November 15, 1954

Kick read in silence, then blurted out, "They found no record of any criminal history for Lacey at the county, state, or federal levels."

"Well that pretty much takes care of the rumors about Lacey," Ray said.

"Do you feel your money was well spent," Kick said.

Ray smiled.

"You've learned a lot more doing the footwork your-self," Kick said.

"You never know," Ray said, still smiling.

Chapter 11

"Hop down off that tractor after you drop that load of fieldstones," Ray told Kick. "We'll go over to farm one and have our picnic in the cove."

It was a beautiful Indian Summer day and this was likely to be the last picnic of the year.

The wooden picnic table had weathered in the ten years since Ray had carried it back to the cove. Other than a few deer hunters using it, Kick and Ray would sit and rest after gathering walnuts or moving fieldstones out of the way of the tractor.

Some of the best times, according to Kick, were just sitting, waiting for dusk when the deer started moving around.

"Here," Kick said, holding out a plastic sandwich bag.

"What is it?" Ray asked.

"Peanut butter," Kick said.

"It's always peanut butter," Ray said.

"Then why ask," Kick said.

"I thought maybe ... skip it," Ray said.

"I told you peanut butter sandwiches don't need to be kept cool," Kick said.

"That's why they make coolers," Ray said.

"Too much trouble," Kick said.

"We keep the beer in a cooler," Ray said.

"Just go on with your story," Kick said, handing Ray a napkin.

Ray wiped his mouth on his shirt sleeve.

"Here's how all the pieces of the crime puzzle fit together," Ray said. "Before I begin, Kick, remember that all this happened twenty some years ago. It's important that you see everything through the eyes of anyone who had some sort of involvement as they were back then."

"I'm listening," Kick said as she leaned back and closed her eyes.

"Remember, times change and people change," Ray said.

Kick opened one eye and looked at Ray, then folded her hands behind her head and let out a deep breath. She knew Ray's story was going to take a while to tell.

"Ronda Jo was a clerk at Sauer's Hardware Store. That's where she first met Cleve Hauser. He was a teacher, he held a position of power and prestige in her eyes; she was impressed. He flirted with her, she flirted back. Ronda Jo was married young, to her high school sweetheart, Stan Brice. When they dated, she liked the idea that she was mostly in charge of their relationship. Eventually, it became boring being married to a 'honey do' man.

"Ronda Jo was a flirt from what everyone says and Stan has always been a 'door mat.' They had trouble conceiving a child, and when they finally did, they were told the baby girl would be their last. As with most couples with children, the children become the common denominator, sometimes the only thing to hold their relationship together. Ronda Jo and Stan loved and protected — no, make that over-protected — their daughter, Trudie. But there's always a person's individual needs, or wants, weighing on them."

Ray looked over at Kick. "Are you awake?" he asked.

Kick fluttered her eyes at Ray.

"What I don't know is if Cleve was Ronda Jo's first adulterous affair, but that really doesn't matter for now. Cleve returned from the war in Vietnam and, like many vets, he was restless and into drugs, mostly marijuana. After all, killing leaves gaps and spaces in one's thought processes. Like I said before, I also don't believe Cleve's problems began in Vietnam, but I'll come to that later.

"An innocent flirtation sometimes develops into other things, not always sexual. Sometimes it's just about having a confidant — someone to share thoughts and feelings with. Many affairs end, but the searching out of a soul mate continues on," Ray said.

"How do you think Ronda Jo and Cleve's fling ended?" Kick asked.

"Well, it was Reverend Hummock who accidentally tipped me off," Ray said. "When he came to town as the new preacher, it gave Ronda Jo the perfect excuse to end things with Cleve. We found out that Ronda Jo and Stan not only became members of the Church Board, but they also became good friends with the Hummocks. They had dinners together at each other's homes and, of course, hung together at the various church functions."

Kick sat up. "So she tells Cleve that she's found God and wants to change her ways?"

"Yes. And it's an old story, but he buys it hook, line, and sinker. Maybe Ronda Jo even believes it herself," Ray said.

"Then what happens?" Kick asked.

"You ever read *The Scarlet Letter*?" Ray asked.

"Back in high school," Kick said.

"Well, I don't mean to sound sexist, but I'll tell you that, psychologically, many women like the comfort and security that a man of God brings along with his vocation. You and I know that Ronda Jo took the preacher in as her confidant. As for the sex part, we keep hearing the same rumors from the locals. Reverend Hummock's gotten himself caught up in his lies about Ronda Jo and the murder itself. She definitely confided in the preacher.

"In fact, by his own admission, Reverend Hummock was once a suspect," Ray said.

"But he was cleared by the Sheriff's Department when he had proof he was out of town at the time of the murder," Kick said.

"Cleared as a suspect, but not as Ronda Jo's lover," Ray said.

"He said that he loved little Trudie," Kick said.

"Case in point, what if one of the times Cleve was peeping he saw the Reverend tucking Trudie into bed. Or maybe a different time he saw an innocent hug between Ronda Jo and the Reverend when the preacher made one of his frequent visits to the Brice home alone," Ray said. "There's no doubt in my mind that Cleve sat in that old place for hours."

"Just like what the school librarian said about Cleve being in the library — sitting and watching the school children," Kick said.

"Yes, and whatever else happened, Cleve's affair with Ronda Jo ended," Ray said. "He probably even bought her religion excuse, but he couldn't stop his voyeurism. It's a sickness."

"A vacant house was perfect cover," Kick said.

"Remember how when I put the map and time frames together, the question as to where he parked his truck baffled me," Ray said.

"The vacant house held plenty of answers, even in its absence," Kick said.

"I think the incident that set Cleve off wasn't anything to do with the preacher," Ray said. "The times that he spied on the preacher only led up to the last straw for

Cleve, the thing that set him off the day of the murder."

"The Olds in the driveway," Kick said.

"Right, with Mitch Wiersma waiting in it while Ronda Jo dropped off some pizza for Trudie's lunch and stoked the wood burning furnace."

"Why'd she take up with Mitch Wiersma?" Kick asked.

"You tell me," Ray said.

Kick nodded. "Oh, I get it, he's another authority figure, same as a teacher, or a minister, but Mitch had another thing going for himself. He was a lawman, Ronda Jo's protector," Kick said.

"Yes. And Cleve wasn't about to give up that easy. He's a person who wants his way, a typical stalker. Ronda Jo was rightly scared of him, as are most of the locals," Ray said. "Hand me that flask of whiskey and get yourself a cold bottle of beer."

"Aren't you going to continue with your story?" Kick asked.

"Right now I'm going to fire up a cigar and watch that sunset," Ray said.

Within moments, the bright red sun disappeared behind the apple orchard.

Chapter 12

It was time to make a move.

Kick left a voice message for Cleve Hauser at Bloom High School:

"Hi, this is for Mr. Hauser. I'm Kick Jetton. I'm the publicist for a writer, Ray Krouse. I don't know if you're aware, but for the past two years, Mr. Krouse has been researching the murder of Trudie Brice. He's writing a novel and has interviewed almost everyone involved with the case in any way, except you. We understand you were the passerby who tried to revive Trudie. Mr. Krouse would like to have you take him through what you did that day. I'm calling to arrange an interview. You can reach me at the toll-free number

*I left with the secretary who put me through to your
voice mail."*

Nothing happened. Ray and Kick spent several days once
more going over their notes, both playing Devil's advocate, trying to poke holes in their own conclusions. They
couldn't find any. They plotted how they ought to talk to
Cleve, how to make him feel safe enough to open up. They
wanted to give him enough rope to hang himself.

Monday morning, Ray walked into the front office
and handed Kick the phone.

"The time has come to dial up Cleve Hauser again,"
Ray said.

"Me?" she said.

"You'll get more out of him," Ray said. He pulled a
chair up to one side of the desk and watched.

Kick shook her head as the phone continued to ring.
Finally, someone picked up. "Mr. Hauser ..."

Kick introduced herself, then said, "I left a message
on your voice mail over a week ago, but wasn't sure you
got it."

Cleve told her he was surprised to get the message,
especially at school. "I saved it," he said.

Kick told him that Ray had been researching the Brice
murder for over two years, and since he was the passerby who discovered the fire and returned to the house to
resuscitate Trudie, Ray wanted to interview him.

"Being an educator, I have to document everything.
I have to know who I'm talking to, plus know something

about him," Cleve said.

Kick told him she would give him Ray's website. "As long as it doesn't take me to a porn site," Cleve said. He chuckled, then added, "I'm just kiddin', ma'am."

Kick disregarded Cleve's comments and assured him it wouldn't take him to a porn site. She thought this was quite remarkable. Cleve Hauser must have known that he was going to have to do a lot of explaining, even if he was innocent. Yet, he still found it in himself to make a tasteless joke.

Hauser asked Kick to fax him the information on Ray instead. Cleve told Kick that a few months earlier, he heard from someone that a book was being written about the Brice murder. He paused, then said he asked the individual if the writer was going to use real names. Kick thought to herself, if he was indeed a hero that day, as he claimed, why the concern over names being used? Cleve told Kick that since no one had the answer, he put the story out of his mind.

Kick said, "It's no secret what Ray's been doing, he thinks the murder can be solved." Then Kick looked at her notes, the straw man that Ray set up for her to use on Cleve, so he would hang himself without knowing.

"It wasn't the Englishman that the Sheriff's Department fingered," Kick said. "And Ray knows about Mitch Wiersma's Olds Cutlass being parked in the driveway the day of the murder. He even found out about the old vacant house across the street from the Brices."

Cleve was silent, so she dropped "the hook."

"Ray even talked to a former student of yours, Junebug Davenport, the first firefighter on the scene." Kick stopped talking and waited.

Cleve took the bait.

"Yeah, he's the first one I remember seeing there," Cleve said.

"Ray knows a lot more, and he'll be glad to share it with you," Kick said. "Ray always says there are many sides to every story, and in all fairness, he'd like to hear your version."

"I'm a teacher, I always have higher-ups, principals keeping me busy and my students keep me busy with school work." Cleve told Kick he could never quite catch up and continued to "water bug." Kick couldn't get a commitment out of him.

Ray drew his thumb across his throat, motioning for Kick to end the conversation.

"I'll fax you the information on Ray," Kick said. "Can I call you back to see when might be a good time for you to talk to Ray?"

"You can if you want," Cleve said.

Kick hung up. "He did what you said he'd do, Boss. He put himself smack dab in the crime scene with his Junebug remark," Kick said.

"That's why I wanted you to end the conversation. We got what we wanted," Ray said.

"He's just like the people described him. The guy jumps all over the place. I don't get a good feeling about him," Kick said.

"We need facts, not feelings, Kick," Ray said.

"Just the same, that porno comment was weird," Kick said. "It gave me a bad feeling. I'm afraid there might be a bad fact to back it up."

The next day, Kick faxed Ray's background information to Cleve along with a note thanking him for his time and consideration.

A call came in a week later from Cleve Hauser. He told Kick that she gave him a lot of homework, and that he'd been checking out Ray's website. He said he'd also checked with some of his own sources who suggested that Ray might be guilty of harassment, which was criminal.

Cleve told her that he wouldn't be available for an interview with Ray. He told Kick he was advised that it was up to him, so it was his decision not to talk. Kick tried to get him to tell her who gave him the advice. He resisted, so Kick continued on. Kick told him that Ray was going to write about Trudie's murder, and in all fairness to him, Ray just wanted him to be able to tell his side of the story of what happened that day.

Cleve said he appreciated her and Ray's concern, but his mind was made up. "I struggled with my decision, but I'm not interested in contributing to, or being represented in any book," Cleve said. The word "represented" sounded like lawyer talk to Kick. She wondered which lawyer Cleve had talked to.

More than twenty years ago, Cleve had told a newspaper about his act of heroism. No, he hadn't saved the girl, he acknowledged, but he'd done everything he could, everything anyone could do. And he'd saved the house from burning down, helped the family who had already lost a daughter from losing everything else as well. Cleve liked that picture of himself, the good citizen, the hero.

"That's that then," Kick told Ray.

"Not exactly," Ray said. "He's already contributed. Maybe by now he really does think of himself as a hero. But heroes don't struggle, they're admired for their achievements and noble qualities by the very definition of the word hero itself. And he misspoke. The *struggle* was with an eleven-year-old girl. Typical Freudian slip on his part."

It was a chilly night, one perfect for a campfire, Ray thought. He tossed a couple more logs on the already blazing fire. Kick moved her chair closer to the flames and rested her boots on the fieldstones that surrounded the fire pit.

"Where'd I leave off?" Ray asked.

"With Cleve spotting Wiersma's car in the Brice's driveway," Kick said.

"Right," Ray said. "Ronda Jo ran some pizza in for Trudie, set it on a plate on the kitchen table for her and left. Cleve watched as Mitch and Ronda Jo drove off together."

"Where do you think they went?" Kick asked.

"Don't know, don't care," Ray said.

"Do you think anyone besides Ronda Jo and Mitch

know?" Kick asked.

"Maybe either Tammy Lemel or Reverend Hummock knows, or both," Ray said.

Ray continued. "Cleve didn't mind waiting. In fact, he enjoyed it. He opened his black metal lunch pail, took out his thermos, unscrewed the lid and poured some hot coffee. He ignored the packed sandwich and fruit. He was too worked up to eat.

"As Cleve stared out across the road at the Brice house, the Olds Cutlass passed back by. He grabbed his binoculars from the windowsill and followed the car. It was Mitch and Ronda Jo, headed back to town. Their lunch hour was over. Cleve checked his watch; forty-five minutes had passed. Cleve looked around, the road was desolate. He jumped into his truck that he'd parked in the old barn, back behind the vacant house."

Ray looked over at Kick. "You want something to eat or drink, Kick?" he asked.

Kick shook her head. "Not now," she said. "Finish the story."

"Cleve drove a mile into town to a public telephone and made his call to the Brices. The little girl answered the phone. He hung up, then drove back to the vacant house, hid his truck in the trees, went back inside and sat before the window, waiting. His eyes focused on the road, anticipating Ronda Jo would come and check on Trudie.

"He figured that Trudie would call her mom at the hardware store to tell her about the obscene phone call.

And according to the newspaper, Trudie did," Ray said.

"How did the newspaper know?" Kick asked.

"Must have been from Ronda Jo. Nobody else knew. The paper said he just breathed into the phone," Ray said. "Another fifteen minutes passed."

"Okay," Kick said, "and so Trudie ate lunch, fooled around with her dog, Tuffy, then went upstairs to find something to wear because she was still in her bed clothes. After she called her mom from the phone in the bedroom upstairs, she came down, filled the bathtub, left her bed clothes on the floor next to the tub and hopped in."

"Cleve was on edge as he hurried across the street to the Brices' house," Ray said. "He heard Trudie's dog barking as he reached for the doorknob. It was unlocked. He let the dog out and stepped inside, closing the door behind him.

"Trudie heard the dog and called out to it. She got out of the bathtub to see why her dog didn't come. Entering the kitchen, she came face to face with Cleve Hauser. His eyes scanned her body. 'Get out,' she screamed. Cleve grabbed her by her shoulders, shaking her. He wanted to know where her mother and Wiersma went. Trudie didn't know. 'I hate you,' she yelled. Cleve started groping at her body. Trudie hit him. Her arms were flailing. Cleve grasped her arm, pulling her toward the stairway leading upstairs. Trudie broke loose and ran toward the phone on the wall near the door. 'I'm telling my Mommy,' she screamed, as she grabbed the phone. He seized the telephone receiver from her hand and whipped the phone cord around her neck. She started to bite and kick. She couldn't breathe. With every last ounce of her strength she broke loose, heading for the door, but the floor was wet. She slipped. Cleve reached down and slung the cord around her neck a second time. She clawed at Cleve's hands, trying to loosen his grip. He pulled the cord tighter and tighter. Her body went limp. Trudie was dead."

Kick let out a deep breath.

"But Cleve wasn't done yet," Ray said. "He took her upstairs and raped her on her mother's bed. By the time it was all over, he was out of breath, his chest was tight. He wanted to carry her outside, but he couldn't lift her, so he dragged her by her hair back downstairs, picked up her body and put it back in the bathtub face up, but at the wrong end — the faucet end. He was in an excitable state of mind, but thought methodically. He reached into his Carhart coveralls, pulled out his work gloves and soaked them in the water. He put the wet gloves on and opened the door of the wood burning stove, grabbing a couple of blazing logs. Cleve carried them upstairs, holding them upright, and tossed them on the bed, in the middle of the mattress — Stan and Ronda Jo's bed. He just as well left Ronda Jo a calling card, add to that the way he raped Trudie.

"Once downstairs, he scanned the kitchen, walked over to the phone on the wall and ripped it from its connection," Ray said. "He took the phone with him."

"That bastard. I'll bet that's why he forgot his lunch bucket in the shack, he was worried about ditching the phone," Kick said. "Someone had to have seen his truck."

"No, the highway was empty. Remember there was a Christmas program going on at the Hampton School," Ray said. "Most every parent in town was there. And if they weren't, it was because they had to be at work."

"Where did he go then?" Kick asked.

"I believe that he was in and out of the vacant house up until the fire started burning through the Brices' roof," Ray said. "Then he went to the Shackleys."

"Do you think Cleve originally intended on killing Trudie?" Kick asked.

"No," Ray said. "Cleve's always been a peeper. But this time was different. He might have roughed Trudie up, even raped her, but killing wasn't originally on his mind. If he thought of killing her, he would have used something other than a telephone cord."

The murder scene was too chaotic. Cleve, a control freak himself, lost control and he knew Ronda Jo couldn't tell on him; she'd be too ashamed, too emotionally shattered.

Ray continued. "Besides, in Cleve's mind, there were others — though not directly involved in the murder — who were just as responsible for Trudie's death as him. That's the way psychopaths think."

Ray had made his mind up. He was ready to take his research to the next step. Ray stopped by Rudy Fisher's law office. He was the current Prosecutor of Penn County.

Ray could tell by the Prosecutor's demeanor that he had kept informed on the progress of Ray's investigation.

Ray outlined what he'd found since Kick had originally spoken with him some months back. Ray told Fisher that he knew about certain evidence obtained in the original investigation, such as Cleve's lunch bucket found in the old vacant house. Fisher said, "What do you want me to do, give it back to him?"

"I'd like you to look at the facts," Ray said.

"Facts? Most of what you have is just your opinion," Fisher said.

"And you want to be a judge?" Ray said.

Fisher told Ray to write him a brief, or send him the manuscript when he finished, he'd take a look at it. Fisher added that maybe Ray should send a copy to Cleve Hauser, but on the other hand, maybe Ray would get a lawsuit filed against him. Fisher shifted in his chair and fiddled with a paperclip.

"I would welcome a lawsuit if that would bring this case to court," Ray said. "Remember, that lawsuit door swings both ways."

The conversation was going nowhere. Ray placed a copy of his map on Fisher's desk, then got up and walked out. Ray heard something slam against Fisher's office door as he walked down the hall. He figured it was the overflowing wastepaper container next to Fisher's office door, an excellent object for a drop kick.

Ray and Kick drove to Junebug's office in Keysville on a

Saturday. None of the usual police staff worked on week-ends, so there were fewer people to notice the visit. They'd arranged the meeting on short notice and were glad that Junebug was willing to talk.

Ray's eyes scanned Junebug's office. There were so many knick-knacks and what-nots in the small space, it was hard to stay focused. Ray looked over at Kick. She continued to browse as Ray talked with Junebug.

After fifteen minutes, Junebug's friend, Dana, arrived. She was a spiritualist who had worked on a number of crime cases. Dana revealed things that came to her in visions. Ray was often surprised how frequently the police relied on diviners and seers in their investigations. He thought that information wasn't widely known because the public might imagine it was a waste of good taxpayer dollars. Ray, of course, approved of spiritualists.

Junebug locked the door and lowered the lights. In a file on Trudie's case, Junebug had found, in an envelope, a little twist of hair from the girl. Something, he supposed, the Coroner had asked for and then forgotten to pick up. He opened the envelope and shook the hair into Dana's hand. Kick couldn't help but be amazed that a life could be reduced to something so small and trivial.

Dana held the knot of hair flat on her palm with her thumb. Junebug, Kick, and Ray remained quiet as Dana disclosed information on what happened that day over twenty years ago. Dana got in touch with Trudie. She said that Trudie's spirit got irritated whenever Junebug was around. She said Trudie thought Junebug wasn't vocal enough as the first official on the scene. Dana said the killer didn't want to talk to law enforcement officers, but she believed he would eventually confess to Ray.

Dana said Trudie was confused by her mother's silence in the investigation. She didn't know why Ronda Jo wouldn't help and be more truthful. Dana said the killer had been inside the Brice house at other times.

Dana felt that the killer and the lead detective on the murder case had some sort of relationship. She said they were good friends. The killer placed Trudie backward in the bathtub, her head facing the water faucets. The killer never attempted to resuscitate Trudie, the spiritualist said.

Dana saw that Cleve startled Trudie when he entered the house. She said Trudie had been in the bathtub. She saw Cleve pulling at Trudie, shaking her, trying to get Trudie to answer questions about her mother that Trudie didn't know the answers to. Dana said that the killer had every intention of dragging Trudie's dead body outside, into the field, but he was physically unable to. Dana thought his chest was very tight, either restricted by asthma or a heart problem at the time. Instead, Cleve dragged her downstairs, thinking he could make it seem like she drowned.

"He wants this over, he wants to confess, he was close to talking about the murder with you," Dana said, pointing to Ray. "But an attorney, or some sort of coun-selor, gave him bad advice."

Dana asked about a name — Warren — she said he

was part of a cover-up.

Ray and Kick knew Warren; he'd been working with his dad, the local Coroner when Trudie died.

"Isn't a teenager awfully young to be a crime scene photographer?" Dana asked.

"Kids are better at that sort of thing," Ray said.

"Doesn't hurt your chances if your dad's the County Coroner," Kick added.

They sat quietly for a while and then turned the lights back up. Junebug held the envelope open and Dana slid the hair inside. Kick noticed that Junebug was pale and his hands shook slightly. She understood Junebug knew that what Dana said — what the spirit had told her — could be true. Maybe he should have taken charge, put pressure on the police ... something that would have pushed them, or shamed them into going after the murderer.

Dana noticed, too, that Junebug was upset. "It's all right," she said, "You're taking care of things now."

On Monday morning, Kick sorted through the day's mail and found an envelope addressed to her from Ethel Coughlin. She opened it and walked into Ray's office.

"Boss, do you want to read the letter Ethel wrote me?" Kick said.

"No, you read it to me," Ray said.

Kick sat in the chair next to Ray's desk.

"Dear Kicky ... she calls me Kicky," Kick said.

"She's entitled," Ray said. "She could be your granny."

Kick continued:

"Dear Kicky,

I apologize for the long delay. This is one of the poems about Trudie. I have another one that is in scribbles. I'll clean it up and send it to you. I was cleaning out an old jewelry box & I found this little friendship pin Trudie had made and gave me. A little voice in me said "Send it to Kick." I know better than argue so here it is. The little pins were to string your shoe lace through and wear on your shoe. I think that you and Ray are the best friends Trudie has right now.

Thanks again, Ethel"

Kick lifted the scotch tape that held a piece of cotton to the bottom of the letter. Beneath the cotton was a small, gold safety pin with several tiny colored beads. Kick held it up. "Trudie made this with her own hands," she said.

"Let me see that," Ray said.

Kick laid it in his palm. She noticed the way Ray looked at it. It was as if he'd seen it before. Kick got up and went into her office. She came back with a velvet covered ring box Ray had given her.

"Let's keep it in this," Kick said.

"She'd like that," Ray smiled.

The following Monday morning, Ray had noticed one of his tires was low, he turned the wheel and noticed a bald spot on the inside, one of those secret signs the front end was out of alignment. First thing, he took the truck in and decided to wait the half hour he was told it would require.

But after forty-five minutes they weren't done and he got impatient. He called the office on his cell phone to see if there was any news. There was.

"I made a call to the Penn County Sheriff's Department about getting copies of all the radio logs from the Brice file," Kick said.

"When will we get them?" Ray asked.

"It's not that easy. A clerk there told me that they just moved into their new building, so a lot of the files were shredded," Kick said.

"So we're out of luck," Ray said.

"Not exactly," Kick said. "When I told her it was about the Brice murder, she said they would have kept that information since that case is still open."

"You really think the Sheriff's going to give you anything?" Ray said.

"The lady said all I have to do is send a written letter to the Sheriff requesting them. It shouldn't be a problem since the logs are available to the public under the Freedom of Information Act," Kick said. "I'm also going to ask for any other official logs or files we're entitled to."

"Don't count on any fast service, or any service at all for that matter, from the Sheriff," Ray said.

"It's the law," Kick said.

"All I'm saying is you waited six weeks for the Coroner to send the Brice reports," Ray said. "And that was after you wrote the state on him."

"And if I don't hear from the Sheriff within a month, I'll write another letter," Kick said. "Maybe to the Attorney

General this time."

"Just keep me posted," Ray said.

"I've already put a note in my binder," Kick said.

Later in the morning, Kick, with several folders under her arm, drifted to the door of Ray's office. She'd been tossing out duplicate evidence and putting things in order according to an outline he'd given her for his book.

"We never got a chance to talk about what all Val White told me," Kick said.

"I have a few minutes now," Ray said.

"Where do you think Cleve ended up after Val's house, if he was ever there in the first place?" Kick asked.

"Maybe he gave Val a hand with some farm chores. That way he could explain any scratches on him," Ray said. "All he'd have to do is tell his wife he got them from clearing out some briar plants. Of course, I'm not so sure he even stopped at Val's house."

"Maybe Cleve went straight home so he could be there and clean himself up before his wife and kids got back from the Christmas program," Kick said.

"Let's take a look at some of the things Val told you," Ray said. "First of all, he said he saw Cleve let the dog out. So once again, Trudie's protector, Tuffy, pops up with her murderer and his goofy friend, Val. Cleve tells the lie that he heard the dog barking when he doubled back to the crime scene and Val swears to this lie. For some insane reason, Val decides to put himself at the crime scene too, making himself an accessory after the fact."

"I made Val mad when I asked him what the dog looked like and where it went," Kick said. "He snapped, 'That was a long time ago, lady.' He never saw that dog, did he?"

"Well, we know what Val says is a lie, because the killer let the dog out when he first went into the Brices' house and it was someone the dog knew. If Trudie's dog would have been inside that house, it would have attacked Cleve when he started his struggle with Trudie," Ray said.

"Then Val said, 'I'll bet no one told you that the water was left running all over the kitchen floor and it was coming out the door, maybe that's why Cleve went in,'" Kick said.

"The water he let overflow from the bathtub flowed out of the Brices' house when he fled from the murder he'd just committed," Ray said, pausing for a moment. "Which brings up another question that should be answered. Reverend Hummock asked me if I knew about the water faucet still running when the firefighters arrived."

"And?" Kick asked.

"The only person who knew about the water overflowing was Cleve. Val and the Hummocks found out secondhand. The Hummocks had to have gotten that information from Ronda Jo, which means that she had to have confronted Cleve after the murder," Ray said. "Cleve was the original source of that information, because Junebug said there was no running water, only a wet, muddy, kitchen floor."

"Val said Cleve told him to stay outside on the porch," Kick said.

"That's another lie," Ray said. "Because in the same conversation, he told you that he grabbed a hose off the fire truck and started dousing the flames coming from the roof. That means the fire truck would had to have been at the scene before Val, and even Cleve for that matter. That being the case, Junebug would have already been guarding the bathroom door in order to keep the crime scene intact. Then Val says that he got his picture taken fighting the fire by *The West Bend Press*. The picture we have shows a person in fire gear, not a civilian."

"You're right, and the newspaper photographer wouldn't have gotten there until at least twenty minutes after Junebug radioed the Sheriff's Department," Kick said.

"Exactly," Ray said. "Plus Val got himself caught up in another of his lies when he said the fire department sent the wrong truck. That means, again, the fire truck was already at the scene when Val first saw it."

"Did Junebug ever say anything about the wrong fire truck being sent out to the fire?" Kick asked.

"No. But he did finally remember who his partner was in the truck with him," Ray said. "The guy Hugh Dixon said it was — Shawn Harvey."

Kick looked at her notepad. She had good notes but Ray had a memory like nobody she'd ever heard of. "Wasn't I supposed to be tracking this guy down?" she asked.

"Funny you should ask," Ray said. "I'm going over to his place of business tomorrow. You finish up on that information request to the Sheriff's Department and I'll take you to the Hampton Grill."

Kick expected their lunch conversation to have a topic. It seemed as though they were finally narrowing their search after all this time. But Ray was turning something over in his mind and he didn't want to talk about the case. Instead, he talked about football. Ray was an inter-mittent football fan though, like all people who live in the no man's land between two major franchises (in this case the Chicago Bears and the Indianapolis Colts), Ray had to be on top of the game, to know who was a fan of whom, and how to maintain friendships on both sides. Ray didn't usually talk about football to Kick. Today was different.

Next day, Ray took his truck, his new tires humming on the roadway, out into the country. He pulled into a small lot and got out. He walked up to a man resetting a fence post next to a drive leading to a lawnmower business.

"You must be the owner," Ray said.

"How'd you guess?" the man said.

Ray laughed. "This is owner's work you're doing."

The man stood up and wiped his hands. "Shawn Harvey," he said.

Ray extended his hand. "I'm Ray Krouse. Got a couple minutes?"

"You the fellow I talked to on the phone about the

Brice murder?" Shawn said.

"Yes," Ray said.

Ray listened as Shawn told him that he and Junebug were the first to arrive at the fire. "There were no cars, no trucks, and no people when we pulled the truck into the Brices' driveway," he said.

Shawn explained that they hadn't taken the wrong truck, rather it was the fire truck that they usually took on brush fire calls because it was the quickest response unit the department had, and it was always ready to go.

Ray asked Shawn if he knew Val White. Shawn said he did and assured Ray that no civilian would have been allowed to handle any of the Fire Department's equipment.

"Besides," Shawn said. "I was using the hose."

When Ray asked Shawn about the picture of the fire-fighter that was in the local newspapers, Shawn told him it was Nick Schwin fighting the flames coming through the roof from the upstairs bedroom. He said Nick was at the side of the house opposite to the door that led into the kitchen.

Shawn said he took the fire hose through the kitchen, up the stairway to help put out the fire out from inside. Ray asked if he saw the Brice girl. Shawn said he did, she was in the bathtub and she was dead. He also saw the deep strangulation marks around her neck, something he never forgot.

"Junebug immediately blocked off the bathroom door and stayed there until someone from the Penn County

Sheriff's Department got there," Shawn said.

"Do you remember the deputy?" Ray asked.

"It was Mickey Wayland," Shawn said.

"You remember a lot," Ray said.

"When you run a business, you train your mind to remember out of necessity," Shawn smiled. "And this was the kind of thing that don't happen every day, thank God. I hope you get this case cleared up. It's gone on for too long."

"You want to grab some lunch?" Ray asked.

"I'd like to, but this here post won't let me. Last week a customer backed his truck over a piece of my equipment," Shawn said. "Once I get this post back in place, I can forgive him and get on with my life."

Ray and Kick sat at a table towards the back of the lounge away from the blare of the widescreen TVs. It was Friday and, as usual, the bar was packed.

"Smell that fish cooking?" Ray said.

"Ugh," Kick said.

Ray grabbed a menu from its holder next to the wall and glanced at it. "What are you having?" he asked.

"Chicken," Kick said.

"I mean to drink," Ray said.

"Brewski," Kick said. "You?"

"Whiskey ... Crown, if they have it," Ray said.

"Why wouldn't they?" Kick asked.

"Last time I was here, one of the bartenders told me there's a late crowd — a bunch of young ones — that have been drinking Royal Butts," Ray said.

"What's that?" Kick asked.

"Crown and butterscotch," Ray said, laying the menu down.

Kick made a face.

The waitress came for their drink order and as she walked back to the bar, something caught Ray's eye.

"Don't look now, Kick, but there's a guy at the end of the bar ..." he said.

Kick turned her head.

"Damn it," Ray said, "I told you not to look. I think it's Mitch Wiersma."

"He didn't see me," Kick said. "It looks like he's sleeping."

Ray slid his chair back and took a step toward the bar.

"Hey, Ray," a voice called out.

Hugh Dixon came up from behind and put his hand on Ray's shoulder, motioning Ray back down in his chair.

"Mind if I plop down for a couple of minutes," Hugh said. "Hi, Kick," he nodded.

The waitress returned and set the drinks on the table. "You ready to order?" she asked.

"Not yet. Give us a few minutes," Ray said. "But bring Hugh a..."

"A beer," Hugh told her. He turned back to Ray. "You don't want to go over by Mitch. He's drunk and doped up."

"I thought you said he's all right," Ray said.

The waitress came back with a beer. Hugh waited for her to leave before answering.

"He's been living out of state for a while. I thought he kicked the habit, but he's worse now then he was back in the eighties," Hugh said. "This time he's not only dealing, but doing the shit, too. Guess it runs in the family."

"Explain that," Ray said.

"Back then ... Hell, even now, some of the good ol' boys on the department were using. More than one buddy of mine told me Mitch's uncle was even dealing himself back in high school," Hugh said. "Don't quote me on that though."

Hugh dumped the rest of his beer down and got up to leave. When he reached the door, he looked back at Ray and shook his head, then glanced over at Mitch and gave Ray a thumbs down.

"That was close," Kick said.

The waitress walked over again. Ray looked up at her. She had her pad and pencil out.

"Give her chicken," Ray said. "I'll have the bluegill, fries, and salad. Blue cheese dressing on hers, Italian on mine. And another round."

Kick shook her head at Ray.

"Make it one drink then," Ray said. "Whiskey on the rocks."

Ray slid the menu back into its holder.

"I've been hearing more and more about Mitch and drugs," Ray said. "Del Pitt even said something about it when I stopped by his farm last week."

"You didn't mention that to me," Kick said.

"It slipped my mind," Ray said.

If it had, it was a first.

Ray sat alone in the study of his lake house. He leaned back in his chair and looked out the window, watching the clouds move in — a perfect morning for thinking. His two-year investigation was coming to an end. He pondered over what he might have left out of Trudie's story before he finished with the resolution. Collecting facts was only part of it. He'd discovered that there were a lot of loose ends and conflicts in the history of an event. But a story was different. A story had to tie things up, it had to have an ending.

He took his notepad from the end table, at the same time turning on the table lamp. It was getting darker outside. Did his story tell enough to interest the reader, to make them care? Did he stay with the facts, as well as the truth? Ray disliked loose ends.

Of course, the passerby was a key suspect — the only suspect, in Ray's mind. Cleve Hauser made himself one by placing himself at the crime scene.

Ray watched the water on the lake turn to small whitecaps. He closed his eyes and sorted through those individuals who he, at the very beginning of his investigation, gave serious thought to either being involved with or actually being the little girl's killer. There were the parents, Ronda Jo and Stan, other relatives that Ray eliminated either because of alibi or circumstance. Then there were those individuals who were indirectly involved: the preacher, the cop.

Ray thought about the people who wanted to bring closure to Trudie's tragedy and those who didn't. Why didn't they? Some even wanted to hinder Ray's investigation; the Sheriff was one of them. Was there a cover-up? By the Sheriff? By Trudie's family? If there was, who stood to gain by the murder remaining unsolved?

Sheriffs are elected. In order to win elections, the candidates must prove their worth and ability to their constituency. In Penn County, there had been too many unsolved murders. In Ray's mind, even one unsolved murder was one too many. Ray knew that the owner of the Olds Cutlass in the Brice driveway the day of the murder was not only a Sheriff's Deputy at the time, but he was also a relative of another Sheriff's Deputy. Mitch Wiersma didn't do the crime, but he knew where Trudie Brice's mother had been that day. She had been with him. That and other reasons eliminated both Ronda Jo and Mitch as the killers, but not as people who might have known why the murder took place. Mitch himself might have stepped forward and been accounted for, if it weren't for the bad advice he'd gotten from others, namely the current Sheriff of Penn County, who happened to be his uncle — Chip Wiersma.

Reverend Hummock and his family eventually left town. He had an alibi, so why didn't he cooperate? Ray knew it was to save his own reputation; after all, Reverend

Hitt confirmed that. Reverend Hummock cared a lot more about his personal reputation than he did about the truth. Ray thought it was a good thing he left town. By Ray's lights, Reverend Hummock was a bad pastor, and a bad citizen.

Ray was down to the names of four people that could be of major importance in breaking the case. These four had answers, answers that had been kept under locks all these years.

The Sheriff was still covering up the murder by not sharing information with Ray. Ronda Jo knew who the killer was. Reverend Hummock knew key individuals who knew who murdered Trudie. Mitch Wiersma knew about the mother's affairs. Why then, Ray thought, didn't these folks cooperate?

The answers were there. Sheriff Chip Wiersma had more elections to win. Ronda Jo was still overwhelmed with guilt and grief, and believed the scandal would be too great to bear. Reverend Hummock wanted whatever secrets he held to remain. Revealing his part might cost him his ministry. Mitch Wiersma fell victim to his own family tragedies; he just didn't care. Mitch was fighting his own demons. Then, of course, there were the two detectives that were assigned to the murder case but didn't investigate properly.

At times, Ray thought that maybe he was being too hard on Detectives Skipper and Fowler, but he decided in the final analysis that he wasn't. The lead detective was not only a fellow war veteran of the killer's, but Ray had also dug up that their wives were school chums since high school and through college. The detectives should have worked together, they should have cared.

Detective Skipper took no names at the crime scene. Instead, he mostly drank beer and shared war stories with the killer down at the American Legion.

His partner, Detective Fowler, was full of resentment. He and Detective Skipper didn't work together on the murder case — they did worse. They worked against each other. Time proved out their contempt for one another when they eventually ran against each other in a Sheriff's election.

All these years later, many of the locals still felt bad. Some of them felt they didn't do enough to help bring Trudie Brice's murderer to justice. Others were still turning their heads away.

The biggest joker in the deck was the Englishman. Not only did some of the locals have two different Englishmen in mind, but the Sheriff's Department itself pointed their misguided finger at two separate Brits. Secrecy amongst everyone made that possible. In this environment, you might almost expect someone to blame Trudie's death on any out-of-towner. Ray knew that with the tidbits of information they brought him, the individuals concerned with bringing the murder case to closure would understand why the Sheriff Department's interrogation of Cleve Hauser went haywire.

For the hundredth time, he replayed the events. In Ray's

mind, the original map he'd drawn had taken on extra dimensions and complexities. The fire alarm in Hampton went off at 3:09 p.m. Police and firemen from Hampton were the first to arrive at the scene. The police and fire station in Hampton are approximately one mile straight down the highway from the Brice house.

The law enforcement agency with jurisdictional rights was the Penn County Sheriff's Department, which is approximately fifteen miles from the Brices' house. The estimated arrival of the first fireman on the scene was at approximately 3:11 p.m., according to the first firefighter in the Brice house. That was Michael "Junebug" Davenport. He guarded the door of the bathroom where the Brice girl lay dead in a tub of water.

How many officials from Hampton that came and went in and about the house is unknown. Junebug radioed the Sheriff's Department and a Sheriff's deputy finally arrived and took over the crime scene between 3:30 p.m. and 3:35 p.m. The lead detective, Lou Skipper, arrived shortly thereafter.

Ray talked to six retired firemen from the town of Hampton and a half dozen retired policemen, as well as the two main witnesses — the first firefighter guarding the door of the bathroom where Trudie Brice lay dead, and Mickey Wayland, the first Sheriff's Deputy, who took over the crime scene until the detectives arrived.

From 3:11 p.m. until approximately 5:16 p.m. (sunset on December 11, 1986, according to the *Old Farmer's Almanac*), no one called the passerby, Cleve Hauser, who said he saw black smoke and flames shooting from the roof of the Brices' house as he passed by, then stopped at the Shackley house where Mrs. Shackley called to report the fire.

No official from the Sheriff's Department interviewed either Mrs. Shackley, or her husband, until three days after the murder. Ray guessed that sometime after sunset a detective finally phoned Cleve at his home and requested him to come back to the crime scene. By then, it was dark and lights had been set up outside the Brice house.

The crime scene was compromised by water, mud from official's boots, smoke, and the less than professional handling of the Brice girl's dead body. By the time the Coroner arrived, Trudie had already been taken from the bathtub, her nude body covered with a dirty kitchen throw rug and moved from the bathroom. Latex gloves were probably not used. At no time that day did the Sheriff's Department interview any of the officials on the scene, nor had they been interviewed since — that is until Ray began his own investigation.

The passerby was declared a non-suspect in the local newspaper by the prosecuting attorney less than twenty-four hours after the murder. How could the Sheriff Department's detectives conduct an interrogation without any information?

Ray couldn't feel sure about the story until he'd checked all the facts. The facts had not one, but two virtues. In the first place, they got Ray as close as possible to the truth. They couldn't get him all the way there because there were too many versions, even amongst people with nothing to hide and no axes to grind. But the sifting of the facts, the judgment, came from Ray's confidence that he'd gone down every alley, contacted every player, shared out every secret. Only God could ever know exactly what happened that day. Ray couldn't hope to know so much, but he could come as close as humanly possible.

He'd brought a folder inside from the truck. Kick had typed up the notes he had written by hand. He'd imagined what must have happened when the detectives questioned Cleve. It was as close as he could come. He shifted the floor light to the desk and started to read the scene he had written, the one he would put in the novel.

The Penn County Sheriff's building had a special room reserved for questioning persons of interest. The room was stark, containing only a wooden table with four chairs.

Detective Lou Skipper pulled out a chair as Cleve Hauser stood across from him. "Have a seat, Cleve," Detective Skipper said. "Can I get you some coffee?"

"No," Cleve said, taking a seat.

"How's the wife and kids?" Detective Skipper asked.

"Fine," Cleve said.

"You're probably as anxious to get this business over as I am," Detective Skipper said.

Cleve's eyes shifted from the blank walls to the wooden table top. He scooted his chair closer to the table.

"How come you didn't wait at the Brices' place until

someone from the Sheriff's Department got there?" Detective Skipper asked.

A couple minutes pass.

"Like I told you before, the boys on the fire department ran me off," Cleve said.

"Anyone in particular?" Detective Skipper asked.

"No," Cleve said.

"What exactly did they tell you?" Detective Skipper asked.

"That I'd just be in the way," Cleve said.

"Couldn't you have waited in your truck across the road?" Detective Skipper asked.

"Look, Lou, we've been over this before," Cleve said.

"Not on record," Detective Skipper said.

"I'd rather be having a beer down at the Legion," Cleve said.

"Me too buddy, but I have paperwork to do, so let's just go on and get this over," Detective Skipper said.

"The sooner, the better," Cleve said, leaning back and folding his arms across his chest.

"So why didn't you wait for me in your truck," Detective Skipper said.

"It was awful seeing that Brice girl laying dead in the tub," Cleve said.

"Dead?" Detective Skipper said. "I thought you said ..."

Cleve cut him short. "You know what I mean," he said.

"Tell me," Detective Skipper said.

"*After trying to bring her back, the look in her eyes, I was so upset. You know I used to teach kids not much older than her,*" Cleve said.

"*So, where did you go after you left the Brice house,*" Detective Skipper said.

"*I went home. You already know that, you called me there,*" Cleve said. "*It was so late, I was starting to think you weren't going to.*"

"*Let's take it from the time you first spotted the flames coming from the Brices' roof. Where were you coming from?*" Detective Skipper asked.

"*I was in town, talking to a couple of your boys,*" Cleve said. "*Sheriff's deputies.*"

"*Who were they?*" Detective Skipper said.

"*Can't remember their names — one was short and stocky and the other one had a mustache,*" Cleve said.

"*You don't remember their names, but you remember their faces,*" Detective Skipper said.

"*Lou, I told you before they were a couple of your new guys. They're still not part of ...*" Cleve hesitated. "*Wait ... one of them was George, George Hanson.*"

"*See, if you just stop and think about something, it usually comes to you,*" Detective Skipper said. He could see Cleve was establishing an alibi.

"*I was talking with them a couple minutes before I spotted the fire on my way home,*" Cleve said.

"*Now we're getting somewhere,*" Detective Skipper said.

"*I drove past the Brices' and stopped at the Shackleys',*"

told Jeanne Shackley to call the fire department, then I went back to the Brices' to see what I could do," Cleve said.

"So that's when you heard their dog barking?" the Detective asked.

"Yes. The door was unlocked so I went in. The little girl was in the bathtub," Cleve said.

"Did you see the marks around her neck?" Detective Skipper asked.

"I guess I was too excited to notice anything. I gave her artificial resuscitation," Cleve said.

"Did you take her out of the bathtub?" Detective Skipper asked.

"What do you think?" Cleve said.

"You tell me," Detective Skipper said.

"Like I said before, I don't remember. Once I left the house, I went blank," Cleve said. "Kind of like back in Nam. You were there, you know."

"Take your time," Detective Skipper said.

Eventually, the Sheriff's Department found a black metal lunch bucket with Cleve Hauser's name stenciled on it. It was found in the vacant house across the street from the Brices'. With that evidence, the Detective set up a couple more interviews with Cleve Hauser.

At one of the interviews, Cleve recalled that he had been doing some field work for Ben Shackley and forgot his lunch pail at the old place. Cleve thanked the Sheriff's

Department for finding it. Cleve's nature at each interview held true to form. He'd go blank with a stare to match, or rattle on, or sometimes talk normal.

Cleve mentioned to Detective Skipper during one of the interviews that he remembered seeing a car in the Brices' driveway around lunchtime, a little after noon. He said he had been headed to one of the local diners in town to grab a cup of coffee.

A few weeks after questioning Cleve Hauser, Tammy Lemel came forward and said that she thought her husband was the one who probably killed Trudie Brice. That's when the Sheriff Department's sights were set on the Englishman — Peter Lacey.

The car in the driveway was never pursued, partly because Ronda Jo became uncooperative with the Sheriff's Department, but mainly because the owner of the car was one of their own.

Ray took off his glasses. He looked up at the window. It was dark outside. There were critters out there. Things growing, things dying. No one could ever keep up with it. But Ray liked what he'd written. He thought it was as close as he, or anyone, could get to the truth.

Chapter 13

The next morning, he hadn't changed his mind.

"Kick, get Cleve Hauser on the phone," Ray said.

"Why?" Kick asked.

"To set up an appointment," Ray said. "You and I will meet him at the Indiana Agriculture College Library at his convenience."

"Am I missing something here? What makes you think he's going to go along with that," Kick said. "Remember what he told us about his quote, unquote 'sources'?"

"Just a hunch. He admitted that he'd been poking his nose around Penn County asking questions. Tell him I have the answers he's looking for and be sure to emphasize that he don't have to say anything. He listens, I talk,"

Ray said.

Kick made the call and left the message. She knew that Cleve had to think everything over — maybe a couple of times. He finally called Kick back a couple days later, agreeing to the meeting with Ray, but stressed the point about him being able to remain silent. Kick reassured Cleve that this would be the case. Kick relayed the information to Ray. Cleve seemed to be confident that he could hear all of Ray's story without giving himself away.

The Indiana Agricultural College was located approximately half way between Cleve's home and Ray's office. The semester had ended and the school hadn't started registration for the next semester. Ray was pleased with the timing — the traffic, as well as the movement of students about the campus would be sparse.

Ray had previously visited the library to check out the surroundings and the facilities before talking with Cleve. The library was perfect for such a meeting. It even housed a small coffee canteen that stayed open throughout the year serving coffee and rolls.

Ray dressed casual — sport coat, T-shirt, pleated slacks, distressed loafers. Kick always looked good. Cleve showed up in an ill-fitting gray suit with a flowery necktie that hung halfway down a telltale grayish-white shirt.

Ray spotted him immediately. Cleve looked around the library, his eyes shifting as if he were picking out someone he knew who'd mixed in a crowd. Ray knew what Cleve looked like from the descriptions of him, but also from the nervous manner of the man in the tie. Ray waved him over to an open study area near the windows.

"I'm Ray Krouse. This is Kick Jetton."

Cleve nodded. They sat down.

"I'll get right to the point," Ray said.

Ray went on to share much of the information he'd gathered, including the map that he laid out on the table in front of Cleve.

"Take your time and look at the time frames and the statements you gave the Chief Prosecutor," Ray said.

Cleve leaned in toward the table.

"Kick, why don't you get Mr. Hauser and me a coffee, and whatever you want," Ray said.

"You want anything in it?" Kick asked, looking at the men.

Cleve shook his head.

"Nothing in mine," Ray said.

"Then black it is," Kick said.

Ray glanced at his watch. It took Kick ten minutes to get their coffee. Not much was said. When Cleve looked puzzled, Ray would explain one aspect or another on the map. Cleve never gave a hint of what he was looking at, or whether Ray's explanations addressed his concerns. Another five minutes had passed when finally Cleve shoved the map back toward Kick. He stared at Ray, then back at Kick. He was expressionless.

"I want you to know that I'm not the least bit interested in you telling your story to the Sheriff," Ray said. "In fact, he doesn't want to do anything with this case, other than say it's still open and point his finger at an Englishman ... make that two different Englishmen, neither of whom was in town the day of the fire."

Kick smiled at Ray using the term "fire," instead of murder.

Cleve blew on the hot coffee, and set it on the table.

"Let's say you finally admit to the crime," Ray said. "I wouldn't be interested in you going to jail. My interest is telling the story, whether I do it as truth or fiction. I'd like to know how you've been able to steer clear of an arrest for over twenty years."

Cleve still said nothing. It was not clear to Kick, at least, whether he was playing dumb or whether he was paralyzed.

In any case, Ray decided to push the interview to another level, to let Cleve know how far his investigation had gone. Ray shared with Cleve how he came to the conclusion that Cleve's problems and personality changes came not from Vietnam, but rather started way back when he was in grammar school at St. Mary's. Ray looked Cleve in the eye. "And your problems with the Catholic religion began with a priest when you were an altar boy," Ray said.

Cleve started to reach for his coffee cup on the table, but had second thoughts. Ray noticed Cleve's hand quiver.

"Oh, I don't have any solid facts. Kick tells me all the records at St. Mary's have been destroyed. However, you haven't been to church there in the last twenty-

some years. I know your father was a devout Catholic
— most everyone in Penn County knows that," Ray said.
"Something must have happened. It might be worth the
trouble to look further."

Ray picked up his cup, took a drink, and looked over
at Cleve. Cleve picked up his coffee and smiled, then took
a sip.

"Are you aware that the Sheriff's Department, as well
as a few county officials and professionals — make that
un-professionals — are doing their damnedest to keep
this Brice case under wraps," Ray said.

"Why's that?" Kick blurted.

Ray turned to look at Kick. He raised his eyebrows at
her.

"I'll tell you why. One reason is that Mitch Wiersma's
car was seen in the Brice driveway that day," Ray said.
"Sometimes solving a case isn't so much about justice as
it is about winning elections."

He continued: "It's a shame that most of the folks in
Penn County believe you killed that little girl, but the officials who could see to it that justice is served are hiding.
It's a joke Cleve. The good ol' boys of Penn County think
less of me, the one who's been investigating the Brice
murder for the past two years, than they do of you," Ray
said.

"That can't go on for ever," Kick said. "Tell him about
divine intervention."

Cleve loosened the knot in his tie. Beads of sweat
broke out on his forehead.

"Okay, I'll just do that, Kick," Ray said. "See Mr. Hauser, we don't want to forget the eleven-year-old ... Oh, you didn't go into that house with murder on your mind. You went in to find out what Ronda Jo had been up to. I'm still at a loss if the struggle began when you saw the young girl naked, or when you started saying things about her mother."

A young lady holding a tray of baked goods and a coffee pot approached the table. "Anyone want a refill or a roll?" she asked.

Ray put his hand over his cup. Cleve shook his head.

"I'll have that brownie," Kick pointed.

The young lady sat the tray down on the table and handed Kick the brownie with her latex gloves.

"What's with the gloves?" Ray asked.

"School rule," she said. "With all the students coughing and sneezing, it's a wonder we don't have a cold going year round."

When Cleve at last got up to leave, the young lady returned to pick up the coffee cups and walked away.

Kick went into the restroom and when she came back, Ray was alone at the table, staring out the window.

"Did he say anything?" Kick asked.

"I asked him to think it over and meet me again," Ray said.

"And?"

"He left without a word."

Ray needed something that would break through Cleve's defenses. So far, his conclusions hadn't budged Cleve. Not even Kick's reference to divine intervention. He still thought that line of reasoning might haunt Cleve. People may grow up and lose their faith, or deliberately walk away from it, but it doesn't give them peace of mind. Old patterns of guilt and shame never die. Ray thought that fear of punishment awaiting him might have an effect.

That night, there was a noise outside Ray's window, a raccoon, or a cat more likely, knocking the lid off a trash can. Ray checked the clock. It was a little before 11:00 p.m. There was no point going back to sleep, he knew he would wake up again in eleven minutes.

There were still a few embers on the fire. Ray stirred them up and added another log. It was dry and it caught fire right away. Ray sat looking at it and waited. He took off his wristwatch and laid it on the side table where the firelight fell on it brightly. He didn't turn on a lamp. He listened. All of a sudden, the fire flared up. It was as if it had hit a pocket of pitch. But it was bigger than that. Ray looked down at the watch. It read 11:11. The fire flamed high for a minute. When the second hand touched 11:12 and no seconds, it died down again. Ray felt more at peace than he had in a long time.

Ray thought now that there might be one story, one irrefutable statement, that might make Cleve fear he was bound to be revealed.

"I'm still trying my best to make sense out of Val White's story," Ray said. "Let's start at the beginning again. Val told you that he saw Cleve on the road, coming back to the Brice house from the Shackleys'. Then he watched Cleve pull into the Brices' driveway, right?"

"Correct. Then I asked Val if he pulled in behind Cleve. He said he didn't, he pulled in front of the Brice house," Kick said.

"Then as Val got out of his car, he told you he saw Cleve letting the dog out of the house," Ray said. "So, Cleve is on the porch opening the kitchen door to let out a barking dog as Val just stands there."

"Right," Kick said. "I asked Val to describe the dog and asked him where it went. That's when he got a little hostile and said, 'That was a long time ago.' He didn't remember."

"From the distance where Val said he parked his car and where he said Cleve parked, they would have been at the Brices' door the same time. And if not, Cleve already would have been in the house," Ray said. "Mind you, a house that was on fire."

"What's your point?" Kick asked.

"Just this — Val said he saw Cleve open the door and let the dog out and that water was running out from all over the kitchen floor. He said that's why Cleve went in the house in the first place. Val didn't say Cleve went in because the house was on fire, but because water was running out the door. By the way, he'd have to have been pretty close to see that water. But yet they both claim they saw flames shooting through the roof. We know for sure Cleve did, because he reported the fire to Mrs. Shackley, who in turn called the fire department at about 3:08 p.m.," Ray said.

"Val also told me that the fire truck wasn't there as quick as Junebug and his partner Shawn claimed. He also said they brought the wrong fire truck," Kick said.

"Now you're telling me Junebug and Shawn were there, but with the wrong truck," Ray said. "Did Val say they had to take the truck back and get the right one?"

"No," Kick laughed. "But wait, it gets more confusing. Val said he grabbed a hose himself and started putting out the fire."

Ray leaned his head back for a moment, then looked at Kick.

"I asked him what hose? The garden hose?" Kick said. "Then he tells me, 'No, the one off the truck.'"

"So he grabbed the hose from the brush truck — the wrong truck — out of Shawn's hands?" Ray said.

"It's hard to imagine, isn't it," Kick said. "Why would a regular firefighter hand over his hose to some fruitcake bystander?"

"Shawn told me he followed Junebug inside the Brice house with the fire hose," Ray said. "Junebug stopped at the bathroom door when he saw Trudie lying dead in the bathtub and he told Shawn he was going to radio the Sheriff's Department and stand guard so others that would be coming along wouldn't go into the bathroom. Shawn pulled the hose up the stairs to where the fire was and started dousing it. By the way, Junebug and Shawn didn't bring the wrong fire truck, they brought the fastest and the most ready piece of equipment the department had."

"Then where was Val all this time?" Kick asked.

"If his story's true, he's right beside Shawn, who only stops for a moment to look in the bathroom, then he sees Junebug guarding the bathroom door with Cleve inside trying to resuscitate a little girl who's been dead nearly two hours in a bathtub filled with water," Ray said.

"That's the nuttiest thing I ever heard," Kick said.

"No, that's just one of the lies that Val tells you," Ray said. "Here are some more. How could Cleve get his vehicle out of the driveway if he was at the Brices' before the fire truck? Shawn said he parked the fire truck in the driveway. And wouldn't Junebug and Shawn have seen Cleve and Val? After all, they both knew them. For that matter, why didn't the police see either of them? They would have still been at the crime scene."

"Not to mention that everyone who saw Trudie in the bathtub remembers her lying face up, at the wrong end of the tub. How could Cleve give her artificial resuscitation in the bathtub? Would he have taken her out, then put her back in a tub filled with water, in a burning house?" Kick said. "All in a matter of seconds?"

"That's the trouble with lies," Ray said. "The people telling them always get caught up in them. Plus Cleve was never seen by anyone. He wouldn't, nor did he, have the time to do what he said he did."

319

"If you're right with what you're saying, then the stuff with the dog being let out and the water running out the kitchen door happened when Cleve first went in that house and killed Trudie," Kick said.

"Exactly. And if what Val told you were true, that he saw Cleve coming from the Shackleys' house after Cleve had Mrs. Shackley call to report the fire, then why didn't Cleve ask his friend Val call the police when he found Trudie inside? Cleve had to have seen she was strangled to death with those deep marks on her neck," Ray said. "We can assume that Val wasn't really upstairs playing fireman. He must really have been standing around with his thumb up his ass."

"You're right. Val told me that Cleve wouldn't let him come inside the Brice house, so Val said he stayed outside on the porch," Kick said.

"No one, and I mean no one, is going to believe Val White or Cleve Hauser. There are too many facts that contradict their lies," Ray said. "Val was never there."

"When I asked Val why Cleve wouldn't tell you his own story, he said that Cleve was a very private person and that Cleve had a lot of emotional stress from Vietnam," Kick said.

"That might be the only true thing Val told you," Ray said. "The rest of the story Cleve made up and told Val at Val's house after Cleve ducked out of the vacant house. Once he saw the fire truck and the confusion that was about to take place, he hit the road, working up his story the whole time."

"Val said Cleve could be a little off sometimes," Kick said. "He thought we ought to cut him some slack."

"That would be charitable, wouldn't it?" Ray said.

"So do you think he went to Val's right then, or later on?" Kick asked.

"Your guess is as good as mine," Ray said.

"It's a ridiculous story," Kick said. "I wonder if Val knows it ... I wonder if Cleve knows it."

Kick liked it whenever Ray decided to take the Gator out to the farms. The ATV not only went twenty-five miles an hour at top speed, but it was open and rugged with its roll bars and big wheels. They'd had a wet spell and the brush was coming back fast. Anybody who has ever given serious thought to the possibility that humankind has conquered nature, has never visited an Indiana farm. All the vines and grass you'd just as soon never see again, come back in force every chance they get. They grow as though no two-footed creature had ever been there or even been invented.

"Here's the plan, Kick," Ray said, backing the Gator out of the garage into the driveway. "When we get to farm one, you can run the tractor since the brush mower is ready to go. First, we'll cut the path down to the cove on farm one, then we'll finish up on farm two. This time I want to cut a trail down to the apple orchard and turn on the spring fed spigot to make a watering place for the deer. They'll need it if there's another hot summer."

"Won't that kind of set them up for the hunters next

fall?" Kick said. She looked to make sure they had every-thing they needed, then hopped into the passenger seat.

"They come to eat the fallen apples in the orchard anyway," Ray said. "Besides, the herds need to be thinned out and Paul doesn't kill for trophies, his family eats the venison."

"Are you going to follow behind me in the Gator?" Kick asked.

"Yes and I want you to have your sidearm with you," Ray said.

Kick unfolded the towel she'd tucked inside the glove box, revealing the .38 caliber pistol. "I don't trust him either," she said.

Kick remembered reading the article about Cleve Hauser teaching gun safety along with a couple of the county's Conservation Officers. The C.O. Ray was friends with thought that Ray was worried too much about the danger that Cleve posed. But it was pretty clear they thought that Cleve was a not a nice man; maybe not even a trustworthy one. Nothing that was said made Ray feel that he could trust Hauser in the woods.

"After we mow, we'll have our lunch in the cove," Ray said, pulling out onto the gravel back road leading toward Hampton.

"I'm hungry now," Kick said.

Ray glanced down at his watch. "It's only ten o'clock," he said.

"My stomach doesn't tell time," Kick said.

Ray sat at the picnic table looking over the freshly cut grass. He took in a deep breath, smelling the mixture of smells from the land.

Kick poked at the fire she'd built inside a circle of fieldstones.

"What are we eating?" Ray asked.

Kick handed him a couple of small tree limbs. "Shave these to a point for the hotdogs," she said.

After lunch, Ray propped his feet up on a log and fired up one of his favorite stogies.

"You want your iced tea refilled?" Kick asked.

Ray nodded.

"Did you ever write that letter to the Sheriff requesting the radio logs from the day of the murder?" Ray asked.

Though Ray had pretty much been able to establish his time frames through his numerous interviews, the radio logs would verify his conclusions.

"Yes," Kick said. "I called and wrote both. And I pointed out that you were entitled to them under the Freedom of Information Act."

"Good," Ray said. "Otherwise we could count on not getting them." It was pretty damn depressing, he thought, when you had to count on a law from the federal government a long way off in Washington to get some information that any right-thinking, compassionate local person should have been glad to give up freely.

It had not been a good beginning to the day. When Kick came into the office, there was a message waiting on her answering machine. It was time dated at 11:15. Cleve's voice said he wouldn't be meeting again with Ray. He said there was no point in it. His "sources" had told him Ray could be cited for harassment. Kick remembered that Cleve had brought up the issue of harassment before. It was turning out to be one of the few arrows he had in his quiver. But why had he waited until the middle of the night to call?

Thunderstorms were forecast and this time of year there could be hail as well, so Ray and Kick decided to dedicate a few days to organizing records in the office. Kick went through her written requests for information, sorting through what she'd received and what she hadn't.

"It looks as if I'm going to get the same type of service from the Sheriff as I got from the Coroner," Kick said. "What did you call it when officials ignore the law?"

"I don't remember what you're referring to," Ray said.

"I wrote Sheriff Wiersma requesting the County's radio logs from the day Trudie was murdered," Kick said.

"And?" Ray said.

"The Sheriff sent me a letter back that his department received authorization from Penn County's Old Records Commission to destroy radio logs up to, and including, December of 2003," Kick said.

"That's strange since the Sheriff was so adamant to emphasize that the Brice murder case was still open ...

you know, no statutory limits on murder," Ray said.

"I think the word is *stonewalling*," Kick said.

Ray raised his eyebrows.

"Yes," she said. "Stonewalling is what you called withholding information, or using delay tactics."

"I wonder if the county tossed out all the Brice records, including the evidence," Ray said. "That's if they ever got any. I wonder if the Old Records Commission approved of that."

"I'm not giving up," Kick said. "The Sheriff ended his letter by saying he's not giving a final decision and we can be assured of his cooperation."

"Sounds like he's just covering his butt," Ray said. "But I tend to think he's lying."

"I know he is, because — remember? — the clerk in the Records Section told me over the phone before I made the written request, that records in an open case wouldn't have been thrown out," Kick said. "Especially not the Brice case. She said that file was a thick one."

"I'd like to give the Sheriff the benefit of the doubt, but he's sure made it difficult," Ray said. "It's almost as if he's getting territorial."

"Territorial with the truth?" Kick said. "There's a concept."

"Isn't it?" Ray said. "Like politicians everywhere."

It had cleared up a few days later. The sky was relatively clear and the air didn't feel as heavy as it had before. Ray and Kick stood on the shoreline of the lake with their new fly rods. Ray decided he'd teach Kick how to fly cast. He knew learning to use a fly rod could be tricky, especially if the instructor didn't have the patience or take the time the student needed. A poor instructor was enough to make anyone give up on fly-fishing.

"Watch me, Kick." Ray took the rod in his right hand and loosened a three-foot loop of line, letting it hang down. He whipped the rod so the line laid out on the lake, then he quickly pulled the rod behind him, letting out a couple more feet as he whipped the rod back toward the lake. Kick sat on the ground next to the cooler. She took out one of the ice-cold beers and watched Ray.

"What you need to do is keep working the line and rod in rhythm. It'll take practice, but I know you can do this," Ray said. "And remember to start with, we'll always be casting out into open water."

Ray finally stopped casting and motioned for Kick to take her place on the shoreline. He pulled a bottle of beer out of the cooler. Kick looked back at him.

"You watched me while you drank your beer, now I'll watch you while I have one," Ray said.

A couple hours later, Kick had the hang of it. "Let's take the boat out," she said.

"After I have another cold one," Ray said.

The lake was still, though a slight breeze came from the south. Kick tied two fly poppers on their lines. Ray smiled. Although Kick said she was after bluegill, he knew she had bass in the back of her mind. She figured she would surprise him. She didn't have to wait long.

"I got one," Kick yelled out.

"Play the fish, don't try to horse it in," Ray shouted.

Ray felt like a kid as he watched her fight the bass. It wasn't going to be easy for her to land this fish. It had already broken water twice and bent her pole under the bottom of the boat.

"Damn," Kick yelled as the line snapped back empty. "He got my popper, too."

Ray lit a cigar as Kick dug around inside the tackle box for another fly. Ray knew the feeling.

"You know, Kick, at times I've wanted to give up on the Brice case," Ray said.

Kick sat still and listened.

"Some folks might wonder why Trudie's murder is more important than any other girls' and boys'. It's not," Ray said. He thought of all the young children in the world that had died tragic deaths by bombs and bullets in political wars; and others who were once alive and well in their homes, or out on a playground, when all of a sudden it was over for them because of a drive-by shooter. Even those kids you see in the paper with birth defects and chronic hunger or disease.

Kick cut the newly tied popper's line with her teeth. "So tell me ... never mind, you're thinking about all the murders and kidnappings on the nightly news again," Kick said.

"At least the police on the late news seem interested. I can't help but think that there's a cover-up in the Brice murder," Ray said. "A very conscious cover-up. Look how the Sheriff went out of his way to get retired deputies to dummy up."

He was quiet for a while. Both of them watched the glassy surface of the water.

"You know, it could be a mistake to give these guys too much credit. Maybe they're not trying to conceal the names of the deputies Hauser said he was talking to just before spotting the fire," Ray said.

"Then why would they try to keep all their deputies quiet?" Kick said.

"Because they don't know and they don't want to be shown up. Maybe they figure that if they if they admit they don't know who the deputies are ..." Ray said.

"...Or even if they exist at all ..." Kick said.

"It makes them look stupid," Ray said.

"They sure try to make us look stupid," Kick said. "The thing that burns me is how the Sheriff said in his letter that the radio logs may have been thrown out. He didn't know one of the ladies in their Records Department told me they would have kept all the records in an open case file, no matter how long it's been."

Ray liked the sound of the lure popping as Kick snapped the line back.

"I got another one," Kick yelled.

"Bring it in easy. It's a bluegill," Ray said, knowing bluegill rarely break water.

Kick eased it toward the boat and lifted it out of the water, holding the line.

Ray knew she wanted him to take it off the hook. He

recalled the one time she tried and got her hand barbed.

"I told you I'd get you a glove," Ray said as he removed the lure from the fish's mouth.

"I know there are times you get discouraged, but think how hard it must have been for the folks of Penn County to open up to you about Trudie's murder," Kick said.

Ray released the fish and watched it swim away.

"Come to think of it, I only had one person that gave me a hard time," Ray said. "The guy that said, 'It's about time, ain't it?' when I told him I was researching the case. Then I told him I was a writer, not a lawman. He said he liked writers even less then he liked the law. He had some kind of animal nickname."

"What did you tell him?" Kick said.

"I hung up on him," Ray said. "Who needs his bullshit."

"I think I remember the name," Kick said.

"Well, keep it to yourself," Ray said. He sighed, acknowledging that nothing was going to change. "This is a useless conversation. I have no intentions of letting Angel-puss down, nor the good people of Penn County."

"It's really not just for the people of Penn County, it's for people no matter who they are, or where they are — even in Great Britain," Kick said.

"Rig me up a frog popper. I'll show you how to dig a hawg out of the lily pads," Ray said.

"Okay, so now you want to make a bet," Kick laughed.

"With you? I don't think so, I remember when you

thought a bottle bass was really a fish," Ray teased.

"Very funny, Boss."

Kick spent some time on the Internet researching the science of forensics. As usual, she was very thorough. She not only read the scientific papers, but also the biographies of the half dozen television stars who played forensics experts on TV. Forensics had become a very attractive sort of police work in modern culture, she thought, maybe because it combined science and danger — both of which were missing from the everyday lives of most people. After she'd gotten some background, she printed up the most interesting and technical articles to show to Ray. She noticed there were many ads for home forensics kits. It was hard to imagine what people would use these for — checking up on spouses and co-workers? Trying to imagine gave her a queasy feeling.

Ray took some time to read up on crime-scene investigation tools that Kick printed off the Internet. Ray called her into his office.

She came to the door with a pile of papers in her hands.

"Get rid of that stack and have a seat," Ray said. "I want to discuss something with you."

"It's about DNA, right?" Kick said.

"You taking up mind reading full time?" Ray said.

Kick laughed. "No, but remember I'm the one who brought you that forensic blood information. I could have researched a little clairvoyance on the side."

"I have to get into the old Brice house," Ray said.

"I assumed that's why you wanted to read up on forensics. But remember Agnes Mann said it freaked her husband out for you to go inside," Kick said.

"I only need to be inside for twenty minutes max," Ray said.

"With me or without me?" Kick asked.

"Either way," Ray said.

Ray explained how he would take some latex gloves and a sterile scraper, collect the killer's blood sample from where he thought it might be, and leave.

"Would Agnes or her husband be inside with you?" Kick asked.

"Of course not. No one knows where I'm going to get the evidence from but you," Ray said. "So it can be you or me inside. I prefer both, but if it takes someone to wait outside on the porch, I guess that would be me. I'll keep Agnes busy with small talk."

"The question is how you going to convince the Manns to give you the okay," Kick said.

"Money," Ray said.

"How much?" Kick said.

"I'll leave it up to her," Ray said.

"Her?" Kick said.

"Yes, I'm betting that with a girl-to-girl phone call from you, she'll go for twenty minutes, especially if you talk about doing the right thing, instead of money," Ray said. "Only bring up money after you've given her all the other reasons she should cooperate."

"You got it all figured out," Kick said.

"I've been mulling it over ever since her husband said no," Ray said.

A couple of weeks passed before Kick was even able to make contact with Agnes Mann — both she and her husband worked. Kick also figured the Manns were screening their calls. With five kids, it wasn't likely they would be away as many evenings as she'd called. Though Ray remembered Agnes telling him that her mother babysat for their large brood of kids.

Ray made sure that when Kick called to set things up that she went with the angle of Ray obtaining actual physical evidence from the house, rather than him going in to get a spiritual feeling of what went on the day of the murder. He didn't want Agnes to start thinking he might aggravate the spirit.

When Agnes finally called, one late afternoon, she explained when she knew her husband would be away for several hours. Kick got Agnes to okay the plan and they agreed on a figure.

The next day, Agnes called back. She had somehow managed to get her husband to go along. He said he just didn't want the kids, or himself, to be there and left everything else in his wife's hands. Kick wondered if the promise of money had had anything to do with him changing his mind.

The visit was arranged for the following morning, when the house would be empty except for Agnes. When the time came for them to leave, Ray told Kick he wanted to bring the photos Keith had sent them. She retrieved them from the safe and handed them to Ray as they walked out to the truck.

"I'll drive," Ray said.

"Okay," Kick said. She opened door and got in.

Ray handed the photos back to her. "Study these," he said. "Remember what I told you."

Ray slowed the truck as they approached the Manns'. "I don't see a car in the driveway," he said.

"She's home," Kick said.

As Ray turned in, he spotted the kitchen curtain pull back.

"So, who's going in?" Kick asked.

Ray handed her the latex gloves, zip bag, and the plastic scraper.

"Put the pictures under the seat," Ray said.

They got out of the truck. Kick went up to knock on the door just as it opened. Agnes stepped outside. She seemed a little unsure, a little uneasy.

Ray pointed to a pile of old building materials that sat at the edge of a field, a little ways past the side drive.

"Is that pile from the fire?" Ray asked Agnes.

"I'll be out in a few minutes," Kick said as she went inside the house.

Agnes smiled. "What pile?" she said.

"Follow me," Ray said.

As they walked up to the burnt boards and shingles, a couple of critters scurried away from beneath the debris.

"You know I've never noticed this stuff as long as we've lived here," Agnes said. "But this isn't on our property." She pointed to a large fieldstone. "That's where our property ends."

"You know who owns this land?" Ray asked.

"No," Agnes said.

Ray talked about Agnes's children — their ages, and who was, and who wasn't in school yet. The conversation stretched out. Agnes talked a long time about her husband, how they feared the economic slowdown might cost him his job and how worried they both were. It was pretty scary to be living on the edge with a big family to feed.

Ray turned to look back at the house just as Kick came out the door.

"I'm finished," Kick yelled, waving at them from the porch.

Kick eyed Ray and put two fingers to her lips. Ray peeled off two hundred-dollar bills and handed them to Agnes.

"No, I said one hundred," Agnes said, leaving her hand with the money in it extended.

Ray patted her shoulder. "Buy those kids a couple surprises," Ray said.

Agnes stood on the porch, waving goodbye with the money clenched in her hand as Ray pulled out of the drive onto the highway. He smiled.

"What are you grinning about," Kick said.

"Just remembering back in time," Ray said. Remembering what it was like to have kids. What a relief it was when they got old enough to take care of themselves.

Kick waved to Agnes out the truck window as they headed toward town.

Ray went into his office and sat down. It wasn't that the conversation, or even the research, had worn him out. He knew that he was about to sew the case up and the responsibility of it seemed like a heavy burden. He looked at the two baggies. One with some dark red scrapings and a splinter of wood, the other with the cotton swabs. "Kick, I want you to get this sample to your uncle and see if we got a DNA match," Ray said.

"You think that cotton swab will work?" she asked. When the young lady had taken Cleve's cup at the agricultural college, Kick had swabbed the inside edge of it carefully with cotton swabs she'd hidden in her purse. When she was finished, she put the swabs in a zip lock bag and put that bag in the safe, along with the photos. Kick had a pretty good idea that this was a reliable way of getting DNA and the reading she had done on the Internet recommended this as an effective way of collecting evidence.

Kick went back to her desk and e-mailed her uncle. She hadn't any doubt he'd help her out and so she carefully labeled the two sample bags, rolled them in bubble wrap, and put them in an envelope.

It was hot. Anybody with any sense was indoors lying low. Kick was typing letters. The air conditioning was cranked up to the maximum and still the air was oppressive. The weather matched Ray's mood and Kick's as well. They were in waiting mode. Waiting for the rain to fall and clear the air. Waiting to hear about the test.

Ray had gone into his office and nodded off. He'd been up late, working on the ending of his book. He awoke to what sounded like three people running up the stairway. It was Kick, waving a paper as she whistled and half sang part of the song, *On the road again* ... Ray rubbed the sleep from his eyes.

"It's a match," Kick said. She moved around the room, holding the report as if it were her dancing partner.

"Tell me," Ray said.

"I got a written report from my uncle. Well, from an associate of his," Kick said. "He tested those samples I sent ..."

"Tell me the details," Ray almost shouted.

"To put it in the simplest of terms, the DNA that we collected from Cleve's coffee cup, and the blood sample that I took from the house, is Hauser's," she said.

Ray knew that meant that they now had solid evidence that Cleve Hauser was Trudie Brice's murderer. No hearsay, no conjecture, not even a map.

Kick threw her arms around Ray's neck, hugging him. Once she'd calmed down, he spoke.

"Now comes the more difficult part," Ray said.

"It's solved, Boss.... It's what we always thought," Kick said.

"But first, how do we handle this evidence? It's really

not official," he said.

"What are you talking about?" Kick said.

"For starters, we've had no cooperation from law enforcement," Ray said. "And if my map didn't get their attention, no DNA is going to either."

"I guess I'm not on the same brain wave as you," Kick said.

"Sure you are, you just need to be reminded," Ray said.

Ray refreshed her memory on how Cleve told her that he struggled with his decision of whether or not to talk to Ray, and how Cleve made reference to his "sources."

Ray thought, at the time, Cleve was all but telling him that his lawyer, or a lawyer who worked on the murder case back in 1986, advised Cleve that he didn't have to talk to Ray at all. Ray could tell by the way Cleve explained himself that lawyer talk was exchanged between Cleve and his mysterious source.

But Cleve had met him anyway, sources or not. Ray thought that maybe he could find a way to get to Cleve somehow. Ray thought so because he had always felt that Cleve was ready to confess to the crime, but for reasons, some known and some unknown, he had been, in Ray's mind, misguided. Ray reminded Kick how often others didn't want to be exposed for their sins — he thought of Reverend Hummock, Mitch Wiersma, even the authorities and the newspapers. Cleve's redemption was the furthest thing from their own selfish minds. Cleve was on his own; him and his conscience.

"So what are you going to do?" Kick asked.

"I'm going to think this through real careful and come up with a plan to get Cleve to tell me his own story. I have to convince him that I'm not the least bit interested in taking what we have to the officials. I want the choice left up to Cleve himself," Ray said. "Your job will be to set up another meeting with Cleve at the Agricultural College Library. I'll go over the details with you on how you'll be able to do it."

Kick let out a deep breath.

Chapter 14

Ray stood in the doorway of the sunroom. Kick sat on the tile floor with tackle boxes, fishing rods, and lures of all types spread out around her. She had on her favorite fishing cap, her Hemingway hat. Once Ray came to the conclusion as to what she was doing, he spoke.

"What weight line you putting on your reel?" Ray said.

"Number eight monofilament," Kick said.

"Green?" Ray said.

Kick looked up at him and smiled. "It's the latest," she said. "The fish can't see it as well as that other stuff I had on here."

"But eight weight … you going after bigger bass?"

Ray asked.

"No, you backlashed all the number six last time we went out," Kick said.

"Funny, Kick. Very funny," Ray said.

"Where you coming from?" Kick asked.

"I drove by Bloom High School," Ray said.

"May I ask for what?" Kick said.

"I wanted to make sure that the high school was closed for the summer," Ray said. "When you're finished rigging that up, I want to talk to you about Cleve Hauser."

"I thought the school was closed," Kick said.

"Yes, but one of the teachers told me that Cleve's teaching a special summer class on farming, animals, or gun safety," Ray said.

"Which one?" Kick said.

"Beats me, but I'm getting a feeling that now's the time for you to leave him another phone message or send him an e-mail," Ray said.

Kick laid the rod and reel aside.

"When he gets back to you, I want you to break our good news and his bad news to him," Ray said.

Ray told Kick that she would have to fill Cleve in on the DNA results, slow and methodical. "I want you to be non-threatening," Ray said. He wanted Cleve to know that he, at least at the present, had no intention of sharing the results with the law. Ray knew, based on his attorney's advice, that he was in no way obstructing justice. His lawyer said that when authorities from the Sheriff's Department refused to use Ray's map and additional information as to witnesses, they, in essence, had either shut down or covered up the Brice case. Kick had managed to get these refusals, in one form or another, on paper. She even had tapes of phone messages, in case they became necessary.

Ray made it clear that the only thing he wanted Kick to do was get him an interview with Cleve, preferably at the Indiana Agricultural College library again. "He'll be the most comfortable there," Ray assured her. "Just set up the meeting, Kick. No threat, no explanations, just the day, time, and place."

"I got it," Kick said.

Ray knew she did. She'd never failed him before on this kind of business.

"Who's all going to be there?" Kick asked.

"Hauser, you, and me," Ray said.

A week and a half passed before Kick heard back from Cleve. She arranged the meeting, telling Ray it was a slam-dunk. Ray knew she had the right to brag a little. Dealing with a psychopath was never easy, nor were there any guarantees.

In general, Ray was not the kind of man to put on airs. He didn't push, he didn't presume. He avoided drawing attention to himself. He dressed nicely but not in any showy way. Nor did he dress down to create an impression. He would never, for example, have gone to an interview wearing a jogging suit. That wouldn't have been Ray.

But this time was different. He gave some thought to how he dressed. He was more casual than usual. He wore a short-sleeved shirt, some light khakis, and loafers. Kick did the same. She wore a plain summer dress. She pulled her hair back and didn't use much makeup.

When Ray and Kick walked into the library, they didn't have to wait for Cleve Hauser. He was already sitting at the same table where Ray and Kick first met with him. He'd also dressed less formally this time. His baseball cap was pulled down to his eyebrows. He had a strange sort of grin on his face.

They walked over to the table. Ray shook Cleve's hand and smiled. He remembered it was Del Pitt who'd first described Cleve's expression — he'd called it a "shit-eating grin." Now maybe they were going to see one of those other sides of Cleve they'd heard about: the joker, the ironist, the wise guy.

Ray and Kick sat down with Cleve.

"I suppose you have a tape recorder with you," Cleve said.

"Yes, my memory is a little faulty," Ray said. That was not true, of course. Ray had never used a recorder. But this time he wanted absolutely no doubts about what was said.

"Good try," Cleve said. "Put it on the table."

Ray pulled the recorder out and set it in the center of the table. Cleve picked it up, removed the tape and put it in his pocket. Cleve laid the recorder on the empty chair next to him.

"It's empty," Ray said.

"Then you won't miss it," Cleve said.

Ray had had years of experience dealing with all kinds of people and personalities. He knew dialogue took time. Ray had thought about this meeting with Cleve over and over. He knew what his purpose was now. Ray believed he'd be successful in getting Cleve to talk, though he felt slight jitters, and highs of the unknown. The feeling was a benefit for whatever obstacle came forth.

"Our last meeting I did all the talking, if I recollect," Ray said.

"See, you didn't need a tape recorder after all," Cleve said.

Ray bit down on his lip. "You're right, so why don't you ask me whatever you'd like to know," Ray said.

"How'd you get my DNA from the Brice house ... that is, if you did," Cleve said. "Your assistant here said that you had DNA."

Ray didn't like the way Cleve said, "assistant." He thought Cleve probably had trouble with strong women.

"Kick, dig out the DNA lab report," Ray said. He turned back to Cleve who was displaying that grin again.

Kick handed the report to Ray. He flipped the copy over to Cleve. Cleve looked at it. He didn't look up once for the next several minutes.

"Where did you get my DNA from?" Cleve finally asked.

"Your coffee cup the first time we met," Ray said.

"I know that," Cleve said. "You know I mean the

match from the house."

Ray knew he finally had Cleve on the defense. Now, he wanted to keep him there. Ray grinned. One shit-eating grin deserved another.

"So you're not going to tell me," Cleve said.

"I paid to get inside the house," Ray said.

Cleve called Agnes Mann a name. Ray wondered if Cleve and Agnes had ever even met.

"I think you're missing the bigger picture," Ray said.

"And that is?" Cleve said.

"The main question I thought you would have asked is why I became so interested in the Brice case in the first place," Ray said.

Kick shifted her eyes back and forth between the men, wondering who was going to speak first.

"Okay, what business is it of yours?" Cleve said.

Kick remained stone-faced, but smiled deep inside herself. She felt her body tighten.

"Funny you put it that way," Ray said. "'What business.' Ronda Jo asked me the same thing." Ray felt that now was the time to make his case. "In the beginning, I was looking to write a suspense book. They're popular, so why not? There's money in telling a good story. But then money didn't really seem to be the reason since I was spending most of my time and quite a bit of money doing research. Maybe it was justice — that's what I told Ronda Jo. I said murder was everyone's business and, in her daughter's case, the murderer should be brought to justice. But it came down to this, if she believed as I do, that her Trudie's in Heaven, a better place, then the killer had to pay for his sins. And that's the real reason I've spent the last two and a half years trying to solve the Brice murder."

"I'm not sure I follow you," Cleve said. He couldn't lose the grin.

"Do you want to think about it and meet again some other time?" Ray said.

Kick relaxed. She knew the procedure.

"No, I want to know now," Cleve said.

Ray turned his top lip in and wetted it with his tongue — Ray's tell sign. Kick was interested in hearing more.

"I don't want to preach to you, so look at what I'm about to share with you as my life philosophy," Ray said.

Cleve leaned back.

"Kick, would you go get us both a cup of coffee?"

Kick left as Ray continued on with Cleve.

"In the beginning, God created the universe and all living creatures, Genesis 1–3. He created Adam out of dust and Eve in the Garden of Eden and all the subordinate critters in the air, in the water, and on land. The story which took place in the garden is about good and evil. The truth of the story is faith-based.

"At this point the questions could be asked: Why did God create? And what is creation all about? Could it have been that God was consulting with his council of angels and one of the highest ranking challenged Him?

"Maybe Satan spoke up, telling God that he too wanted a part in the creation (perhaps disguised as a serpent) to prove to God that man and woman would defy Him — over the slightest of rules. Maybe all Satan requested was that the serpent look enticing and be able to talk.

"God agreed and made a beautiful garden, one with all kinds of trees and fruits. What God did was set up an almost perfect world. A world where there was no such thing as death, sickness, suffering, sadness, or need. God warned Adam and Eve about one special tree that grew in the center of the garden and forbade them to eat of its fruit.

"The serpent convinced Adam and Eve in their naked innocence to eat of the forbidden fruit — the fruit from the tree of knowledge. When God found them hiding, He asked them why they ate of the fruit. Adam blamed Eve, who blamed the serpent. The serpent probably sneered. Because of Adam and Eve's sin, God placed a curse on all those three involved in the transgression, thus changing life here on earth — men and women do suffer and die. Since the eating of the forbidden fruit, I believe that Adam and Eve brought about free will. Temptation is innate.

"Should we blame God for setting us up? My faith causes me to think not, since we had free will in the Garden of Eden. The story of creation is complex, to say the least. It is an ongoing battle between good and evil. God (good) makes all the rules for salvation, and then allows Satan (evil) to continue to tempt humans to trespass. Creation is only the beginning of this matrix.

"The final judgment of what becomes of God's creatures is addressed in the book of Revelations and has subjective interpretations. Yet I believe, in time, all answers will be revealed in eternal life."

Kick came back and sat the coffee on the table.

"You missed Ray's story," Cleve said to her. The smirk again.

"You know, Cleve, you're letting others off the hook by not stepping forward. Believe me when I say that most of the folks in Penn County know you were the passerby, right?" Ray said.

"I guess," Cleve said.

"Come on, Cleve, you told people that you tried to resuscitate Trudie," Ray said. "This is time for the truth."

"You saying I didn't try?" Cleve said.

"I proved that it was impossible for you to do what you said you did. Plus, I have the word of eyewitnesses who were on the scene," Ray said. "But that's not the point now. The point is, Ronda Jo, Reverend Hummock, Mitch Wiersma, and others won't come forward and tell what they know. Personally, I believe they're guilty — not in aiding or committing the crime, but guilty in letting you face damnation. And it's not because they want to protect you; they have their own selfish reasons. They worry about self-incrimination, pride, and public condemnation, among other things. But guilty they are."

"Mitch Wiersma was doing drugs and selling them too," Cleve said. "As far as the good Reverend Hummock, it was hanky-panky with Ronda Jo. Nobody's clean."

"Now's not the time to name names," Ray said.

"How about Penn County's so-called law enforcement?" Cleve said. "And what was Vietnam all about? Nobody's concerned about my killing people over there. Not even women and children."

"Let it go, Cleve," Ray said. "Your problem started way back at St. Mary's when you were an altar boy."

Cleve turned pale. "How would you know about what happened at St. Mary's?" he whispered.

"You know what a calling card's for?" Ray asked.

Cleve stared at Ray, then glanced over at Kick.

"The fire in the bed and the method of the rape ... you left your calling card," Ray said. "You'd been in that bed before and you told Ronda Jo about what the priest did to you."

Cleve reached for his coffee cup, knocking it over. Kick jumped up as coffee streamed across the table in her direction.

"I didn't mean to kill her," Cleve said. "She pissed me off."

"Here's what I'd like you to do, Cleve. Go back to living your life, but keep this in mind. If you decide that you want to confess to Trudie Brice's murder, call me. I'll get you a lawyer and even attend your trial," Ray said. "And if they send you to prison, I'll visit you."

"Why would you do that for me?" Cleve said.

"I already told you that story," Ray said.

"Something has to be in it for you," Cleve said.

"No, but there's something in it for you," Ray said.

"Salvation."

Ray stood and picked up the DNA report from the table and handed it to Kick. Kick grabbed the recorder from the chair next to Cleve.

"You took a little girl's life, plus everything she had, or would ever have," Ray said. "It doesn't make her happy. It didn't."

"What do you mean, 'doesn't?'" Cleve said. "She ..."

"I've heard from her," Ray said. "Haven't you?"

Ray and Kick started toward the exit. Ray stopped and turned around. "Remember, call me," Ray said.

The weather was eerily beautiful on the way back. "You want to drive?" Ray said.

"No, I only like to drive your truck," Kick said.

Ray pulled his car into Willow Grove Cemetery. "Look, Kick, Mr. and Mrs. Bluebird are moving in," he said.

"Stop the car," Kick said.

"What now?" Ray said.

Kick dug into her case and pulled out her camera.

"They'll be gone time you get ready," Ray said.

"Hold your horses, I want to put the zoom lens on," Kick said, fumbling with the camera.

"They're gone," Ray said.

Ray pulled the car to his grandfather's grave and stopped. It was habit. Ray rolled down his window. "Hi, Will," he said.

After a moment, Ray continued on toward Trudie's gravesite.

"Oh, look Boss, Trudie's flowers are blooming. Aren't they pretty," Kick said.

Ray parked the car and got out. Kick followed him to Trudie's gravestone.

"Well, Angel-puss, it looks like we've come to the end," Ray said. "I promised you that I'd find out who the person was that took your life and I did. I know you think it should have happened faster. But I had to have the evidence. That's how we do things here. If you'd lived longer, you'd have found that out yourself."

Kick bent down to pull a couple of weeds that had grown in between the flowers.

"You ready?" Ray said.

"Not yet," Kick said. She reached into her purse and took out a piece of paper. She unfolded it and began to read aloud:

"Jesus, Trudie, and Me,
Alone I looked toward the Heavens
and watched the white clouds roll by.
I knew that Jesus, my Savior,
was watching from His throne on high.

"I felt His presence so near me,
a warm glow filled my heart.
Though He is many miles away,
we are never far apart.

"I thought of my dear friend, Trudie,
who is also far away.

I know Jesus was watching over her,
as He did me today.

"Suddenly I didn't feel so alone,
as I stood by the old willow tree.
I felt their presence very near;
there was Jesus, Trudie, and me.
— Ethel Coughlin
December 11, 1986"

Ray reached back into the truck and found a tissue. He handed it to Kick.

"It's so sad, Boss," Kick said.

"She likes that poem," Ray said.

On the way back to the lake house, Kick pulled something out of her purse.

"Want to hear what he had to say," she said, holding a miniature recorder.

"Did you get it all on that tiny thing?" Ray said.

"It's the latest," Kick said. "Digital."

Ray shook his head.

Kick held up her hand and laughed. "High five," she said.

Seasons passed — summer, fall, winter. Ray and Kick still thought of Trudie and continued to visit her grave, more often during the Christmas season.

One early spring morning, Ray stood at the edge of the pier, casting his spin bait out onto the rippled lake. A light rain began to fall as a bass struck the lure. Ray set the hook. He could tell this was a big fish by its pull. He looked toward the noise up near the house.

"Boss, Boss!" Kick came running outside, holding the phone. "It's Cleve Hauser ..."

EPILOGUE

I stood at the gravesite of a young girl I did not know. I walked away only to return. I began to wonder why and how it was she died so young. In time, I was drawn by the little girl's spirit.

I found out that there were a number of cold case murders in Penn County. This girl's unsolved murder caused me to spend the next two and a half years of my life searching for her killer.

In the beginning, I thought that her story should be told. As a writer, I believed the reader could benefit from whatever lesson there was to learn. One, for example, was that law enforcement, locals, and others won't always cooperate on a murder investigation. And, of course, a good story is not only rewarding work, but it also answers questions that have remained secret for years. However, storytelling eventually lost out to a call for justice.

So, I asked myself what business of mine was this girl's death? After giving it some considerable thought, I came to the conclusion that, here on this earth, in whosoever's lifetime, murder is every citizen's business. Though the soul is judged by the Almighty in the hereafter, justice on God's green earth is in our charge. My second reason, though seeming reasonable, was not my final reason to write this story. For one to understand my decision, one must seek out his or her own faith.

For those who believe, you already know that there has been an ongoing battle between good and evil since the beginning of time. Ultimately, this struggle is for our souls. God makes all the rules for salvation and allows Satan to continue to tempt us to trespass. The final judgment of what becomes of God's creatures is laid out for all in the Good Book. However, forgiveness for our sins is measured by Him by our faith alone.

You, the reader, deserve no less than the true ending of this story. Trudie Brice's killer still walks the streets and drives the back country roads of Penn County. He wants to confess to this little girl's murder, but he can't. The officials of Penn County won't let him.

After more than twenty years, Penn County is through talking about Trudie Brice. Again.

Young Trudie's killer still has time to redeem himself. He should step forward and forget about damning advice from outside and instead do his own soul searching.

Trudie wanted me to tell you her story. I have. Now, may she rest in peace.

West

Fire truck

Passes DeHann at 3:11?

Brice house

Barn built 30 x 40

Passing

FD Arrives 3:11

DeHann House

X

FD

3:05
Passer by

PASSING B

suspicious
vacant old fa___
house

FD

approx .4 mi

Vacant farm
house w/loot bldg
demolished 1991

the smetu____

North Hampton
Town receives Alarm
3:09

A Passerby found in bathtub face down

Passer by

B What door did passerby enter? (side door)

Firefigh___

C Passer by moves body to outside

D Firefighter Davenport found girl FACE UP
   in bathtub

E other fireman know Trudie lies in bathroom

F Why doesn't passerby call police while in hous___

G No one sees passerby

H Firefig___